Jo

Manuel

The View From Kleoboulos

First published in English worldwide by
Lulu Press, www.lulu.com

Typeset in 10pt Garamond by the author.

Front cover photography and design by the author.

ISBN 978-1-291-11462-1

To answer before listening—
that is folly and shame.

-Proverbs 18:13 N.I.V.

Also by John Manuel

The "Ramblings from Rhodes" series:

Feta Compli!

Moussaka To My Ears

Tzatziki For You To Say

A Plethora Of Posts

All of the above available from Amazon worldwide
in paperback or Kindle format
and from the publisher, www.lulu.com

More information about the above titles can be found on
John Manuel's blog:
http://ramblingsfromrhodes.blogspot.com

The View From Kleoboulos

Part One

A Coming Together

1. Alyson – Lindos, January 1st 2007

I don't know why I come out here. Well, I do, but I know it won't accomplish anything. It's too late to change things now. But there is some solace in sitting here with old Kleoboulos, although he's been dead about two and a half thousand years. He won't answer back, that's a cert, anyway.

At this time of the morning in mid-January you do need a warm jacket on. Later, when I make the forty-five minute walk back to Lindos beach I'll probably have to take the jacket off and sling it over my shoulder; but now, with that keen wind, it's necessary. I so remember that wonderful feeling when we arrived here and decided to stay. It would have been a kind of catharsis to leave my overcoat in the Sue Ryder shop before leaving the UK, knowing that I'd have no need of it living out here. That wasn't to be, but never mind.

"Catharsis". See, now that's a Greek word. From the limited amount of Greek that I've learned I know it means something like "cleansing" in the sense of a release. I felt like my whole life was being cleansed of addiction to material things when we came over here. So liberating, so exhilarating.

If only I'd known quite how it was all going to turn out.

Is it really only six months ago? Seems like it may as well have all happened in old Kleo's era, it's that distant. Things like this only happen in novels, don't they? Ahem, well, evidently not.

2. Bath, UK – October 1997

"They look a bit tasty." Said twenty-one-year-old Dean, a youth too beautiful for his own good, long flowing locks that he always kept immaculately clean partly obscuring his face.

"Who do? Where?" Asked Malcolm, who was staring in the other direction at some street musician attempting a Radiohead song with nothing but a beaten up old acoustic guitar. It was something from their brand new album, OK Computer. A bit ambitious for a one-man band, but he was doing a pretty good job nevertheless.

Malcolm hadn't been at school on the day they handed out the good looks. Not that he was ugly; he just didn't have any features of note. He was built well enough, if anything slightly stronger of frame than Dean, his friend of seven years, yet he usually got the other girl when Dean selected which one of the two he'd fancied when they'd met a couple of people of the other gender on whatever particular outing they'd been engaged in at the time.

"Over there, by the colonnade. Yours even looks half-decent this time!"

"Yea, well, thanks. Where do you think they're off to, anyway?" Dean was driving his father's runabout, a Mercedes A140, their "little" model. His dad's other drive was an all-singing all-dancing Jag. He always liked Jaguars did Dean's father. Forget the fact that they were now foreign-owned (by Ford). They had "pedigree" he always said. They were distinctly English by tradition. Dean's father was one of those who could afford to say such things; after all, he could also afford to purchase a top-of-the-range limo any time he liked.

The two friends were out on the prowl; both of them recently single after having ended relationships which had lasted for several months. Dean was a bit miffed because his ex, a tall blonde girl called Carolyn, had been the first to raise the subject of a split. He'd also begun to feel that they were going nowhere, but she got it in first. What he needed, what he and Malcolm both needed, was to find a couple of new girls and get started on a possible new relationship a.s.a.p. So Dean had picked his dad's keys up from the telephone stand in the ample hall of his parent's home on the outskirts of the city of Bath and then gone and picked up Malcolm from his "pad" in one of the city's Georgian terraces and they'd gone off for a pint or two and a "reccy".

"It's your turn." Said Malcolm.

"OK, OK," replied his friend. "Watch and learn, sucker." Swinging the car around to bring it alongside the two girls in question, Dean pressed the electric window button and the glass quickly disappeared downward into the door. Leaning ever so slightly out from the window aperture he hailed the girls.

"Excuse me!" They turned to look at the source of the voice, which was apparently hailing them, "Excuse me!! I don't know Bath very well. Which way's your place?"

The response which this elicited from the "quarry" wasn't exactly what Dean had hoped for. Instead of a giggle and some body language that may have indicated a modicum of interest, the two girls turned in disgust and marched arm in arm into the colonnade of pillars, an area where cars couldn't follow.

"Well, I certainly learnt something THERE." Declared Malcolm. "How not to impress a couple of women I've never met before. They were actually pretty tasty too. You blew it, know-all."

"Yea, well. It's not my fault if they don't have a sense of humour. Probably wouldn't have been our types anyway."

"You would say that, NOW, wouldn't you, dipstick!"

It's funny how things turn out. An hour later Dean and Malcolm could be seen sitting in a trendy backstreet bar with subdued lighting and blues music playing over the sound system. To the sound of Albert Collins, they were engaged in an animated conversation with two other girls with whom they'd been friends for a couple of years. For reasons which none of them could probably cite, they'd never "got off" with these two, merely become chums on the same social scene.

Dean was going to become a graphic designer now that he'd finished his course and achieved his BA Hons degree. His days at college had finally come to an end during the summer just past and now he was to be thrust out into the real world to try and actually use what he'd learned to make a living. Not that it was going to be easy. He often recounted to his friends how, on the very first day at University, one of the lecturers – an American bloke who bore more than a passing resemblance to that sidekick of Robert Vaughan's in the ancient TV series "The Man From U.N.C.L.E." had shuffled into the room, plonked his loafers on the desk in front of him, stared at the thirty four students facing him and declared: "I hope you all know that if five of you end up actually working as designers and not cleaning windows it will be a higher than average success rate for a class of this size."

Dean was always going to be one of the five if it was the last thing he did. His father would be livid anyway if he didn't make it. His

Father, in fact, didn't really even approve of his doing "design" as a course. "It's a bit airy fairy," he'd declared when Dean had told him what he really wanted to do.

"It's not really a proper job is it? Why don't you study architecture? That's a little bit arty, whilst also being far more likely to earn you a decent crust. You needn't think you're going to live off your parents for the rest of your life my boy."

"If I studied architecture, I'd spend my entire working life having to swot up on all the new regulations, new building materials and all that stuff and then sit ever more exams until I retired early from boredom or exhaustion after a few decades of continually feeling guilty over not having done my homework. It would be like staying at school forever. If there's one thing I looked forward to when I left school, it was an end to that continual guilt over homework half-done, or not done at all, or the prospect of half the coming weekend being taken up with sitting in my bedroom swotting. Best years of our lives? I don't think so!"

"You know *nothing*, son. This world doesn't owe you, you know. The sooner you learn that the better."

This was a typical conversation between Dean and his dad toward the end of his teens and on into his twenty-second year. Mrs. Waters, Dean's mother Julia, was usually the one to bring a halt to such arguments. Addressing no one in particular, she'd march into the kitchen, jodhpurs on, and throw a horsewhip on to the table whilst declaring, "You two are always at it. One of these days you'll both admit that you love eachother. Hopefully before it's carved on to your father's gravestone Dean."

It was Dean's turn to go and get a couple of drinks in. After ascertaining what the girls wanted, he wrestled his way to the long narrow bar and tried to attract the barmaid's attention. Before he could do so though, he spotted about ten feet along the bar a face he recognised. It was only one of the two girls they'd tried to "pull" from the window of the car earlier in the evening! By the time Dean had returned to their table, his and Malcolm's backs to the table behind, he'd realised that the two were still unattached and sitting right behind the two young men.

"Malc," Said Dean, "since I got it all wrong and failed abysmally with those two up by the Abbey Church Yard, I'll happily defer to your superior wisdom in all things romantic and allow you to have a go this time. They're right behind us, still just the two of them! Get in there my son and I'll follow at a safe metaphorical distance." After having explained the situation and this second chance which they'd be given to the girls with whom they were sitting, and been told that they ought to go ahead, the girls wouldn't mind, Malcolm did a quick silent run-through in his head. Turning around on his stool, he proffered his packet of cheese and onion at the closer of the two girls and said, "Want a crisp?"

3. Lindos, Greece – 2005

Brian always thought he'd make it as a singer-songwriter. To be fair, he's good, mesmerisingly good in fact, when he picks his acoustic guitar. The problem is, in every town in every county all over the UK there are others equally as good. There's just too much talent in this world, sad fact though that is for the many who never "make it".

He's not really complaining though. Born in Bath in 1950, Brian grew up with the hippy movement, the Beatles versus the Rolling

Stones, jamboree bags, and conkers in the autumn. Raw knuckles but an unbeaten forty-sevener and he didn't even cheat by putting it into his mum's oven to harden it off. That delicious smell that only a fresh, shiny conker gives off when you've liberated it from its spiky green shell and polished it whilst sitting under a huge horse-chestnut tree in a British Autumn's leafy lane.

It's funny what goes through your mind when you're laying on a sunbed on the small beach at the far end of St. Paul's Bay and it's touching forty degrees Celsius. If he takes one of the earpieces of his iPod out from it's snug little home in the side of his head, he can marvel at the intensity of sound that the cicadas make during high summer on a Greek island. Or perhaps he can tune his ear into the deep hum of a boat's engine as it passes just the other side of the rocks to his right, those rocks which make this bay so sheltered from the swells of an angry sea during the winter months.

When was it, now, that he'd first got a gig playing guitar and singing in the corner of a bar? Oh yes, that's it, it was Bath circa 1976-8. He'd particularly enjoyed doing his extended version of *Seamus*, the acoustic blues song at the end of Pink Floyd's Meddle album, where the dog whines along in the background. Of course, there were no dog sound effects in Porky's Bar on a Friday night in a Bath backstreet as 1976 drew to a close, but a rapt audience, fingers tucked lovingly around pints or – in the case of the females in his audience – gins and tonic or bloody marys, was what gave Brian a huge lift. Never failed to get a huge round of applause that one.

Now here he was doing something similar a mere twenty seven years further down the road; this time, though, just about 2,000 miles South East of Bath. The bar in Lindos where he'd managed to persuade Tsambiko the owner to let him do his set once or twice a week was going from strength to strength and his original two nights had extended to four. Cash in the back pocket. Life was good. He even managed to slot in one or two of his own songs occasionally. To be honest though, it did rattle him when some bright spark of a tourist asked if one of his own songs was a pared-down version of something by Guns and Roses. He'd be too embarrassed to tell them the truth. Whether that was embarrassment for himself or for the ignorant tourist with a half consumed glass of draft Mythos in his hand he was never sure.

Never mind, the Euros, which he tucked into his faded army fatigue shorts at around 3.00am several times a week, more than compensated for the odd irritation. Some Greek bloke whom he'd met through a mutual friend and who had a recording studio up in Rhodes town had promised him when he'd been living up there that he'd get him in for a session some time next winter so he could record a CD and flog it to the tourists at the bar while he took his intermission each night. Must ring Kosta and find out when that's going to happen. Tomorrow, I'll do it tomorrow.

Brian re-inserted the iPod earpiece just in time for the Bellamy Brothers' *"Let Your Love Flow"* to begin. He usually had the MP3 player set to shuffle. He liked to think it was like listening to a really good rock station on the radio. He even did the DJ comments in his brain during the brief gaps between songs, talking subliminally over the intro of the newly-started track before the vocals began, assuming that it was a vocal track that is. "Now here's a fab golden oldie from probably the best summer the UK has ever known, the Bellamy Brothers with *"Let Your Love Flow!"* He had to be brief with this one, the vocals come in quite early, just a couple of power chords and zap, a Bellamy brother comes in with *"There's a reason for the sun-shiny sky…"*

Music can do incredible things with the senses. As soon as the song began, in fact within the first thirty seconds, Brian's brain was back there in Porky's Bar in Bath. He was behind the bar with Christine, who worked with him for a couple of years, starting with that incredibly long hot summer of perpetually blue skies and high temperatures.

Christine was only sixteen, but she looked older. Born in 1950, Brian was ten years her senior and had developed a kind of fatherly protective thing for her. He'd much rather have developed an intense relationship to match the temperatures that the weather was creating, but it seems she never saw him in that light. Perhaps to a sixteen-year old a twenty-six year old looks ancient. Whatever, it never happened and he always took pains to try not to let her see what he really felt. He was perpetually being wrung out emotionally that summer owing to Christine's screwed-up life. Born in 1960 to a single mum at the buffer end of the social strata, she'd already had a son, George, earlier that year and her mum was George's surrogate carer. He probably thought his grandmother was his actual mother, the amount of time he was in her care. Christine's mum lived off the state and had no intention of changing things. Christine was very intelligent. She read Jean Paul Sartre and stuff, but her disadvantaged background, perhaps her mother's way of raising her, thought Brian, had made her a vulnerable person who was always being taken advantage of. She wanted to do something more with her life, but so far working as an under-age barmaid was the peak of her career possibilities. Not a great CV, it had to be said.

What really pained Brian was seeing her going off at the end of the evening so frequently with some bloke or other. He knew what they were after and he also knew that Christine's lack of self-worth meant that they'd probably get it. It was as though she thought that she had to keep doing penance simply for being who she was. If only Brian could get her alone over a coffee some day and give her an impromptu amateur session of therapy. Perhaps he could help her get her life on to some sort of more noble, more satisfying track. If she'd just look at him with something resembling affection, he just knew he could make her happy and give her a better prospect in life.

Give her a better prospect? Who was he kidding? Brian Worth, now there's a joke in itself. What a surname. Here he was at twenty-six washing glasses and playing guitar in the corner of a pub, whilst his years for getting noticed by some A&R man slipped through his fingers. Here was Brian Worth thinking he could give this poor, beautiful waif of a girl a better life. Quite how many different partners he saw her going off down that be-darkened Bath backstreet with on those torrid evenings he shuddered to think. He worried with some good reason that maybe she'd catch something. Poor Brian, to be standing next to someone so precious and see her being treated like something you throw away, which is exactly what these men did with her, once they'd had a bit of fun.

"Just let your love fly like a bird on the wing
And let your love bind you to all living things
And let your love shine
And you'll know what I mean, that's the reason…"

The song faded and he realised that he'd not really heard it. He'd been back there in Bath all those years ago and he now sat up with a start and tore out the earphones. He realised that he was feeling very hot and unsettled and it wasn't due to the Greek summer heat.

4. Alyson – Lindos, January 8th 2007

It's such a tranquil place. Before last summer I loved being out here. Now? Well, now I suppose I still do love it, but I hate it too. How can it all have ended up revolving around old Kleoboulos' final resting place?

Resting place. At least you can call it that in your case Kleo. Can I call you Kleo? Good. How are you today? With all this sunshine, even in winter, you must be well pleased with your resting place. If only everyone could find rest like you my friend. If only.

5. Christine – Bath, summer 1976

There are worse places to work. I'm not going to stay a barmaid forever. That's about the size of it. My life-plan: to not remain a barmaid forever. All the "T"s crossed and "i"s dotted, …not. Still, at least I do have work and me mum looks after baby George.

George, my baby. He's only five months old and I love him so much it hurts deep inside me, yet I wish I'd never been dopey enough to have him. His father? Just some stupid lawnmower salesman from the London Road who I was daft enough to let slip me a few quid for the privilege. I didn't go any further down that route though, oh no. I'm not going to live my life with people saying things like, "She's on the game," oh no. I do have some pride. Though where it's hidden at the present is a well-kept secret, even from me. But I'm sure going to find it, dust it off and show off a bit of it again some day soon. I've promised myself that, at least.

I don't know where I'd be without Brian to look out for me. Such a nice guy and so much like the father I never had. I don't know exactly how old he is, but he must be thirty-odd I'd say. What a guitarist. He's wasted playing in Porky's and that's for sure. I'd so love to see him get a recording contract and become famous. I know one thing, there are plenty of less-talented guys out there who are on the telly all the time who don't have anything like Brian's talent. When he plays it's like an orchestra in the room, not just one man and six strings. How he does it I'll never know. I mean, the only thing I can play is the fool, usually with some stranger who I'm never going to see again.

Please don't judge me too harshly. I really would like to meet Mr. Right. OK, so I knew that Jake Carey wasn't him, I don't see myself welcoming home to domestic bliss every night someone who's going to tell me all about why a Qualcast is better than an Atco, or the other way around, whatever. It's not me. I want someone who thinks, someone who uses his brain. Someone like Brian, but he doesn't seem to see me in that way. Probably sees me as a stupid child. Such a shame. I think an older man would be good for me. Give me a steadying influence. Still, no good daydreaming. It isn't going to happen any time soon, more's the pity. Brian talks about such interesting things. I think all musicians must be thinkers. I mean, they're creative aren't they. They're passionate about ideas and all that stuff. It was Brian who first gave me *Nausea*. What a book. It made so much sense, yet it also made me a defeatist. There's really no hope if you listen to old Jean Paul. Just throw up at the pointlessness of it all and then go and top yourself. Still, at least he's not subjective. He doesn't swallow all the propaganda we get rammed down us by the Church and school that so many seem to accept as a framework for life.

I'm sixteen years old and I'm staring at a brick wall. Oh yes, there have been one or two men who come into the bar after work and look like decent types. Trouble is, the best ones are usually married, or in a long-term relationship. I don't want to steal someone else's fella. What would that do for my prospects? If he's going to cheat on the one he's with now, what will he do with me if another girl flutters her eyelashes at him when I'm not around? There I'll be, one baby at my breast, another tugging at my skirt while I stand in the kitchen stirring my husband's dinner and there he'll be chatting up the girl I used to be just a few years earlier. No, I couldn't cope with that.

So, where do I stand? At least I've got a council house, well, maisonette actually. It's up three flights of stairs on the edge of town and I only got it because I have George and the bloke from the council helped me out because I was willing to do him a favour, ...or two. Haven't seem him in a while either, but at least I have a nice view out over a lawn and there's only New King Street between me and the city centre. I don't need a car. Not that I could afford one anyway and I'm still not even old enough to drive one legally.

What time is it? Curses!! I need to get ready for work. Got to drop George off at mum's on the way so I'll have to get moving.

Still, at least it's a great summer. I've never been there, but it almost feels like I live somewhere like Greece, the weather is that good this year. Maybe some day, yea? I can dream.

6. Brian – Lindos, Greece – 2005

It's twenty-seven years since I worked at Porky's Bar in Bath, just around the corner from The Hatchets pub, which, if I remember correctly, was on the corner of Queen Street, just across the junction from the Salamander. Twenty-seven years is a long time, but I don't feel any older. I'm fifty-five now and still hoping to "make it". I know, sad isn't it? But I shouldn't complain because here I am living on a Greek island, albeit without much to my name materially, but what does a bloke on his own really need? How may things have turned out if I had managed to get together with Christine? No good crying, the milk was spilt too many years ago.

But here's the odd thing. If I remember correctly, and it is all a bit of a blur I have to admit, the last time I saw Christine was in January of 1978, when I left Porky's to go to London and try to get some recognition playing in pubs and on street corners in "the smoke". Someone was bound to spot me and say, "You know son, you have something really special. Come into my office, have a cigar, you're gonna go far."

Which reminds me. Ages ago, a couple of years in fact, Kostas told me that he'd fix it for me to record some tracks in his mate's studio when I lived in Rhodes Town. Must ring him about that, maybe tomorrow.

No, see, here's the strange thing that happened last night. From my calculations, Christine would be about forty-five now, 'cause I'm quite sure that she told me she was born in 1960, which would make her ten years younger than me. So here I was playing some mellow songs in the bar last night when in walks this girl who made me go hot and cold all over, all at the same time. If I didn't know better I'd have sworn that it was Christine. Now, logic tells me that it couldn't have been her, because this gorgeous raven-haired beauty in a white cotton top and very skimpy shorts, revealing legs that went on forever (not that I really noticed, honest!), came in with a couple of people and looked only about twenty five or thereabouts.

At first I thought that she must have had a picture in the attic.

But then reason took over and I thought: no. It's just a coincidence. But all the time that she remained in that bar I couldn't take my eyes off her. I hope she didn't notice, but she probably couldn't fail to have. It's not just that she was the image of Christine Wright, it's more the fact that as she laughed and played with her hair, as she smiled in such a familiar way, as she sipped her drink through a straw, she did all those things exactly as Christine used to. Am I losing it? Is all this sunshine finally doing my head in? Maybe I'm becoming delusional. Perhaps I'm cursed to have Christine as my "muse" forever. If I'm brutally honest I haven't passed a day since 1978 without thinking about that girl. What became of her? Where did she go? Did she finally meet her Mr. Right? Perhaps she went off to tour the world and write poetry or something.

Not that I believe in all that stuff, but what if she were the daughter of Kleoboulos back among the living after two and a half millenniums. Old Kleoboulos did have a daughter, I've read about her. Her name was Cleobulina and she apparently became quite famous as a poet in ancient Greece, composing riddles as well. Her dad, apart from ruling the village of Lindos for a few decades during the sixth century BC, was also a bit of a poet, apparently. He even became famed as one of the "Seven Sages" of 6th Century BC Greece. It seems he also travelled extensively and studied Egyptian philosophy. I wonder if there was an ancient Egyptian equivalent of Jean Paul Sartre. I used to read him avidly when I was younger. In fact, I think I gave a copy of *Nausea* to Christine as a gift one time. Yes, I did, as far as I can remember.

I had to rub my eyes a few times last night to be sure that I was seeing this girl properly, not just through hopeful or idealistic eyes. I could almost have marched up to her and asked, "How did you get on with *Nausea* then Christine?"

I'm going doollally. I must be. Still, wonder if she'll be in again tonight?

7. Dean and Alyson – Bath, October 1997

"Trust Malcolm to succeed with such a crappy intro as that." Thought Dean as he studied the face of the girl beside him at the table in the trendy backstreet bar.

Indeed, "Want a crisp" had worked, at first to Dean rather annoyingly but, now that he was engaged in conversation with this vision of beauty, who apparently was called Alyson Wright, he'd decided that forgiveness was in order. It already seemed that Dean was with Alyson and that Malcolm was with Nicky. Dean inwardly had drawn a huge sigh of relief, since he'd been drawn to Alyson even when they'd seen them in the street a couple of hours earlier.

Alyson Wright was nineteen and had a generous mane of rich raven hair, which fell to just between her shoulder blades. It was quite thick, beautifully brushed and had an ever-so-slight natural wave to it. Like the sea on a moonless night, Dean thought. Her dress sense could best be described as "nouveau hippy chic," which was perfect for Dean, who felt that dress sense gave away much about what kind of intellect was to be found inside that person's head. She leaned slightly forward, allowing him to take surreptitious glances down to the space where her blouse (Laura Ashley, or perhaps vintage Oxfam, but either way, OK) fell forward from her chest and he was hooked, line and sinker. Alyson's skin was of a kind of perfect Mediterranean Olive tan, making her seem perhaps Spanish, Italian, or Greek. She was none of those as far as *she* knew, but again, it scored her heavily on Dean's scale of one to ten. He found it difficult to follow any of the conversation between the four of them and was relieved when the two couples ended up just conversing one-to-one.

Am I really this lucky? He thought. I can't imagine having found a better looking, brighter, more intelligent girl if I'd manufactured her using weird science, like in that 1980's movie.

"So, tell me all about yourself." He found himself asking her.

"Like, what exactly? That's a very broad brief." She replied.

"Well, for a start, where do you live? Do you have brothers and sisters? What do you make of the cosmos and our place in it? You know, all the usual stuff a guy wants to know about a girl."

"I don't think I'm going to tell you all that stuff about me and my family. I have to retain an element of mystery, now don't I?"

This didn't faze Dean at all. In fact it indicated strongly that she was finding the experience of having met him as positive and exciting as he was, having just met her.

"All right, then. Is there stuff you'd like to know about me? Fire away."

"Music?"

"Music. Like, yes or no, do I play an instrument or what type do I listen to?"

She told him that she'd like him to explain all of the above. So he told her that he was well into guitar music, preferably blues/rock, plus some of the experimental bands like Radiohead. He also liked delving into older prog rock and heavy rock from the seventies, his parents' era. The odd singer-songwriter too, but he told her not to even go there in the field of "manufactured" groups like the Spice Girls. "I get so annoyed" he told her, "when they call these groups of girls or boys who all take it in turns to sing their little bit to kind of justify their being there a 'band'. No way are such pathetic groups 'bands', a 'band' plays instruments, they don't just stand around trying to look mean whilst waiting for their line."

He was in danger of going off on a rant at this stage, but, amazingly, she told him that they had a meeting of minds on the subject and that her favourite album of the time was The Verve's "Urban Hymns." They both talked on about the tragic death of Princess Diana, the two of them agreeing that it was very fishy, since the British Crown was in danger of getting a Moslem man as a step dad to the two heirs to the throne, William and Harry.

At well after midnight, having dropped Malcolm and Nicky off at her place, Dean pulled up at the non-descript corner in Twerton to which Alyson had directed him, not the most upmarket area of the city of Bath, and asked if he could take Alyson right to her front door. Alyson made excuses, insisted that she could walk the last couple of hundred metres and gave Dean his first downer since the moment they'd met. She did allow him to kiss her, and not just a quick peck either and then, having promised that she'd meet him the following evening in town, she got out of the car and strode off into the sodium lit street of council houses.

Dean sat in the car, engine quietly ticking over, and wondered. Was that a rebuff? "No, you can't take me home or I'd have to refuse if you asked to come in." But then, if that was so, then why the lingering kiss which smouldered with positivity?

He put the car into gear, tilted the arm on the steering column to indicate and pulled slowly away to make the drive home to his parents' house. Tomorrow would be Sunday and she'd agreed to meet him at eight outside the Empire Hotel. That surely was the best thought to hold for what was now considerably less that twenty-four hours. Then he'd see if he could wheedle a little more out of her about where she lived and what kind of family she came from.

Next morning, Dean entered the huge kitchen to see his mother, standing at the "island" over which was suspended a vast array of utensils on a huge stainless steel rack, preparing scrambled eggs on toast. She knew he always applied lashings of tomato ketchup and so slid a full plate towards him with one hand whilst plonking the ketchup bottle in front of him with the other. Heinz, of course.

Julia Waters was born Julia Abrahams in 1954 and, at forty-three, was still a stunning woman. Exactly the same shape as she'd been when she and Francis, her husband of twenty-three years, had met, she still attracted whistles and the blowing of vehicle horns from passing male motorists when she jogged the country lanes around their Limpley Stoke residence, which she did almost daily.

"Coffee son?" She asked. Knowing what his response would be, she picked up the glass coffee jug from the coffee-machine's hot plate and poured some freshly brewed Douwe Egbert into a "Best Dad in the World" mug. "So, are you going to tell me about her then?"

With a mouthful of scrambled egg, toast and a slurp of black coffee, he replied "vers nh mash tmmph ell." Swallowing the contents of his mouth, he repeated, "There's not much to tell, really. I'm not sure how much I know about her."

"You know you really should practice the art of showing interest in the other person, Dean. Nobody likes someone who rattles on about themselves all the time you know."

"Mum. Don't pass judgment before the jury's heard all the evidence. I tried, I really did. But she had a way of turning the conversation around so that I didn't get many of the answers that I'd have liked. I tell you what, though. It may sound a bit twee or trite, but there really is something about this girl. I can't remember feeling this weird about any girlfriend before."

"Aah, young love. So, have you set a date yet?"

"Ha ha, bloody ha. You'll see. She's got something this girl. You won't believe how much we've got in common."

"Aha! So you did get something out of her then."

"Yes, s'pose I did. I at least know that our musical tastes coincide really well. Dad about, is he?"

"A more observant son would have noticed the lack of golf clubs in the hall when he came down the stairs."

"Aimi in bed, is she?" Here referring to his younger sister, who was born in 1981, thus she was just sixteen and therefore obnoxiously precocious. She'd come along a little later than Francis and Julia would have liked, but at least they managed to produce her in the end, thus achieving the "one of each" which they'd planned on having.

"Staying at Penny's up at St. Catherine's for the weekend. Not that you'd have noticed of course.

"Dean. I do hope that this girl's got a good pedigree, for your sake. You know how your father is about the kind of girl he wants you to end up with."

"Only too well mother, only too well. But Dad's still to learn that, oddly enough, I'm living *my* life not his. Neither is *he* living my life. I've never met anyone so stuck in the past when it comes to 'class and breeding' as my flipping father. I've got my degree, I've got a new job to start the week after next and I'll be doing what I wanted to do. He ought to be proud of me."

Francis Waters was a snob, pure and simple, though he had no right to be, having come himself from very humble beginnings. But, having also worked his way to the top as an independent financial advisor to some very rich and very famous clients, helping them to avoid tax, *"not evade it"* he'd always quip, but avoid legitimately paying the government too much of their hard earned cash, he felt the need to mix in genteel circles. For this reason alone he encouraged his wife to own a couple of horses and liked to boast about the time that they'd taken tea at Highgrove. When sounding off about the occasion, he'd always omit the fact that this was owing to his tenuous link to an entire cricket team who'd been invited to dine with HRH after having enjoyed a particularly successful season. Only once during the entire evening had he stood face to face with the Prince, and that was when they were all being introduced on their arrival at the estate.

Even Dean didn't know at this point quite how different were their circumstances from those of Alyson Wright.

At eight o'clock sharp Dean was standing in front of the old Empire Hotel, in Orange Grove and staring eagerly in all directions for Alyson's approach. So it made him almost jump out of his skin when she tapped him on his shoulder, having made her approach by walking around Grand Parade from Pulteney Bridge. Turning to take a look at his prize he was stunned to see she was wearing sneakers, a pair of tight jeans and a figure-hugging woollen sweater, which dropped off of one of her shoulders. No bra strap was in evidence. This is the kind of thing a bloke notices. Not that it necessarily proved anything about the underwear situation, bit it excited him nevertheless. For an October evening it was pleasingly warm, so her coat was draped over one of her arms.

"So, where do you want to go then?" He asked, trying to contain his elation.

"How about The Huntsman? It's only just around the corner from here. Not sure if we'll catch anything live tonight though, but never mind. We can just talk."

"The Huntsman it is." So off they set and she slipped an arm through the crook of his elbow, like they were already an old-established couple.

"If you don't mind my saying so, you talk a bit posh. Does your family have money?" Alyson asked, once a gin and tonic had been placed before her and Dean slid into his place beside her with his pint of real ale.

"Nothing like going for the jugular eh?" Seeing her expression turn to one of dismay, he quickly continued, "It's OK. Just joking. Actually my dad's family were very working class, but my dad was a social climber right from day one and he always pressed onward and upward. He's very ambitious and likes to flash his wallet around now he's what he likes to call himself, a 'self-made man'. A 'driven man' is what I'd call him. He's hardly ever at home, often working late on weekdays and usually on the golf course for most of the day on Saturdays. He does try to spend some time with my mother on Sundays, when they'll usually go out for lunch to some swanky restaurant way out in the sticks somewhere. That's mainly so that he can drive really slowly into the car park, making sure that anyone around gets a good eyeful of his Jag XK8."

"If you're trying to intimidate me, you're doing a really good job." Alyson was now having serious doubts that this relationship would ever work out.

"Alyson, I'm doing nothing of the kind. I don't like my father's morals and, although I do confess to loving him as my dad, we don't see eye to eye on very much at all. I believe that intellect is always a much better measure of a person than the thickness of one's wallet. Someone who cares about the important issues is a far more valuable member of society than the bloke who flaunts his Callaway gear on the fairway."

"But then, you do have the luxury of being able to say that while enjoying a measure of financial security which, I'd imagine, most of us only dream about." She was worrying Dean now. He had to make her see, had to put her at her ease somehow.

"Look, Alyson," he took hold of both of her hands, "I would gladly give up everything that my dad ever could or would give me, if it was a choice between that and a girl I'd fallen in love with and wanted to spend the rest of my days with. You may not believe that now, but stick around. Plus, if we're going to give each other a try, and I desperately hope that we are," he was now staring straight into her deep brown eyes, "we're going to have to be honest with each other. BOTH of us. Understand?" She nodded, ashamed that she'd doubted his sincerity.

"So," Dean continued, "tell me about YOU."

She looked at him, eyes searching for something to tell her whether it was going to be worth the frankness. If she told him about her mother and how she had no idea who her actual father was, the fact that a succession of "uncles" had been around while she was growing up, would he bolt like a hound out of the traps? Surely his family would never accept her. A gold-digger would be what they'd brand her, not to mention a few choicer words too no doubt. Why are people so judgmental? Why do so many people make decisions about others based on a wrong premise so often?

The expression "like mother like daughter" was continually bouncing around in her head. By the time her mother was her age she already had George, Alyson's older brother by two years. George was a slightly different colour from Alyson and then there were her two younger sisters, born in 1980 and 1983 respectively, Shirley and Gemma, the latter of whom was always being called "black" because the dominant gene in her cells was most definitely from her father, who'd been a West Indian. He'd gone the way of the others though and her mother's current partner was number who-knows-what? Nice bloke though he was. Christine Wright never seemed to keep hold of a man for long. They'd always leave their calling card though, another sibling for George and Alyson it seemed.

Despite all this, she dearly loved her mother and her three siblings. Once you've been brought into this world, you're a person with the same feelings, rights, and aspirations as all the rest. You're not to blame for the route you took in order to get here, or rather the route your biological parents took which produced you as the after-effect.

What, though, would Dean think if he actually saw her mother's house? At least her mother now lived in a house. It was better, but only just, than the maisonette she'd moved out of when Alyson's second sister was born. But it had no front fence, that having rotted long since and all that remained were a few decaying pieces of wood with dangerous rusty nails protruding from them, as a pair of bookends to the front end of the "garden", which was more mud than grass, covered as it was too with all kinds of detritus from the road. Plastic wrappings, old cigarette packets, drink cans and paper bags all graced the area which in another time was intended to be a garden. The cracked concrete path leading from the pavement to the front door was uneven enough in places to sprain someone's ankle if they approached the front door during the hours of darkness. Old mould-ridden window frames, which now retained precious little of the paint that once covered them, added to the sense of despair which the property exuded.

Of her three siblings, George, Shirley and Gemma, only Gemma still lived at home with her mum. She was still only fourteen and at school. She smoked, not only tobacco but a few other substances too, and had several earrings already decorating each ear, around the top parts that is, not the lobes.

At least her mother, Christine, still retained her looks and figure, although how she did this was a complete mystery to Alyson. On the rare occasions when they actually went anywhere together, they still could be mistaken for sisters, since Christine had been only eighteen when she'd given birth to her first daughter and their hair and features were strikingly similar. For all the fact that her home rather stereotypically represented the "lower under-privileged class" in the

UK's strata of society, Christine was very intelligent and, but for the way her own mother had lived and raised her, she could have been something quite different. She could have lived a very different life from the one that she'd been stuck in for so many years now.

Alyson was her mother's favourite, although Christine often told herself off for even having one. She truly did love all the children, but perhaps because Alyson was so much like her clone, they had an affinity that the others were never privileged to develop with their mother. They saw eye to eye about almost everything. Why, Alyson even liked all of her mother's favourite music and Christine almost always approved of the bands and artists that her daughter introduced to her as well. Christine had been raised with Pink Floyd, Led Zeppelin, the Who, Deep Purple and Jethro Tull. She also had virtually every album ever recorded by John Martyn. Alyson would borrow her mother's CDs perpetually, as she would her books too. Alyson was into Tori Amos, Morrisey and Blur. She liked the Cranberries and the Beautiful South. When she would put one of these artists into the CD player her mum would enthuse and the two of them would either sit cerebrally and listen with respect, or perhaps dance around the kitchen table with wooden spoons or hairbrushes for microphones.

These girls got on like a house on fire. Christine had an aversion to all established religion. Yet she retained a deep conviction that there was a creator up there somewhere. She just didn't know quite where, but hoped to find out before it was too late. She used to say that God was the great employer and that all the churches were like bogus reps, all selling their wares on his patch and sullying his reputation with inferior products. Sooner or later a company MD worth his salt would take measures to get rid of such counterfeit pests and Christine seemed to remember a Jehovah's Witness or someone who came to her door once and told her that this was going to happen one day. "Roll on: she'd say, "roll on."

She read philosophy and Freud. She was particularly proud of the fact that she had a copy of his work *"The Psychopathology of Everyday Life"*, which he'd produced in 1901 or thereabouts. Alyson would take paperbacks from her mother's shelves and devour them. Her mother had first started her off down that route by giving her the Penguin edition of Jean Paul Sartre's *Nausea*. She had read it several times and carried it around in her bag everywhere she went. When Christine had first handed it to her, on a kind of "permanent loan" basis, Alyson had been intrigued by the message scrawled across the title page, which read:

To my little "spiritual daughter" Chris. I hope this won't depress you too much, but it certainly opened my eyes!"

Love you – do you hear?

B.

"Who's this 'B' then mum? An old boyfriend maybe?"

"No," her mother had replied, "Though if I'd had my way he would have been. Brian was a bloke I used to work with in Porky's Bar. He left not long before you were born. I was pregnant with you when I last saw him. I've never seen him since. So it would have been about January of 1978, 'cause you popped out in August."

"Right, so there's a chance that he may be my father then?"

"No, absolutely not. I told you, I never had a relationship like that with Brian. He was much older than me. He went off to London to seek his fame and fortune. He was a very good musician. He used to play in the corner of the bar some nights. I suppose he never actually found what he went off looking for, or else I'd have seen him on 'The Old Grey Whistle Test', but I never did. I've told you sweetie, I don't really know who your father was. It's not a time of my life that I'm very proud of."

This was the only aspect of her mother that really frustrated Alyson. She could not believe that her mother wouldn't remember whom she'd slept with about nine months before she'd given birth. After the age of about nine, she'd begun to be consumed with curiosity and a desire to find out and meet this man face to face. Her mother always stonewalled her interrogation, so she couldn't make any progress. It would be good to find this Brian fellow, but what were the chances of that happening?

In the Huntsman's lounge bar, she stared Dean out, decided to trust him to a certain degree and started to talk. "I'm afraid that you and I are a bit like Romeo and Juliet, Dean. Our families may not be feuding yet, but once your parents find out where I'm from they'll declare war. I just know it. Trust me to find a fella I actually do want to go out with, only to find that he's so far above me in our so-called 'classless society' that it'd be a miracle if we ever made a go of it. Perhaps I should go."

Dean's hand once again shot out and covered Alyson's. "Look," he said, "I'm starting a new job the week after next. I told you last night that I'd just completed my Ba Hons in Graphic Design and, contrary to the prophecy of one of the lecturers at college, I got through an interview at Street's, the out-of-town chain in South Wales. I'm going to be working in a studio for the first time and I'll be moving to Cardiff." Dean saw the look of alarm that registered in the face of this vulnerable, sweet girl whom he was so taken with, so he quickly continued:

"No, don't get me wrong. What I'm saying is, stuff my dad and all his class-based hang-ups. I have a job. I have a salary. Well, I will have at the end of next month. Alyson, I can stand on my own two feet.

I've got a small pad sorted out in Roath and what I'd really like is for you to come with me."

Now her expression changed to one of shock.

"I'm sorry." He said, "I suppose I am being rather too forward now, I've only known you for just under twenty-four hours and yet the thought of moving to the other side of the Severn Bridge and leaving you behind is unbearable. What about if we made a deal to share the flat? You told me you were a hairdresser right? Well that ought to mean you'd soon get some work in South Wales, even if you advertised in a newsagent as a home-visit hairdresser, right?"

Tears welled up in her eyes as she fought with her feelings. Wouldn't this be crazy? Wouldn't it be fraught with perils? Wouldn't her mum disapprove? They hardly knew eachother and yet she had to admit that she felt this affinity with him too. Something she hadn't felt before. She may be young, but she'd had quite a few boyfriends. This relationship definitely had something that the others had lacked. But was it enough to take this kind of plunge for?

There was only one way to find out.

Part Two

Fading Fast

1. Cardiff, South Wales – June 1998

Dean was pleased with how well the job was going. OK, so it was a journey of more than ten miles outside the city to the office each day and the pay wasn't brilliant, but it was a job and it was a Graphic Design job. The fact was, he was happy with it. He got to design press advertisements, corporate themes for new campaigns, logos for the new departments which were regularly opening up in the branches of the store. He had the feeling that the Marketing Director, to whom he answered, was pleased with him too.

Exciting too was the new iMac which had been purchased for the studio. The days of the parallel motion on the huge drawing board, the age of Cow Gum and typesetting agencies, of paste-up and overlays, were all drawing to their close and Dean's employers were sensible enough to understand this. Soon the darkroom would be dismantled and the production of "bromides" would be something to be consigned to a museum of the history of graphic art. Of course they'd had Macs for a few years, since well before Dean had come to work there, but the iMac was a new and funky update that everyone wanted to get their hands on. He may too have had visions of moving on one day; even of opening his own office and calling it *D. W. Design* or something even more imaginative, but for the present he was happy with how his professional life was going.

His private life was something else.

"When are you going to tell your father about me. Dean?" Was a question that Alyson put to him more and more often. The more she raised the issue, the more ratty Dean would become in response. He knew it was unfair to Alyson, but his own cowardice got to him and so he'd lash back at her to cover for the fact.

On a Saturday morning in June 1998, over muesli and yogurt accompanied by peppermint tea, she raised her eyes from the Daily Mail and looked across the breakfast table at Dean.

"Dean?"

"Yes love?"

"I'm going away for a while."

"OK. See you later then." His eyes didn't lift from the current issue of Q magazine, which he was perusing.

"You're NOT listening. I said, I'm going AWAY for a while. I didn't say 'I'm going OUT for a while."

This time his eyes did leave the page and looked across at Alyson from behind the glossy magazine cover. He studied her for a moment. Trying to focus on quite what she'd said. He responded: "You're doing what? Why? What do you mean 'away'? Away where? What's brought this on?"

"Dean," she said, tenderness evident in the way she spoke his name, but tinged also with desperation, "I have to take some time to think and you have to be forced to confront your dad. If we go on like this I'll get to hate you and you'll resent me. You HAVE to tell him about us. He still thinks you live here alone doesn't he?"

"NO! Well, yes. But I am going to tell him. I just need the right moment. Trust me on this Allie."

"Trust you? Dean, ever heard the expression *'cry wolf'*? Trust ebbs away in situations like these. If going to Greece is what it needs to make you confront your own fears then so be it."

"You're going to GREECE? What ... *THE* Greece? The country? I don't believe it. I know you're upset but, tell you what, I'll ring him today, how's that? OK? I'll leave it until he gets in from his precious round of golf this evening and..."

"Dean, Dean, you know that's hot air. Take some time to plan it, but start now. I've already booked. I'm flying out from Cardiff Airport next Wednesday. I'm going to Kefallonia."

"You CAN'T BE. WHO WITH? HOW DID YOU BOOK IT?"

"It's not that hard, love. I just went into the travel agent round the corner in Wellfield Road. This *IS* 1998 you know, unless you hadn't noticed." Before he could protest further, she raised a finger as if to say: "Hold on" and she continued: "I've booked a holiday in Argostolo-something, the island's capital. I'm going to do some thinking. I'm going alone Dean, OK? ALONE. I don't want anyone else Dean. I want you. But I don't want you any more in these circumstances."

"But, what about the money? How will you manage?"

"My hairdressing business has been going really well. I do try and tell you about it, but you're not the world's best listener, love. I've been putting some money away for several months and I have more than enough to get me to Greece for a couple of weeks and to enjoy my stay whilst there."

The reality now seeping into Dean's brain, he thought for a moment. "Can I ask why Greece? I mean, why not go back to Bath, Bristol, bloody Burnham on Sea for goodness' sake. But GREECE? That's a long way away. What if something happens to you?"

"What you mean is, what if I meet someone? Don't worry, darling, I'm not in the market. If it'll help, look," she lifted her left hand to reveal a gold band on the third finger, "So, we're not married, but no one else needs to know that do they? I'll wear it all the time. I don't need someone else Dean. I've already told you. I need you, but not on these terms.

"The reason I chose Greece is simple. My mum always told me about the hot summer of 1976, two years before I was born. She used to say that it at least gave her the chance to dream that she was in Greece. She always said 'Greece' because she'd read or heard about all the islands, the food, the special kind of light, the music and the culture, the presence around every corner of ancient history rubbing shoulders with modern life. Greece seemed to her to represent something to aim for. 'One day', she'd say, 'one day I'm going to go there. I'm going to walk in the land of the Gods and drink Ouzo or Retsina and watch the sun set over a turquoise sea.' She may have been a dreamer, but it gave me the same dream and I decided that it would be the perfect place for me to think about my life ...our life, and what was going to become of it, of US, Dean. Do try and understand."

The reality now having well and truly sunk in, Dean Waters stared at the girl he'd come to love as deeply as his own soul - and then a little more - and tears welled up in his eyes. He loved her even more for the things she'd just said. How easy it had been for him during all those years while he was growing up. Why, he hadn't even told her yet about the island cruise as part of a flotilla of yachts that his family had taken when he was younger. He was even ashamed now to tell her that they'd stayed a night in Fiskardo, the village right at the northernmost tip of the island of Kefallonia, the very island that his beloved muse was now about to visit, without him. Greece was somewhere you *can* go for a holiday for people like Dean.

For people like Alyson and her mother Christine, it was an ideal to be aimed for, only possibly to be grasped, not even a certainty. Greece, the land of the Gods, the land of dreams, the land of sunshine and souvlaki, of dance and daybreaks with a backdrop of an impossibly blue sea, all things of which he'd taken for granted. Although he felt a deep pain under his ribcage at the thought of Alyson being away from him for the first time in more than six months, he understood. He had been selfish and negligent. Now it was payback time. He either faced his responsibility or he would lose the one woman he'd loved so deeply he couldn't envisage what his life would be from now on if that were to happen. It was too terrible to contemplate.

"I can't talk you out of it then?" He said in the tone of one who was already defeated.

"No, love." She replied, "No."

2. Brian, Lindos, Greece – 2005

Ever since that dead ringer for Christine Wright had walked into the Lindos Bar where Brian played four nights a week, he couldn't get the past out of his mind. The visual image of the girl swam around his brain continually. He had no control over things. All those years ago and he'd let Christine go. Why the hell hadn't he asked her to go with him to London?

Now, let's be honest, he told himself. It was the kids. She had baby George, who was only about two, and she was about to have another. It would have taken some special kind of guy to take on two small children which weren't even his own. It would have meant too many mouths to feed for a struggling musician, especially when he may even end up busking to survive in the capital. No, if the truth were to be told he kind of had a plan. He thought that he'd get spotted in a flash by some record label and before long would send a stretch limo all the way down the M4 to Bath to collect Christine and whisk her away to his mansion in Surrey, kids and all.

That was the real reason why he'd lost her. He never made it and so she never heard from him again. It was better for her. At least, that's how he persuaded himself to see things.

But now here was this girl. She was so much like Christine that there *had* to be a connection. There just had to be, despite the gap of twenty-seven years. Tonight he would be playing again. He was going to do a selection of Bob Marley numbers and throw in his version of Pink Floyd's *"A Pillow of Winds"*, maybe do "*Seamus*" again too. He'd also now rehearsed the Bellamy Brothers' song, *"Let Your Love Flow"* to remind him and anyone who was old enough of the year that the UK had experienced a "Greek" summer. Throwing on a tattered pair of shorts and a sleeveless t-shirt, he slipped on his flip-flops and, grabbing his guitar in its case, set off through the narrow maze of whitewashed streets to the bar for the evening. It was 9.00pm and he was due on at around 9.30.

Just in the middle of *"Redemption Song"* he saw her. Sure enough it was the Christine look-alike again. Why didn't he just sidle up and say hello during his intermission? Yet he froze at the thought, partly because he was fifty-five and she probably wasn't yet thirty. Then there was the fact that she wasn't alone. What a prize chump he'd make of himself if he asked if she knew anyone called Christine Wright, from almost thirty years ago, before she was even born no doubt.

So he had to be content to snatch glimpses of her at every opportunity in an attempt to work out what was happening. Perhaps there was some great celestial divine plan at work here. But no, he couldn't persuade himself of such things. Brian always saw red when anyone said, in response to some tragic event in their lives, "everything happens for a reason." Was that dozy or what? They never think things out such people, do they? I mean, if you asked them if they thought that God or someone was up there making cars drive over precipices, killing the people within, so that "everything could happen for a reason" – what hellish reason would that be then? If they answered, as some did when he challenged them about such a way of thinking, that no, they didn't see it as God, but rather as fate, he'd say: So you're attributing some intelligence to this impersonal thing "fate" then. In which case you really mean God anyway.

Oh yes, well, something drops into place in the life of some dope in the UK and quick as a flash they conclude that it happened 'for a reason,' when half of Africa's starving. Evidently God or fate or whatever, isn't too bothered about all those poor sods out there then, eh? Where was the logic in such thinking? There isn't any and, for Brian, logic has to come first. There was simply no logic in this "everything happens for a reason" way of thinking. It's a fool's way of making some sense of things which don't really make sense. Unless you accept, of course, that it's all a big lottery and things just happen because of circumstances, no cause, no "fate" thinking things out, no hand of God messing around in puny human's affairs would make a logical explanation for what simply *happens.*

If there was a God up there, Brian thought, he certainly wasn't going to interfere in some petty way for some British person's benefit, whilst ignoring the millions in Africa who face starvation on a daily basis, or all those living in war zones who risk getting blown to smithereens while they go out for a loaf of bread.

No. Either this girl was Christine's daughter, or she simple bore an uncanny resemblance. It was as simple as that.

Just when Brian was getting his brain settled to accept that she probably was simply Christine's doppelganger, something made him stop playing half way through…

> *"Won't you help me sing these songs of freedom, all I ever…"*
> …then silence.

Everyone in the bar turned to look at the bloke on the stool behind the microphone in the corner. His right hand hovered above the strings and his left hand showed white knuckles where the fingers were trying to bore into the fret board. Beads of sweat broke out and ran down his face and dripped on to the instrument. Suddenly aware of what he'd done, Brian quickly composed himself and said: "Sorry folks, senior moment!!" and continued with the song, although anyone studying his voice would have noticed a slight tremor that hadn't been there just moments before.

What had been the cause of this strange hiatus in the song? Brian's eyes had been fixed on the girl as usual. Whilst he sang she had riffled in her canvas shoulder bag as if to find something whilst listening to her girl companion. In order to extract what turned out to be her mobile phone, which was lit up to reveal the arrival of a text message, she'd brought several items out and placed them on the bar beside her.

One of these was an evidently ancient copy of Jean Paul Sartre's book, *Nausea*.

3. Alyson, Kefallonia, Greece – June 1998

The book *Captain Corelli's Mandolin* was one of the reasons that Alyson was drawn to make the island of Kefallonia her first Greek experience. Other, more practical, reasons included the fact that one could get a package from Cardiff Airport that included a direct flight.

The aeroplane door opened and the passengers began filing out into the stifling temperature of a Greek summer. Late afternoon it may have been, but the thermometer, had she been able to inspect one, would have shown her that it was 37° Celsius. This was Alyson's first ever trip outside of the United Kingdom and a British summer could never have prepared her for these conditions. Not being a very seasoned traveller she'd boarded the plane on a wet, dull June day. It wasn't a good summer, even by British standards. The temperature at Cardiff Airport had been in the low teens and she couldn't remember when they'd last seen a day without rain. So she was well wrapped up and immediately realised that she'd have to peel off several layers or risk heat exhaustion before reaching the terminal building.

By the time she'd waited in the queue to have her passport inspected by a rather surly man with very dark features and an even darker leer, she was already wondering whether this had been such a good idea. None of the other passengers seemed to notice her as she did her best to appear as though she knew what she was doing.

In reality, she had no idea at all what she was doing. She'd concealed from Dean the fact that she'd applied for and received a passport and rather naively thought that the rest would be plain sailing. Now here she was, a girl still approaching her twentieth birthday and she was over fifteen hundred miles from home in a foreign country, where she couldn't even read the signs, let alone speak the language. Not surprisingly, fear crept up on her.

She broke out into a sweat and contemplated asking someone if she could turn around and go back on the plane to the UK. Panic began to fight with her fear and, just when she was about to cry with fright and anxiety, an older woman, who seemed to be also travelling alone, approached and spoke.

"Hello, are you meeting someone? Is someone waiting for you here, love?"

She was probably in her forties, slim, rather lined in the face from too much sun and evidently a "Bohemian" type. She spoke without a discernible accent. Various earrings of differing colours and sizes hung from each lobe. Her hair was mousy, quite curly and cut very short, to the nape of the neck, around which hung several necklaces of varying coloured and sized beads and flouncy multicoloured robes wafted around her in the breeze as they emerged from the terminal to find the transfer to their accommodation. At least Alyson had worked out how to reclaim her baggage. She'd simply followed everyone else.

"No, I'm here on my own. Alyson, and you are?"

"Claire, darling. I hope you don't mind, but you did rather look a little bemused, if not quite apprehensive. I just thought that perhaps you could use a little confidence-inducing assistance."

Alyson contemplated ways of making Claire go away; but then she decided that perhaps this evidently well-travelled and well-educated woman would be more of a help than a hindrance. She let out a sigh,

"You thought right. Bang on in fact. It's my first time abroad."

"Your first time abroad? Oh, heavens darling, and alone too. You – if you'll forgive me here – you can't be long out of your teens, unless you're still in them perhaps?"

"Spot on again. I'll be twenty in a couple of months' time. The kind of life I've lived, I've had to grow up quite fast. Thank you for your concern Claire. I must admit that I was thinking about trying to get back on the plane and fly straight back. All those signs in that strange alphabet. That man who checked my passport, he looked like he'd like to do things to me or throw me in jail – or both. I felt like I didn't have anything on, the way he looked at me. And the heat, I've never experienced anything like it. Now I know what the turkey feels like when it gets shoved into the oven at Christmas!

I supposed it finally dawned on me what I'd done. It seemed such a good idea, the right thing to do, a couple of weeks back when I booked it. Am I really that transparent?"

"Let's just say, hopefully you'll be glad it was me that spotted you before someone a little more unsavoury did darling. Anyway, where are you staying?"

"Marina Rooms, at Argostololo-something or other."

"Well, that's amazing. Marina Rooms, at Argostoli is where I'm staying too. Let's take a look at your paperwork." Alyson stirred a hand around in her bag and extracted the Tour Operator's folder, which she handed to Claire. With the air of someone who'd done this innumerable times, Claire pulled out a folded A4 sheet, opened it and cast her eyes down it.

"Wonderful!! Simply wonderful darling. You're in room 6 and I'm upstairs in 9. We're going to get along swimmingly. Come on, let's find our coach."

The coach pulled away from the parking area at Kefallinia Airport and climbed the gentle hillside, whilst Alyson, Claire beside her, stared out at a new world. Everything about what she saw was new to her. Chain-link fences surrounded groves of olive trees, others of citrus trees bearing the still-green fruit which a few months later would give away the fact that they were oranges, mandarins, lemons, grapefruit and more. She saw houses with their roller shutters half-closed against the fierce afternoon sunshine and cats and dogs asleep in whatever shade they could find. The occasional donkey, tethered to a tree by a rope; goats, here, there and everywhere. There were lizards basking on top of dry-stone walls and huge shrubs and trees bearing a riot of strange blossoms in yellow, white, pink, blue and red. The landscape was predominantly yellow from weeks of rain-less blue skies and dry grasses swayed along the roadside in the hot afternoon breeze. Now and then a little old lady, all in black with a headscarf covering her head, could be seen hobbling slowly along. Motorbikes and scooters whizzed past the coach to the liberal sounding of horns on both parts.

So this was the land of the gods that her mother had always

dreamed of. Now, here was Alyson, finally here, albeit not under the best of circumstances. She still couldn't decide whether she was going to enjoy this experience, to benefit from it, or perhaps regret it. It kind of all depended upon what was going to happen between Dean and his father. Still, at least the advent of Claire was now affording her a measure of confidence. She knew that this woman would look out for her, would share the benefit of her own years of foreign travel with her. She believed that this woman was essentially good and therefore she felt that she could afford herself a mental sigh of relief. Had Claire not spoken to her when she did, who knows how she'd have been feeling now, just an hour or so later.

Following a few other stops to let off the new arrivals at their accommodations, the coach eventually drew up outside Marina Rooms, which were situated along the seafront just ten minutes walk from the main square in Argostoli.

Now, thought Alyson, a new adventure begins.

4. Dean, Cardiff – June 1998

Alone in the flat for the first time in months, Dean felt an emptiness and a sorrow that he'd never previously experienced. Had this girl really got that far under his skin? The simple answer was that, yes, she had. Home from work on the evening that Alyson had left for Greece, he found himself half-sitting, half-laying on the sofa, glass of wine in his left hand, TV remote in his right, just thinking.

The TV wasn't even on. The evening light began to fade and he realised that he'd been lying there for several hours since he'd come home from work. He had had a bad day at the studio too. The 64-page Sale brochure that he'd been working on was suddenly going to be changed. All the departments that featured in the inside pages were going to move around. Some, which had originally been going to occupy a single page, were now going to be doubles; some doubles were to become singles. The copy date was, of course, still the same and he knew that the number of hours required to make a good job of it design-wise were far too many for the actual amount of time remaining before the whole thing needed to go to print. There was no room for leeway on the copy date as there were huge numbers being inserted into one of the local newspapers and the distribution house needed the brochures by a certain time or they'd miss the deadline, end of story. How often this happened. In college there was never a deadline issue. You had all the time in the world to design something, put it together and present it. In the real world there were always last-minute changes. The MD would sometimes not like the design of an advert, or want some essential "white space", which balanced the look of an ad, filled in with a "bomb-blast" declaring some tacky, deceptive offer. Already, too, Dean was having to correct the English of much of the work done by his colleague Huw, whose first language was Welsh and thus he couldn't even get some pretty fundamental English words spelt right. Huw would do all the large Point-of-Sale and signs. Just last week, Huw had produced artwork for a huge banner to be erected at the entrance to the Hotel, Leisure and Golf complex that the company owned. It was to publicise an upcoming sponsored "Ladies' Day" at the Golf Club. Dean had been asked to drive up to the club to see someone about a brief. As he'd driven into the impressive front gates of the entire complex, he'd almost cried when he saw two men erecting the hoarding. On it was emblazoned in huge vinyl lettering, white out of navy blue: "LADY'S DAY".

What brought his thoughts back to the problem at hand was the fact that the ladies' day in question was being sponsored by the local Jaguar dealer. His father had owned Jaguars for as long as Dean could remember.

Francis James Waters had been born in 1950 to poor parents. He'd been one of seven children and the first job he could remember his father doing was a potato round. It was just his luck that his quick brain had meant that he passed his eleven-plus with flying colours and so had been sent to the City of Bath Boys' School. A few years after he left to go to college, the school was amalgamated with a "secondary modern" to become one of the new 'comprehensives'. But in his day the City of Bath was a Grammar school.

It hadn't taken him long to become aware that most of the boys with whom he was sharing a classroom were from private homes and considerably better off that Francis. The school was a rugby-playing school, in keeping with the long traditional association that the city of Bath itself had with the sport of Rugby Union. In fact, the official Bath Rugby Club was founded back in 1865 and was regarded as one of the oldest and most successful clubs in the UK. Thus, the grammar school was a rugby school. This didn't help Francis because he was a beanpole. He'd always grown upward rather than outward as a child and was six feet tall and less than 140 pounds in weight when he was fourteen years old. The result was that he was always playing on the wing during school "games" and was usually the only boy to return to the changing rooms without a spot of mud on his kit after an hour and a half on the pitch.

Other boys had fathers who ran their own businesses; some were sons of doctors, others of lawyers. Francis was beaten up more times than he can remember and was mortally afraid of any conversation turning to what the boys' fathers did for a living. By the time he'd reached the fifth form he'd learned how to keep out of trouble and had made one or two friendships with boys of like mind, like his friend Geoff, who's father ran his own tyre business. Geoff, however, was a down-to-earth lad and saw this as a pretty working class occupation, even though his dad had a Rover and they'd go water skiing every summer in Scotland, where the family had a cottage way up near Thurso. In all these things were the makings of a boy with a burning ambition.

Francis Waters was going to BE somebody. Francis Waters was going to have the last laugh. He was good at mathematics at school and his English grades were pretty good too. The arts were a total mystery to him and he failed to see how anyone could expect to earn a decent living out of painting pictures or carving clay and stuff. No, you had to know how to earn cash and, what's more important still, how to manage the cash that you earned.

After a spell as an encyclopaedia salesman on British military camps in Germany, where he spent two years after college and was consistently top salesman in the team, he returned to embark on an accountancy course. Geoff would still see him now and again and, in the Crown and Anchor in Upper Weston over a pint one night when they were both about a third of the way through their third decade of life, Francis explained the tricks of the trade to his friend.

"See, it's all about exerting pressure without the punter realising that you're exerting pressure." He told Geoff. "There's nothing like saying absolutely nothing to put the screws on. After you've spent half an hour explaining why this particular little family needs this 14 volume set of encyclopaedias at a ridiculously expensive price, you then tell them how little per day it's going to cost, plus how they couldn't afford not to give their children this essential advantage in life in this cutthroat world. Then you place the contract in front of them, offer them your pen and say: 'Would you be kind enough to tick the box there that says that no high pressure sales tactics have been used in persuading you to buy', then you sit in total silence and watch them sweat. Works every time. OK, not every time, but most times!

"I've sat with some dopes who've taken several minutes, looking first at the document that's going to make paupers of them, then at me, while I smiled and kept schtum all the time. Then, looking at their wives, they've both nodded at eachother and signed away a fortune and put a decent sum into my bank account in the process. I tell you, Geoff, it was a blast!!"

In April of 1974 Francis married Julia, the most beautiful girl he'd ever seen. Had she not been it wouldn't have made a great deal of difference. Her father kept racehorses. She had all the right connections and by this time Francis had a Ford Granada. He took every exam going in the financial field and soon had his own little office, with a couple of juniors setting up mortgages and a girl to do all the typing while he concentrated on catching some bigger fish with a view to showing them that he was the man to ensure that they avoided an excess of inheritance tax when they died, plus paying the government a penny more than they ought to whilst still alive. He was finally able to order his first Jaguar as he approached his thirtieth birthday. By now he and Julia had a son, Dean, who was born in June of 1976, during the middle of the best British summer in living memory.

Francis was very concerned to make sure that Julia never went out to work, so he encouraged her to buy her first horse when she turned thirty, in 1984. By this time they'd moved into a large house with stables and a considerable tract of land out in the sticks to the South West of Bath and things looked like they were all going according to plan. In

1981 they'd had the joy of producing another baby, this time a girl, whom they named Aimi, and so they were able to stop at two, one of each, the perfect nuclear family. Francis didn't keep in touch with his own siblings very often. He knew that they'd never amount to much. No drive, that was their problem. He loved his parents, of course, but somehow he was just not able to get to see them in their little semi-detached council house on a large estate in Twerton. When his father died he did send a large bouquet to the funeral, but had to be on the golf course with some very important clients at the time. Not for pleasure, of course, but he needed them to sign on a dotted line and it was just the way you do such things. In the nineteenth hole later in the day, they signed and he drove home assuaging his guilt with the fact that he'd had to ensure his family's wellbeing and prosperity. Isn't that the sign of a good father and husband?

This, then, was the man that Dean Waters needed to call about explaining his love for Alyson, a girl from a one-parent family in Twerton, Bath.

"Hello? Dad? Dean."

"Hello son, how are things in the depths of coal-mining country?" This was calculated to wind Dean up and he nearly bit. On previous occasions he had bitten, but now he new that there was no point. This was 1998. The mines in South Wales had all long since closed and the place was now peppered with landscaped and grassed former slag-heaps and new metal sheds housing Japanese TV and car manufacturers. The "Valleys" were now predominantly green, as green as they had been before the mining industry had effectively raped them of their dramatic beauty. What irritated Dean even more was the fact that the "Valleys" were twenty miles further north anyway. He lived in Cardiff and worked in the Vale of Glamorgan, an area designated as one of outstanding natural beauty, consisting as it does of gently rolling hills dotted with picturesque villages full of middle-class homes sporting huge wisteria plants and manicured gardens. People here played golf for goodness sake. My father ought to realise that it's his kind of turf. Of course, thought Dean, he probably does. He's just trying to wind me up because he thinks I'm still in the wrong job.

"Tickety boo, Dad." There followed a slight pause, after which Francis asked, "So, come on son. Out with it? You need cash I suppose."

"NO, dad, I don't need cash. We're …I'm managing fine thank you very much. It's just that I want to tell you about my girlfriend." There, he'd said it. Now there'd be no going back.

"I'm listening. I do hope you're going to tell me that she's a Doctor or something. Perhaps from a wealthy family out in the Vale maybe?"

See, thought Dean, he knows what kind of area the Vale is after all.

"I know, she's actually from our neck of the woods, down here in the Bath area, eh son? Son? It's your turn to speak. As I said, I'm listening."

"Perhaps it would be better if I talked it over with you face to face. I'll be over on Sunday and maybe we can go for a pint in the local, just the two of us. Father and son bonding session perhaps."

"Ooh, an olive leaf perhaps? In that case I shall look forward to it Dean. Drive carefully." With that the line was dead.

5. Claire, Kefallonia – June 1998

Alone. I can't quite believe it. This poor child came out here alone. She has absolutely no experience at all of foreign travel. It's quite obvious that something's amiss in that little brief life of hers, poor child. I must, however, be ready to give her some space. I mustn't crowd the girl, Alyson I mean, yes Alyson. She seems to be very intelligent to me. Thoughtful, yes, she's a thoughtful one. Or should I rather say thinking. She comes across as someone who thinks. Such a curse it can be to be such a person. I do so often feel that the simpler people live the happier lives. They don't address the deeper questions and so take pleasure in what life brings them, such as it is. If you think deeply you only end up with more questions than there seem to be answers.

I say 'seem to be' because I do always so live in hope that the answers may be out there somewhere. I just have to keep searching in order to find them. Why do we humans have such an enquiring brain? Well, most of us anyway. There is, of course, a school of thought that suggests that if we can at least do something good for others then that's all the meaning that we can expect to extract from it all. Perhaps I ought to be content with that. Yet I'm afraid I'm not. Here I am, forty seven and not much better off than this young thing Alyson. She's alone. I am too. But at least there's someone for her back in the UK, of that I'm convinced. I'd be very surprised if she didn't begin to tell me the whole scenario once she's ready, once she's decided that she can trust me. Fair enough, we've only just met, so she'd be a fool to do so just yet.

How lovely it would be for me to have someone. I'm not even going to begin to explain to her what's happened to me. It doesn't really matter anyway. Charles is gone and he won't be back. 'End of story' as so many people are fond of saying nowadays. You don't tend to come back from a fall like Charles took. It's a hell of a long way from the

Clifton Suspension Bridge down to the mud below, especially when the tide's out along the Avon Gorge. And I drove him to it. I know I did. It's no good trying to talk me out of it. Had I not been who I was, ...am, had I not virtually persecuted him with my problems I'm quite sure that he'd be here with me now.

I'm so sorry Charles. I am truly so sorry. At least I can make some kind of amends; well, no I can't really. Rather I ought to say that I can do penance by trying to be a good person from here on in. One day I'll get to the bottom of it all, why we're here, what the whole thing's really about. If I don't then my death will catch up with me first and, if it does. it'll only be what I deserve anyway.

"Claire?" Are you OK? You're crying." It was Alyson's voice, waking Claire from a reverie. She was sitting on the bench across the road from the rooms, with the beauty of Argostoli Bay spread about before her, lights beginning to twinkle as the daylight faded rapidly and the night took over. Alyson stood a few paces from her, afraid to approach further for fear of interrupting, yet feeling suddenly very protective of this woman whose protection she herself craved in these unfamiliar surroundings.

They had agreed to meet here at 8.30pm to go out for their first meal on the island since arriving earlier in the afternoon. On hearing Alyson's voice and bringing herself back to the present with a jolt, Claire soon gathered herself, smiled at Alyson and said, "It's all so beautiful, don't you think?"

Indeed it was, agreed Alyson. Yet she kind of knew that there was more to Claire's tears than this. It wasn't her place to enquire though. Give Claire enough space and time and perhaps she'll tell Alyson when she's ready. In a way it made Alyson feel better. It gave her more confidence. Here was this woman, who exuded confidence, coming across as so worldly wise, yet she too had her vulnerabilities, her weaknesses or burdens to contend with. We all do, we all do, mused Alyson.

Setting off arm in arm they strolled along the front toward the centre of the town. Taking a right turn they soon found themselves in a central square which was alive with human traffic, plus a little of the conventional kind was circulating around the perimeter too. Alyson was again absorbed in taking in all the new sensations, especially the smells and sights, like the periptero on the corner. She had to ask Claire what they were called, these 'kiosks', after studying the one in the corner of the square and noticing that they seemed to sell every kind of newspaper and magazine, cold drinks, sweets and chocolates, chewing gum, cigarettes and a host of other stuff. People sat around under parasols and engaged in animated conversations, men sat on idling motorcycles at the roadside and talked with friends who stood and checked out the passing 'talent' all the while. Children ran around, seemingly without any parent or guardian taking much care for their safety. This alarmed Alyson. Surely they could come to some harm, even be abducted or something. Wasn't it past their bedtime anyway?

Everywhere she heard the Greek language rattling on sixteen to the dozen and it made her slightly anxious. Never having been out of the UK before, she felt strangely illiterate in a way, like an infant who hasn't yet learned to talk. She realised with some disquiet that she couldn't even ask someone the time. At this point she hadn't yet found out that so many of these people could speak English to some degree.

Claire suggested that they sit in a bar and take an aperitif. Alyson agreed readily and they were soon seated, perusing a drinks menu. Alyson asked if Claire would mind going to the bar to order drinks, since she'd be scared to death of doing so. Claire replied that there would be no need. A waiter would be along in a jiffy, and he was.

Enquiring in very good English what they would like to drink, an Adonis if ever Alyson had seen one, gave her a warm, flirty smile and walked across the road to the building, which evidently had ownership of these tables, soon exiting again carrying a tray laden with all kinds of drinks. How he managed to carry that many glasses on bottles on a tray supported by just one hand was a miracle to the young nineteen-year-old. Soon he placed a grapefruit juice in front of her and a Campari and Soda before Claire, flashed them another magnificent smile and was off to further unburden his tray at some of the other tables. He'd also placed a small glass dish with some peanuts in it on their table too.

"How are you feeling now my girl?" Asked Claire. "A little more at home maybe?"

"I wouldn't go that far," replied Alyson, "but I'm getting used to the idea that I think I'm quite safe here."

"Don't you believe it, darling. That waiter would no sooner flash you another of his smiles than you'd be underneath him on some secluded beach or other before that night was out." Claire spoke these words with a hint of a smile, but it was apparent to Alyson that there was a genuine warning in there somewhere. Alyson was quite shocked. Her face registering the fact, Claire continued:

"The Greeks are very friendly. Don't get me wrong. But a lot of the males of the species are perpetually trying to practice reproduction at every available opportunity darling. Trust me I know. I'm only sad that it's you they're flirting with these days and not me."

Once again, her words jolted Alyson into the realisation that perhaps she had indeed been very foolish to think that she could have come here alone and get away with it unscathed. Dean's face flashed through her mind and she was suddenly very melancholy. Why was she so far away from him? Why did she go and do such a thing? Why couldn't she have trusted him to speak to his father without doing something like this? Had she been just a little too rash in hatching such a plan as she had? Oh, Dean, she so wanted to be in his arms at that moment. She wanted to hear him breath, to be that close to him. To smell the shampoo in his hair, see the light playing in his eyes as he stared at her in wonder at her beauty. Not that she believed all that about her being beautiful, but he'd never failed to mention that he thought that she was at every opportunity. She wanted to see him dunk his digestive in his tea while staring at the TV and let the wet part drop off, splashing tea all over his trousers. She so wanted to rush for a damp cloth to wipe them quickly, before the tea caused a stain. She wanted to be walking with him in Roath Park, watching the cormorants and shags up in the trees, the waterfowl on the surface of the lake. She so wanted to brush his long hair after he'd just washed it. Could anyone on the planet be more miserable than she at this moment? She couldn't imagine so.

"Alyson?" Claire's voice finally penetrated Alyson's musings. "Do you want to tell me what it's all about? I see you're wearing a wedding ring. You do seem awfully young to have been married and for it all to have gone horribly wrong. If you want someone to sound off to, I'm your girl. I'm hardly going to go blabbing to anyone, since I'm highly unlikely to know anyone you're liable to mention, now am I?"

So, Alyson began.

6. Dean, Limpley Stoke near Bath – June 1998

Julia Waters sat gazing at her son. For once there was a little sunshine and so, here they were on Sunday morning out on the terrace having a drink together. Dean's father had yet to put in an appearance. It was around 11am.

"You needn't think you can hide it from me you know, Dean. I know you've got the world on your shoulders. A mother always knows."

"Is it that obvious?" Asked Dean.

"Only about as obvious as the nose on your face my boy. I know you're totally strung up about talking to your dad." Dean threw a glance at his mother. "Look Dean, I've been married to your father now for twenty-four years. I know him inside out. He's a big pain in the backside a lot of the time, but he does have some redeeming features you know. Call him work-obsessed and I'd probably agree. But no one's ever striven harder to provide a secure home for his family than your father. He's totally dedicated to me and to the two of you, you know. He only wants the best for you and Aimi, although you don't always understand that fact."

"Yes, but, the best in his view may not necessarily be the best from my perspective."

"But who's got the most experience in such matters, Dean?" Francis Waters had walked out on to the terrace behind his wife and son, hot mug of filter coffee in his hand. "A good son, let me tell you, is the one who listens when his father offers a bit of advice about how to handle life."

"Dad," replied Dean, "Have you ever seen the movie *'Dead Poets Society'?"*

"What's having seen a film got to do with anything? Anyway, let's try and get off on the right foot for a change shall we? How's your career coming along?" Dean thought: why is he steering clear of the issue that he knows I want to raise with him? One thing's for certain, he'll have a covert reason if I know my father.

"I'm enjoying the work. It's a bit pressured, but then I suppose that's always going to be the case. Plus it's still a case of adjusting to the real workplace after the easy life at college. No doubt your work is pressured much of the time."

"Of course, son. It's the nature of the beast. Cut and thrust. Dog eat dog. Those who do well don't do it by lazing around all the time, like so many of those shirkers you see lining up to sign on all their lives."

"Not that you'll ever have actually seen any of them lining up, eh?"

"Quite so, Dean. Why should anyone who's remotely industrious end up in such a place? Anyway, who's this mystery girl you need to tell us about? Is it really getting serious? Should we expect an invitation to drop on to the doormat any time soon? Is she well connected?"

"Are we going for a pint? Perhaps we ought to talk about it just the two of us first."

"Whatever you say son. Let's go up to the Viaduct then, at the bottom of Brassknocker hill, as it's close enough."

With relatively little conversation having passed between them in the interim, they were soon sitting in the modest garden of the pub, Dean with his fingers around a pint of real ale, his father swilling the rocks around in his malt whisky. A few clouds had bubbled up and were threatening to cover the sun any time soon. The weather conditions seemed to be a portent of how Dean foresaw this conversation going.

Dean took a deep breath and tried to start. Where to start though, that was the question. Should he perhaps tell his father all about the night that he first met Alyson. Would his description of events, including how wonderful she had looked at the time, sway his father at all? Would it make him see events as though he were Dean and hence be more sympathetic? Would anything make any difference, knowing his father as Dean did?

His father's face demonstrated a degree of impatience. It was quite evident already to Francis that he wasn't going to like what he heard from his son. He decided to kick things off anyway.

"Let me guess, son. She's gorgeous but a bit of a low-life. Am I right? In which case, she'll be a gold-digger and the sooner you see that for what it is, the sooner you'll grow up and enter the real world. I know, you think I'm totally heartless, cold and unsympathetic. Fine, think that if you wish. But if you ever doubt that I've always had your best interests at heart then you may dispel that thought right now. How many times have I seen people ruin their lives for 'love' son. If I had a Pound for every bloke I've known who's gone down the wrong path because his lust led him like a slave I'd be even better off than I am now, which would be rather nice I must admit." Dean's father leaned forward, evidently needing to add emphasis to what he was going to say next.

"Son, please consider this: The world isn't a movie and it isn't a romance novel. The world is a brutal place and there will never be any hint of equality among us humans. It's just how things are and neither you nor I will ever change it. That's why Communism doesn't work, son. Oh fine, the ideals were noble when the Bolsheviks brought Russia's ordered society to an abrupt end back in 1917, but it didn't take long for the elite to start living like kings off the backs of their 'brothers'. Am I right? [Dean's father had a propensity to repeat this expression often. It had the effect of browbeating a listener into acquiescing.]

"There will always be the 'haves' and the 'have nots'. After all, didn't Christ himself say 'you'll always have the poor with you'? Well, I for one agree with him, but I don't want to be one of them or indeed have them at close quarters. It's also a well-researched fact, Dean, that the poor are in that position primarily because by and large they have a lower intellect. Who do you think are the targets of the mass, crappy media, like the 'Red Top" newspapers, the crumby sordid soap operas on the TV, the football madness and pop music? It's anaesthetic for the masses son, pure and simple. Didn't the Roman Governors say, as the Empire began to crumble, 'Give 'em more sport!'? Keep the masses occupied with the News of the World and they'll be happy.

"Look, to further emphasise the point. Walk into a newsagent in one of the less prosperous (I'm being kind here) areas of any city in the UK. Will the Times or the Telegraph be selling well? I don't think so. Will the people in the tatty little council houses be watching Horizon on BBC 2? You know the answers Dean, don't you. So, what am I trying to say? Dean, you're my son and I love you dearly. Yes I'm prepared to see you make some decisions that I'm not altogether happy with, like your choice of career for example. But, a few years from now, I'm not going to see you throw your future prosperity away on a tacky divorce case where some slob of a woman who just happened to be good in bed for a while takes you for half of what you've grafted to earn or own."

This was enough. Dean had been listening quietly up until this point. In fact he could almost have scripted the speech since he'd heard it that many times. But to hear Alyson described in such terms was enough. He exploded, so much so that other drinkers at the other picnic tables around them turned to stare momentarily.

"YOU KNOW NOTHING ABOUT HER! HOW DARE YOU TALK ABOUT THE GIRL I LOVE IN THAT WAY!! YOU'VE NEVER EVEN SEEN, LET ALONE MET HER!! WHY DOES EVERYTHING BOIL DOWN TO MONEY AND STATUS WITH

YOU? EH?!" He stopped here, firstly because he'd noticed the other customers staring and, secondly, he just didn't have any more words, he was so exasperated at his father's stance on everything in life. He suddenly noticed that he was standing, his drink having spilled when he'd shot up, knocking the table violently in the process.

As he slid back down to sit on the bench, his father, who hadn't registered any reaction to this outburst continued: "I think you've proven my point dear boy. Look, Dean, emotions are powerful things. I don't need to meet this, this …girl in order to know what is going to happen a couple of years down the line. Take it from me. I know. I'll tell you what I'm going to do. It's obvious that your feelings are running high and that you think you're in love. At your age a lot of us think such things about the girls we encounter. The older you get, the more you'll understand that love's got nothing to do with it and we never really understand what love actually is. Practicality, on the other hand, is a principle that always applies. Am I right?

"So, as I said, here's what I'm going to do and it's for your own good. I'll give you one month from now to get this girl out of your system and out of your life. Oh, go on, have a little more fun with her if you wish, but by this date next month I want to hear from you to the effect that you've sent her packing, is that clear? If you have done as I ask, then you can carry on as you are, with your dainty little career in graphic design. If you have not complied with my wishes, Dean, then I shall expect that car back on my drive on that very day and I shall be withdrawing your allowance immediately. Oh, and I'll stop paying for that nice comfy pad of yours in Cardiff too. I'm doing this for your own good, son, and the day will come when you thank me for it. Understood? Now, drink up, let's go home for Sunday lunch and we'll hear no more about it."

"I'm not going home with you. I'll walk."

"Splendid idea. That way you can consider the things I've told you. Then perhaps you'll begin to see reason and develop a degree of maturity. I'll tell your mother you'll be a littler later getting back." At this point Francis Waters picked up his car keys, rearranged his Pringle sweater around his shoulders and walked back to his Jaguar.

Dean didn't arrive for lunch. By four o'clock, when his mother walked out on to the gravel drive in front of the house to find out what had happened to her son, although quite what she expected to see she didn't really know, it was to see that the little Mercedes had gone. Dean was already almost across to the other side of the Severn Bridge and driving like a thing possessed. Of course, Francis hadn't told his wife of the ultimatum that he'd presented to his son. He knew that it probably wouldn't have gone down too well. Women, eh? Far too sentimental sometimes. No, he'd just made up something about their son having forgotten some urgent errand or other, which necessitated a speedy return to South Wales. "He sends his apologies, pet." He'd told her.

Dean sat in the darkness, TV burning away with the sound off. He held his fourth can of beer in his right hand and felt extremely sorry for himself. He really didn't care what his father did. He'd find somewhere else to live, maybe not quite as grand, but that didn't matter. He'd get a friend to drive over the bridge with him just as soon as he'd found a cheap old car and then they would deliver the Mercedes back to his father's drive, probably under cover of darkness, although not before he'd pranged it just a little. No, wait, maybe that was a bit too rash. Oh, maybe though. We'll see, he thought.

The most difficult thing was that he couldn't contact Alyson. She was 1,500 miles away and still didn't have a mobile phone. Dean, of course, did possess one. He had one of the new-fangled flip-open types that were just recently on the market and making everyone who owned one pretend to be Captain Kirk asking Scottie to beam him up. If only I could beam Alyson back here right now, he thought. I don't even know exactly when she's coming back. Why did I let her go like that? Why didn't I put my foot down and stop her. Why didn't I plead with her to give me the chance to sort this out?

After all, I've done it now. He knows. Although it means I'm going to be worse off, I feel so much better. I don't care if things are going to be a bit tougher, I really don't, he persuaded himself. But let's be honest here, he continued reflecting, would I have done it if Alyson hadn't done what she's done? Why is everyone issuing ultimatums all of a sudden? What have I done to deserve this? Maybe Dad's right after all; maybe she really is taking me for a ride. But then, I can't believe that she's that type. We may have rushed into this relationship, but the way it's developed since has been just perfect. We fit together. We were made for eachother. Sounds trite, but in this case it's the fact. I know it. Yet where is she now? Who is she with?

Dean almost couldn't bear to think of all the possible scenarios. Was she - right now - getting chatted up by some would-be Greek lover? Maybe she's met an English bloke who's tall and handsome and has a yacht or something. Who's staying in the room next to her? Is she even now making love to some hunk who's made her decide never to come back? His thoughts were taking him down an ever more vicious spiral and his knotted stomach was making him feel unbearably desperate. How would he get through the next few days, weeks? Dammit, he didn't even know when she'd be coming back, always assuming that she would be.

And now he'd blown it big time with his father. Why wasn't she with him to get through this together? Now his desperation was turning to anger. The bitch. Why did she have to go off like that? Hadn't we been good together? Hadn't he promised her that he'd stick with her whatever the consequences? Maybe, after all, Dad was right. She knew he'd lose his father's support and so she did a bunk the only way she could without having to actually come out with it. 'What did Dad say about love? It ought to play second fiddle to practicality. Why didn't I see the sense of it when we were sitting in the pub garden earlier today?' he thought.

Now he had lost both his father and his girl. What an idiot he'd proven to be. There was nothing for it but to call his father, eat humble pie and tell him that he was right after all.

Dean cracked a fifth can of beer. Shall I call Dad tomorrow? He thought. But then he reconsidered. What if he did call his father, only to have Alyson call him the moment he'd hung up and declare her undying love and her desire to whizz home to him, now that he'd been a man and stood up to his father? What if it was all exactly as she said. What if she really loved him dearly and just wanted time to think in the hope that he'd sort it out with his father while she was away? All this thinking was doing his head in. he took a sip of beer and realised that he needed the bathroom.

While he stood over the bowl, head swimming and making it difficult for him to remain standing, the phone rang. Who's that NOW? He thought. Please don't hang up while I finish off here and answer it. But he'd consumed rather a lot of beer and needed to stand over that bowl for several minutes. Vigorously shaking himself, then rushing to pull up his zip to the extent that he got it stuck, he began running for the lounge. He'd barely reached the door when the phone stopped ringing.

A particularly expressive expletive emerged from his lips as he again flopped on to the sofa in the pits of despair. Where are you Alyson, Alyson, ALYSON?" He called aloud as finally his tiredness got the better of him and he began to drift off into some pretty tumultuous dreams.

7. Alyson – Lindos, January 15th 2007

We slotted together like pieces in a jigsaw. Dean and I. I've no idea how it all fell together so well, why it all fell together so well. But that's what happened. Maybe some great celestial plan was at work. No, I couldn't have said that to him, he'd have dismissed that as idealistic twaddle. He'd probably be right. It's the luck of the draw, but I drew the ace when I bumped into Dean. How can you meet someone and within hours feel as though you had spent all the years of your life until then working up to that moment? Yet that was what it had felt like. Those months during which we lived in the flat in Cardiff were so perfect, so comfortable.

I so enjoyed my hairdressing too, bringing in my share of the money. I don't think my poor mother could ever have had such a relationship, however hard she tried to find Mr. Right.

Two Adidas trainers. Placed neatly together. They must have been there to tell me something, but what?

8. Alyson and Claire, Kefallonia – June 1998

"It's all going to sound so idealistic to you Claire; no doubt especially because I'm so young. Yet I met this guy last October in a bar in Bath and I knew instantly that he was going to be the one for me. Don't even ask me how. I was probably wrong to think that way so soon, and yet time has proven that it was the case. We ended up moving together to Cardiff where he'd got a new job and we shared a flat.

"My mother raised me alone. Well, I say 'alone'. She has had a succession of 'partners' in an attempt no doubt to achieve some kind of family stability, but it never seemed to work for her. She lives in a council house on a run-down estate and I have three siblings; a brother George, who's older than me, and two sisters, Shirley and Gemma, both of which are younger. Gemma's actually still at school, but if you met her in Bath on a Friday night you'd never guess she was still only fifteen.

"I can't remember any really happy times during my childhood. Most of the 'uncles' who've shared our home have been non-descript men of varying colours and sizes who didn't take much interest in me. I s'pose that's something to be grateful for. I could just as easily have been a victim of abuse or something, but fortunately that never happened to me.

"I love my mum. And she's very intelligent. It's just that life... well, life just hasn't fallen into place for her. My earliest memories are of mum coming home from working in a bar somewhere in a Bath backstreet. My granny often sat for us when mum worked. She only worked evenings, so at least she was always there when I came home from school.

"Mum never had any skills, apart from serving drinks behind a bar. That's why I did a hairdressing course. I thought that hairdressing was something I could do anywhere and everywhere. Once you've got the tools you can easily find a client or two. Then with word of mouth… well, I thought it would mean I could always earn a bit of cash.

"Anyway, I should cut to the quick, shouldn't I. Dean and I are good together, but he's got a huge problem with his dad. Basically, his dad's a snobby, well-off guy who only believes in money and Dean knows that he won't approve of me, because of where I come from. He hasn't told me everything, but I know his dad provided his car for him and I have my suspicions that he's also helping Dean out in other ways.

Dean's been putting off telling his father about me because he knows it's going to cause a major family row. He's torn. He's been promising me that he'd have it out with his father, but just keeps putting it off.

"I suppose that's why I told him I was going away to think things out. I wanted to force his hand because it's been making the both of us miserable. I told him that I'd be gone a while and that during this time he should get it sorted once and for all with his dad. He needs to stand up to him, he really does."

Claire interjected, "If you don't mind my saying so, darling, he sounds like a bit of a mummy's, or rather daddy's boy to me. Do you think he'll make the stand, now that you've left him to it?"

"I don't know now. I thought I did when I left for Greece. Now, though, …oh, I don't know anything any more. I'm suddenly very aware of my age. I don't have enough experience of life, full stop. I really do think that I love Dean. We share so many ways of thinking, of tastes in music, of tastes in food even! He cares about the environment and the two of us recycle everything we possibly can. He's such a logical thinker that I find him totally refreshing to be with, except for this one area, his father."

"Does he work Alyson, or does his father bankroll him through life?"

"Oh he works all right. He got his degree and is a qualified graphic designer. He's been in a job for, oh, I dunno, seven or eight months. Ever since we moved to Wales. It's the reason why we moved in fact. He's proud of the fact that he qualified in something that he was interested in doing, even though his father wanted him to be a lawyer or an architect or something."

"You poor thing. I really don't know what to say and I'm certainly not going to advise you. In my experience, advising others leads to a degree of responsibility for any action which they may subsequently take. I can't bear such a weight I'm afraid. I'm always willing, however, to be a shoulder for others to cry on. Heaven knows I've needed my share of shoulders and I know what it's like not to have one available when you need it the most."

Over the next few days the women saw eachother frequently and at pre-arranged times. They'd go out to eat together, or perhaps agree to spend a few hours on the beach where they'd talk incessantly, Claire never revealing very much about her history or present circumstances. But then, Alyson didn't ask. She was more in the mood to pour out her soul and was only too grateful for an audience. If nothing else, this trip was proving to be a therapy session and Claire an expert listener.

When she was alone Alyson took to walking for hours. She was in an environment so alien to all that she'd ever experienced that she couldn't drink it all in fast enough. She'd stoop to examine every bougainvillea plant, every Oleander flower or a Lantana, with its tightly packed flower heads, with the peripheral petals being of an entirely different colour to those in the centre, and all this in an area about the size of a large coin. She'd wander the backstreets, running her fingers through the rich, green, luxuriant leaves of a basil plant growing in an old olive oil tin outside someone's front door. She walked out to the headland, passing tiny coves and gazing down through impossibly clear water at the fish darting around beneath the surface. She arrived at a small circular building on the point, a little like a temple or something, but rather small for that purpose really, she thought. She didn't really have any idea what it could have been for, but it looked lovely to her.

She'd watch cats demonstrating the art of relaxation as they hung off windowsills or sat on walls. She found the lizards absolutely fascinating, gazing for ages at huge grey or black ones with prehistoric-looking skin, as they basked on stone walls, or scuttled into the parched undergrowth at her approach. The bright green ones, which ran, heads held high, across the road like lightning, drew her attention and she cursed them for the fact that they always managed to get out of sight before she'd really been able to take a good look. She came across cobwebs of such a gauge of silk that their strength restrained her as she moved through them by accident. The occupants of such webs were of such a size that she fancied that they were really crabs who were suffering an identity crisis.

One day she took the ferry across the bay to Lixouri, where she walked around the central square, all the while looking up at the huge rubber tree in its centre. The only rubber trees she'd ever seen in the UK had been called "plants" rather than "trees" and they'd been just a few feet in height and sticking out of pots in people's conservatories. Here was a tree the size of a mature oak and its huge leaves were rich and shiny on the upper side, varying in colour from a deep delicious green to a wine-red. She had no idea that a rubber plant could grow so big. She sat in a bar and ordered an orangeade. The can that was placed before her, along with an empty glass with ice all over it, sported as brand name that she didn't recognise, something like BAP. What kind of a brand name was that?

She bought hot spinach or cheese pies from bakeries and ate them as she walked, all the while staring at everything around her, trying to drink everything in, trying to register it all so that she wouldn't forget it. She regretted not having a camera to record all that she saw.

When she ate out with Claire she allowed her to select dishes from the menu while she was gradually being educated by the older woman in Greek cuisine, all of which she ate with gusto and loved. She was delighted that everything came with or was cooked in olive oil. She took to drinking Retsina right away and a meal was soon not complete without a bottle. Better still, they liked finding tavernas where they could order the resin-enhanced wine in those little red aluminium jugs. She marvelled at the Greeks' use of herbs, especially oregano, which brought out delicious nuances of flavour in so many dishes.

The only thing that did become slightly tiresome was the fact that seemingly every Greek male wanted to make evident his appreciation of her beauty. Cars would honk as they passed her, men and boys would whistle. Not infrequently someone would actually suggest that she go off with him that very instant and find out just how essential a Greek lover is for a girl. When she broached this concern with Claire, her mind was put at rest to some degree by Claire's assurance that, despite this very outward way which the Greeks had of expressing their appreciation for a pretty girl, she was in no danger of being molested or attacked. It was just the way the Greeks were. A young woman just had to learn to deal with it.

Very soon the end of her holiday approached and she found herself sitting alone on her small balcony, gazing out across the turquoise bay, wondering if she was really going to climb aboard that coach the next day and allow herself to be whisked back to the airport and flown back into Cardiff just a few hours later. What would she be returning to? Even more relevant in her mind now was the question: "Can I really go back to Dean and become responsible for him losing his family on my account? Wouldn't it be better if I just stayed away? However much I love him, she thought, I ought to think first and foremost of what's best for him. I could go back and be with him. I really long to go back to be with him. But that's selfish reasoning, she thought. If I really love him, can I give him up? Will I do so for his sake?

She'd only tried to phone him once in the whole time she'd been here, and that had been very late in the evening and there had been no answer. Was that cruel? Probably, she concluded. But then, she added in her mind, you've got to be cruel to be kind. Later she'd be meeting

Claire downstairs by the front entrance for what ought to be their last evening out on Kefallonia. But was it going to turn out quite differently? Was she hatching the germ of a plan to spare Dean a lot of unhappiness, far more, she felt, than losing her would cause him. He'd get over her one day. He wouldn't be able to get over becoming an outcast in his own family anything like as easily.

Part Three

Far, Far Away

1. Lindos - 2005

There was nothing for it, thought Brian as he sat sipping at his frappe in the Atmosphere Bar the next morning. He'd have to go and speak to this girl. It was just a question of how to go about it. He began to consider the facts.

From 1976 until January of 1978, a frightening twenty-seven years ago, when he'd been a mere twenty-something, he'd worked in a bar called Porky's, in a backstreet of the city of Bath. His best friend had been the beautiful Christine, who was too young to be a mother, yet had given birth to a son, George, earlier that first year he'd known her, 1976. She was sixteen going on thirty-five, poor thing. He'd have given his eye-teeth to have become her partner, but always believed that she only ever viewed him as a father figure. He could close his eyes at any time in the intervening years and describe her perfectly, blessed as he was with an incredible memory.

He stared up at the Lindos Acropolis and thought for a moment. How many others down through the millennia had perhaps sat in this self same spot and wondered about the brevity of it all. Time, once it's passed, is nothing. It's as though it gets condensed like a concertina, leaving only images in the minds of those who'd lived through those moments to prove it ever actually passed at all. 'Here I am,' mused the musician, 'still thinking that I'm young enough to "make it", to be spotted by some high-flying record company exec who's maybe taking a holiday on the island of Rhodes and just happens to breeze into the bar one night. "Wow!" he'll think, "this guy's got something. I'll sign him up now. He'll be a household name within a few months."'

Yea well, a man could dream. To be honest, living in Lindos and playing acoustic a few nights a week in a bar during the summer season was a pretty good life. He had his fair share of female company if he needed it. Yet oddly enough, although he and Christine had never become an 'item', he'd always find himself comparing any woman he'd dated with her.

Now, here he was with this strange occurrence to deal with. A young woman who couldn't be more than in her mid twenties, had come here for a holiday (or did she perhaps even live here?) with friends and there she'd been, seated in the bar where Brian played, looking such a dead-ringer for Christine that he almost had a heart attack. The only thing that proved that she couldn't have been Christine is the twenty-nine year time gap.

Had it not been for the fact that she flicked her head like Christine, that she smiled exactly like Christine, that her face was Christine's down to the last detail, that she laughed like Christine, he'd have dismissed it as some silly fancy.

Then, she walks into the bar another time and pulls *"Nausea"* by Jean Paul Sartre out of her bag, the very Penguin edition that he'd given to Christine all those years ago. There was really only one explanation. Christine had produced a daughter and this girl was she.

Had Christine really kept that book for all this time? If so, how come her daughter had brought it to Greece with her for a holiday? Brian had to figure out a way of approaching the girl that wouldn't faze her, that wouldn't freak her out.

The arrival of a couple of his Greek friends brought him back to the moment, so he cracked a smile as their conversation began to include him.

2. Kefallonia – June 1998

Having now made her resolve, Alyson felt better. Not a great deal better, she had to admit, but better nevertheless. She knew that she'd have to suffer an enduring ache inside over not returning to Dean, an ache that would probably last a very long time, but she told herself that what she was doing was for the best. He would also hurt badly, or so – In a strange kind of way - she hoped, but would eventually come to understand that it was for the best. Dean was better off without her. He'd been the product of a normal, 'nuclear' family, with a dad and a mum and a younger sister. It was all too much for her to ask him to give this up, especially when his father, albeit a bastard, was well off and likely to be able to assist his son at the crucial stages in his life. How could she be the reason for Dean losing all of this security? Plus, even more important, she couldn't bear the prospect of him reminding her as their lives together would have progressed, of how much he'd given up for her, something that he'd be certain to do whenever things got tough for them.

He'd have been right too. She couldn't bear the prospect and so she decided to put a proposition to Claire. No sense not at least giving it a try after all.

They met outside the front entrance to Marina Rooms at 8.30pm. Claire was in an ebullient mood and suggested that they stay out late, perhaps going to one of the two extremely good Bouzouki clubs out around the headland from Argostoli, which would mean their staying out until the early hours. Alyson, now more settled in herself, readily agreed. In fact, it would suit what she had to propose to Claire all the more.

Having eaten in their favourite taverna, they strolled arm in arm along the road leading away from the island's capital due north, which would bring them in a quarter of an hour or so to the first of the two clubs, the Katavothres. Alyson wasted no time, once they were away from the town, in broaching what was on her mind.

"Claire," She said, to which her new friend answered,

"Yes sweetie?"

"Claire, you haven't told me all that much about yourself. But am I right in assuming that you're a bit of a free spirit? That perhaps you don't have much to go home to? I don't mean to pry or anything, but it's important before I ask you something huge."

"Wow, Alyson. What DO you have on your mind my girl?"

"Not going back. Staying here in Greece and seeing what life may bring us if we go island-hopping. I've heard that expression a few times during this past week and it sounds tremendously exciting to me. I know we'll survive. I'm a qualified hairdresser and something tells me that you'll know how to earn a few pennies when push comes to shove. The one thing that is very obvious to me is that you've travelled a lot and not just on package tours. What do you think? I've got a bit saved up which could keep us going for a few more weeks yet anyway, especially if we live cheaply. Already here I've had that many people tell me about rooms to rent that I'm pretty sure that, one way or the other, we'd manage. Well?"

"Well, indeed. And what about this guy you've been agonising about all week?"

"I've decided that I'd be too selfish if I went back to him. He'll lose so much and I'd never forgive myself. I know he loves me. I know that I love him, but that's exactly why I have to let him go. If I go back, he'll sacrifice his family for me, which is something that I just can't make him do."

"Oughtn't that to be his decision, Alyson?"

"Of course. I totally agree. But think about it, Claire. What if, a couple of years down the line, things get really tough for us; then he turns around and says to me: 'If I could ask my father for a bit of help to tide us over, it would be all we'd need. But I can't.' You see Claire; he won't even be able to phone his father up for a bit of advice. He'd probably be cast off so that he couldn't even see his mother or his sister again. Can I really put him in that position, Claire? Even if he decides that it's what he wants to do now, who's to say that he won't later start thinking, especially if we hit a rocky patch, 'Why did I ever do this? Why didn't I listen to my father?' No Claire, I may be very young, but I think I've just learned one of life's lessons. It's that sometimes we have to realise that what's for the best isn't always what we want to do at the time.

"I think too that if I stay away from him for long enough, then I'd perhaps be able to go back one day and find out, with the advantage of more maturity too, whether he's still waiting for me, or whether he's got over me and maybe found some horsey girl his father approves of. From all perspectives, I have to stay away from him for a while. Even though my whole being is dragging me back to his side right now. Am I making any sense?"

Claire's face displayed an expression of understanding and concern. "OK, yes I see where you're coming from. Plus, as I told you the other day, I won't offer you advice. You guessed partially correctly about my circumstances Alyson. I shall now tell you a little more, which with hindsight may just make you think that our bumping into eachother was very fortuitous.

"I don't often take a package to go abroad, but I will occasionally because it's usually just as cheap, if not cheaper, than going freelance when I want to get somewhere in particular. I was married once, Alyson. I had a good man and his name was Charles. I'm not going to bore you now with all the sordid details, but he threw himself off the Clifton Suspension Bridge and left me bereft. I loved that man to distraction and I'm still convinced that my own hang-ups or phobias, my preoccupations, my neuroses if you like, were largely the reason why he did what he did. I spend my life now doing penance for being the reason why a good man killed himself. I..."

"Claire, you don't really think that. He must have been depressed, surely. He must have had a host of other problems crowding in on him to make him do something like that. Maybe even an imbalance in his brain, bi-polar dis..."

"You're such a sweet girl, Darling, but I've been through all this stuff. I've gone over what happened so many times in my mind. I always come to the same conclusion. Look, there's no sense re-analysing all this now anyway. What I really wanted to tell you is this: Much to my own bemusement, I'm a very wealthy woman, Alyson. I couldn't have ever dreamt of all the assets that Charles had to his name and they all came to me. There were several lucrative businesses and all kinds of investments that were raking in the cash. I simply couldn't have imagined what he'd had in his portfolio. It all came to me and I converted it all into liquid capital and stuck it into a savings account.

I'd have to live an awful lot longer than I'm going to, sadly, to have any idea of exhausting it all. Alyson, dear, what I'm saying is this. Let me spell it out. I've been a very lonely person for several years. I want someone to share it with. I don't want another man, although God knows how many well-meaning friends have tried to set me up with someone. But a travelling companion, well, why not?

"I know what you're going to ask me now. How come a man with no cash problems commits suicide? If I knew that then perhaps I'd have been able to head him off before he did it. But the fact is, he did it and I was left with all his assets. I kept thinking that someone would turn up and tell me that he owed them a small fortune, or that he'd acquired all this wealth by illegitimate means, but it hasn't happened. Net result – you're looking at a reluctant millionaire."

Alyson took a moment to register that last comment before exclaiming, "MILLIONAIRE! You're kidding me!"

"Darling I'm not, I can assure you. Mind you, putting things into context; by today's standards being a millionaire isn't what it was several decades ago, but the fact remains that I can't even spend the interest fast enough."

"But," continued Alyson, "Why didn't you say so before? I'd never have guessed, really I wouldn't."

"Exactly my girl. Do you think I'd have been able to trust your motives quite as much as I do now if you'd known my little secret? Now that I've known you for a whole week and you've even suggested this little adventure without knowing my circumstances, I'm a lot more inclined to take you up on it than I would have been if I'd told you before. See my point?"

Alyson agreed and silently considered how lucky she'd been to have Claire approach her at the airport the moment they'd left the plane. Perhaps if she hadn't been looking quite so apprehensive, she'd have spent the entire week on her own. Yet Claire, having spotted her anxiety, had been what led her to this point, where she and Claire had the prospect of exploring the entire country of Greece without financial restraints. Alyson had never in her entire life either had such an opportunity or even the dream that she one day would have. Claire now asked:

"What about your family, your mother for instance? Won't she worry about you?" Alyson explained that she hadn't actually seen her mother for several months, although she had spoken to her by telephone almost every week since moving to Wales. Why Christine didn't even know Dean's surname, only that he seemed to be everything that her daughter had wanted to find in a man, and more. She was happy for her daughter and had her reasons for not expecting her to return home to Twerton any time soon.

What was there here for her, thought Christine? Living in a run-down council house with a mother who was perpetually struggling to make ends meet. Christine had her hands full anyway. Her son George was - at twenty-two - two years older than Alyson, but often in trouble with the Police. Shirley, two years younger than Alyson, was stacking shelves, but at least she had a job. Gemma, the youngest at fifteen, and whose father had been a West Indian, was already into Rastafarianism and rather partial to a puff of 'ganja', something which occasionally led her to justify petty theft in order to finance the habit. Despite Christine's evident intellect, life just hadn't dealt her a winning hand. Perhaps she was a victim of her own upbringing, as we all are. Our insecurities, our phobias, our anxieties and all kinds of other things are so often shaped by the way we were brought up. Christine had settled for her share of satisfaction in knowing that her little girl, her Alyson, had managed to break the cycle and find someone who took her for what she was as an individual. Alyson's man looked into her psyche and saw a bright, intelligent person with a lot to give. He was one in a million and Christine was grateful for that. She didn't care if her daughter didn't manage to see her from one year to the next, just so long as she was living a real life, not a life on permanent "pause" like her mother.

"If it'll make you feel better Claire," said Alyson, "I'll send my mum a postcard from each place we visit. How's that?"

"Well, Darling. I don't suppose it's my business anyway. Just as long as I'm not responsible for anything that may develop at home as a result of your not returning. You may not really know what you're doing, but then, it's your life my girl."

The two women both realised that they'd arrived outside the Katavothres Club, from which floated the sound of a loud bouzouki band and singers, a sound that drew their attention away from the conversation they'd been having. Claire suggested they go in and let their hair down, then continue making plans the next morning. Alyson agreed. After all, it was a celebration of sorts, albeit tinged too with a degree of sadness.

A week later, Alyson was gazing in wonder at the fireflies floating this way and that among the olive trees as they walked in the gathering darkness from their accommodation into Gaios, the largest port (which isn't saying much) on the tiny island of Paxos, a little further north from Kefallonia, and accessed by boat from Corfu, a short distant further north again. Here they stayed for a couple of weeks and Alyson kept debating within herself whether to write to Dean or to simply keep out of his life. She did worry about him though. She wondered how he was dealing with her absence and felt a deep pain when agonising about what he'd be going through, not even being able to get in touch with her.

Her heart said, 'Call him' and her head said, 'No, you mustn't. It will only weaken your resolve. He must get used to the fact that you're gone. Only in this way will he eventually realise that he'd best get on with his life and find someone more suited to his situation and background.' But oh, how it hurt. On occasion Claire would detect that Alyson was having a 'moment' and give her a little space. She'd go off alone and let Alyson work through it. It made Claire feel that in this way Alyson would resolve within herself what she ought to do. If it meant that their 'odyssey' was to come to an abrupt end, then so be it.

But on other occasions the girl seemed content, even excited, at all the things she was seeing for the first time in her life. She was falling in love with the country, this was very evident. They found a really nice taverna, up on the hill to the South of Gaios, overlooking the sea, called Taverna Klis. It was rough and ready, its terrace consisting of a gravelled area, surrounded by bushes and with a circular concrete dance floor in the centre. On this the men of the family who ran the establishment would put on impromptu shows. The younger man (in his late twenties), probably the son, would squirt some fluid from a plastic bottle on to the bare concrete dance floor, which he'd immediately put a lighter to, creating circles of blue and yellow flame, within which he'd hop and leap like a thing possessed, dancing the Zebekiko. He would dance for several minutes to the plodding two-three rhythm of the music, before retreating from the floor to be replaced by the older man, probably his father, who was well into his sixties. While the older man was dancing with equal fervour, his son would place perhaps a knife or a glass of wine in the centre of the floor. In the case of the knife the older man would eventually bend over backwards so far that he could retrieve the piece of cutlery from the floor with his teeth, whereupon he'd receive a rapturous round of applause from the diners around him. If the object was a glass of wine (the small tumbler types so often used for Retsina), the man would place one foot squarely on the glass and momentarily it would bear his entire weight, before he'd leap from it and then pick it up in his teeth, as he had done with the knife before, at once raising it above his head and draining it of its contents in one deft move of the dance. Then his son would appear from the background carrying one of the square wooden dining tables, its check tablecloth still in place, which he'd then put in the middle of the floor. His father, having danced near this table for a while, would then pick it up with his teeth and dance around the floor, the table's weight being taken by his jaw and his chest in equal measure, once again to the delight of the audience, the members of which the women of the establishment would encourage to show their appreciation by throwing heaps of paper serviettes or red flowers from the abundant supply of geranium plants all around the periphery of the dining area all over the man himself, who would eventually come to a finish when the music stopped and take a well-deserved bow and the respect and adulation of his enraptured audience. By the time Claire and Alyson were lilting their way home along the dark lanes among the olive groves, the music still ringing in their ears, the concrete circle, together with quite a large area of gravel around it, was littered with a liberal dusting of paper and petals, to the extent that in places one couldn't see the floor for the detritus.

As they travelled and she witnessed one island or port after another, the spirit of the Greek culture was seeping into Alyson's soul, irrevocably. She was absorbing the ways in which the common or garden Greek would take fleeting recreation and respite from the pain that was daily life. She would muse about how these people must all have their problems, much as did she and every other person on God's earth. Yet the Greeks were able to relieve themselves of the tedium in such soul-appeasing ways. She had yet to learn that the dances told stories which were generated through centuries of toil and heartbreak on both sea and land. For example, when they came to the island of Kalymnos and sat for hours in a small bar with some old Greeks, she found out what a devastating havoc the sponge fishing industry had wreaked on the male population for decades before it was understood quite what "the bends" actually was. She knew as yet precious little of the other empires that had trampled this land over the centuries since even before Christ and his apostles had walked the earth. Yet already she was learning to savour the unbelievably exquisite experience of rising early in the morning and taking a short stroll to the local bakery, the aroma of yeast, flour and stone ovens becoming heavier in the dawn air with every step of her approach, handing over a few coins and then walking back, greeting with a "kalimera" those whom she'd pass on the way, all of whom would crack a wizened and warming smile for her and add, "Na eiste kala!" or "Sto kalo!" in return.

Once, on the mainland, they decided to hire a car and drove from Parga up through the hinterland as far as Meteora. The drive took them through beautiful country areas unseen by the mainstream tourist. They stared at storks' nests precariously perched on electricity poles and wondered at how the birds didn't manage to electrocute themselves, not to mention causing a blackout over a wide area. They slowed to allow tortoises to scuttle slowly across the road in front of their car and they sat in cafes in Ioannina, Metsovo and quite a few small villages along the way, sipping their drinks and staring at all the local people, buildings and landscape that continually widened their perception of the country of Greece. They were amazed to see snowploughs parked in garages behind dusty glass doors and red and white rods often positioned beside the road to measure the depth of snow during wintertime. Alyson was quite ashamed to admit that she had no idea that parts of Greece experienced very harsh winters and that there were popular ski resorts in the highland areas. There were sections of road in the mountains, which sported snow-catching canopies to keep the way open during the depths of winter. Birds of prey, whose species the two companions could only speculate about, circled high above them as they drove ever on into the interior of this fascinating country.

When they reached the small town of Kalabaka they found a small room and crashed out for a while. Then they took an evening meal among a few smiling, crease-faced Greeks who laughed and danced and told them stories about their area's fraught history, using sign language as often as their tongues to communicate their thoughts. Next morning they set out to hike up to the sheer pillars of Meteora, where they marvelled at the audacity of people who could build such retreats in such inaccessible places. In fact, the extraordinary rock pillars upon which are built the monasteries tower over the town's streets like sentinels, or alien giants poised to invade at any second. One could be forgiven for thinking of the H.G. Wells classic, The War of the Worlds, or perhaps something out of an episode of Star Trek. One can't help but stare up at them frequently from the hubbub below. Looking west, away from the hugely impressive Meteora, the region has, in some small way, the air of Denver Colorado, since across a short area of flat plain there are huge peaks rising up to scrape the sky, rather like the High Rockies do just west of that town. For much of the year too there are snowy patches still evident on the towering peaks. This is an area the topography of which puts one in mind of the "Big Country".

Further north Claire and Alyson came, during a particularly fine and pleasantly warm February, to Halkidiki. They stood beneath the old Byzantine Tower on the waterside at Ouranopoli ("heaven-town", or "city of the heavens") and drank in the history that oozes from the town's pores. They walked the short distance south to the 'border' of the land that is owned by the Orthodox Church, which is virtually the entire Athos peninsula south of Ouranopoli. Sitting on a low stone wall and staring at the coastline running south in the crisp clear light, they found themselves asking questions about the place.

"See," started Alyson," I can't get my head round how a religion that claims to follow a bloke who only had the clothes he stood up in can need to acquire so much land and material wealth. I mean, there's no disputing the beauty of some of those buildings down there, but what has all of this to do with Jesus Christ? I seem to recall, from my admittedly very sketchy knowledge of the subject, that he said something once about not storing up treasures on earth, but rather treasure in heaven. I see this as an ethic to encourage his followers to live the kind of life that builds up a good record with him upstairs."

"I'm with you a hundred percent on that one kiddo," replied Claire. "I couldn't be called religious by any stretch of the imagination, yet I do think that what I have heard about the gospels and how they depict the main man as far as 'Christianity' is concerned strongly indicates that his self-appointed 'reps' don't do a very good job of selling him. I rather think that if I were Jesus now, I'd be sacking the lot of them; giving them their P45s. There's no logic to me at all in how they carry on. Seems to me that he'd turn in his grave a few thousand times over at what the 'Christian' religions purport to be his system of belief, or conduct, or whatever it was he wanted to teach people. Bears no resemblance."

"My mum used to read the Bible sometimes. Not because she wanted to see the light or anything like that. She says a lot of the things that you do though. She just used to say that it was one of the World's great works of literature. She told me that H. G. Wells had once said, or written, or was quoted as saying – whatever - that unless someone had a working knowledge of the Bible they couldn't be called 'educated'."

"I suppose that makes a bit of sense. Better get ourselves a copy then."

"Yea, well, not before we've found a decent café for a coffee, agreed?" Her companion didn't need much encouragement and they eased themselves off from the wall, dusted off their jeans and strolled back toward Ouranopoli to find a suitable pavement table.

Later that same year, In Skiathos, one of the Sporades Islands, they happened upon a beach bar on a southern peninsula about half-way down the island's south-east coast, about fifteen minutes walk down a lane from where they'd got off the bus which ran up and down the island's only road of note. They'd studied the map and decided to try a beach called Vromolimnos, which was situated on a peninsula. Arriving with aching feet at the bottom end of the beach they were at first dismayed at the sight of a volleyball net near what appeared to be a trendy bar. To get to the beach one had to first walk around a small rush-filled lake, across which darted various small birds, which would also move furtively among the reeds, and you'd then walk up on to the soft sand, which brought you out on to the beach itself. It was evident that this beach could become very crowded, but the women were fortunate enough to have arrived early in the season and the beach was only occupied by a handful of thinly scattered sun-worshippers. The beach bar toward their right was situated behind a low whitewashed stone wall and consisted of a courtyard area of varying types of chair, most of which were very comfortable-looking. Beside the bar was a taverna, which looked like it was probably owned by the same people. It was an attractive taverna because the tables all sported the traditional-looking blue and white check tablecloths and those upright, raffia covered wooden chairs.

Once the two women had been slouched in a couple of low chairs for a while, their fingers drawing patterns in the condensation on the outside of their glasses and their sand-covered feet resting on the horizontal wooden bars which ran between the piers on the wall which separated the bar from the beach just feet below, Claire ventured the question:

"So, Alyson, any regrets? I mean you haven't said much of late about what you're running from…'" This last comment elicited an immediate response from Alyson, who made as if to reply with some annoyance, but Claire corrected herself and went on, "…Sorry. Poor choice of words there. I should have said, 'whatever or whoever it was you left behind."

Alyson breathed in deeply, as though to allow herself time to reflect. Then answered,

"Regrets? I suppose if I allow myself to think too deeply, I can still find myself thinking that I ought to run to a telephone and call Dean. Then I think, ah well, it's been a couple of years. He's bound to have shaken me out of his hair by now. Probably made it up with his dad, that's always assuming he actually told his dad all the details, which I still doubt he ever did." Here the conversation lapsed, as Alyson went into a reverie about possible scenarios in Dean's life. Claire was happy to leave it at silence for a while, thinking as she was that there was no nicer beach bar anywhere on the planet, so why not simply close her eyes, lean her head back and enjoy the sensation of having nowhere to go and no one to see.

Alyson again went deep into her thoughts. She had been keeping her mother Christine updated about her travels with Claire. She'd sent a postcard each time they arrived anywhere new and she'd phoned her every couple of weeks or so. But Dean, what was he doing? At moments like this she almost allowed herself to become morose about having lost him. It was as if she needed to hurt her own feelings as a kind of penance for having handled things the way she had done. She'd imagined that with time her desperate loss, that huge void deep within her, would heal, would close up. It hadn't. If she gave herself a few moments anywhere, any place, any time, she could very quickly feel it all welling up inside her. How could she have met the man she really believed was just right for her and then let him go? Why did his father have to be such a huge fly in the ointment? Did he still yearn for her, or had he decided that she was a right bitch to abandon him as she had? If the latter were true, she thought, he'd have every right. Now that she'd allowed so much time to elapse, there really was no point in trying to get him back. It would only throw his life, whatever direction it had taken since she'd gone, into unacceptable turmoil. It would be even more cruel than the initial act of abandonment.

No, she had made the right decision. She'd done the right thing for Dean. She'd just have to move on and perhaps one day there would be someone she could relate to who'd finally take the pain away. Yet here she was, a couple of years down the line, still not able to face even the idea of going out with anyone. She'd had plenty of opportunities too. She was grateful that Claire had never tried to intervene. If some bloke had been chatting Alyson up, Claire would always retreat and leave it up to the younger woman. As she'd reminded Alyson on many occasions, she would never offer advice, only friendship. As she was so fond of saying, offer advice and then you accept responsibility when the person you advised does what you suggest, gets into a pickle and then you're to blame. Yet each time some eager young man had clapped eyes on this raven-haired beauty with the melancholy air about her, she'd found herself making excuses and fending the guy off. She was still not ready for a relationship. Feeling like she did right now, she mused, would she ever be again?

OK, so she was still very young. She was only twenty-two. Yet why did she feel like she was going on sixty? In her short life so far she'd had enough emotional upset to age her, or so she thought. Still, at least their travels were effective at keeping her mind occupied for most of the time. She'd truly been gob-smacked by all that she'd seen so far in their Grecian travels. How grateful she was to have bumped into Claire at Kefallonia airport back in June of 1998. What on earth would have become of her had that chance meeting not taken place? How she appreciated Claire and her philosophy about life, not to mention the fact that she turned out to be so well-heeled. Not that Alyson ever considered the idea of never paying Claire back in some way. She still felt that sooner or later she'd stop wandering and start earning. She'd hone up her hairdressing skills and begin to show Claire that she didn't intend to be a freeloader forever.

Eventually, after having visited innumerable islands, many of which Alyson had great difficulty remembering by name, they came in May of 2001 to Rhodes, island of the Colossus, one of the Seven Wonders of the ancient world. This statue, which was forged of bronze and stood immense at Mandraki Harbour for a mere fifty-four years, from 280 to 226 BC, had stood over thirty metres high, making it one of the highest structures in the ancient world. It lasted for such a brief time because a huge earthquake brought it tumbling down unceremoniously after so short a while. The legend today says that it stood astride the two piers which formed the entrance to the harbour, but the fact is that it probably did not stand there at all, but rather to one side of the entrance. A sad fact is that had it been made of stone, the ruins would no doubt still be in evidence today, along with the rest of the island's abundance of relics and archaeological sites which pepper the modern city and much of the remainder of the island too. But, because it had been constructed of bronze, and although the remains lay where they'd fallen for around 800 years, the bronze was eventually carted away for scrap. Such an ignominious end to what had been such an artistic engineering wonder.

After drinking their fill of the Old Town, built by the Crusader Knights between the twelfth and sixteenth centuries, they found themselves accepting an invitation from another ex-pat British couple to come down to Lindos, on the island's East coast. It was here that Alyson first attempted to dance the Tsifteteli, the sensual dance based on the Turkish belly dance and usually danced alone or in groups by the women. It's not a dance in line, but rather a dance in which the woman will gyrate her hips to a driving and percussive beat, often to the accompaniment of the men clapping, whistling in appreciation or occasionally joining in. In recent decades the men have joined their girls on the dance floor more often and the dance has become one of flirtation. Very frequently this will result in any girl who takes the fancy of a watching Greek getting lifted on to a table, where her male admirer may also attempt to get up and dance with her. Not infrequently does this also result in the table in use collapsing under the kind of weight that it wasn't ever built to withstand, although usually without either party sustaining serious injury.

Alyson soon discovered that she was very good at this dance and began going to the few bars and clubs in the Lindos area, which would not get going until after midnight and the clientele of which would wend their way home toward the end of the small hours. This didn't worry Claire at all, since she delighted in having a little time to herself, to read or listen to old jazz music whilst sitting in the courtyard of the "Captain's House" which they'd taken on as a rented home for an indefinite period. She would sip a Metaxa on ice and reflect on things. She gradually realised whilst doing this that she didn't really have the wanderlust any more, at least not to the extent that she'd had it before. Perhaps she'd been running away from things. Perhaps now that she had

Alyson to 'look out for' she'd achieved a degree of penance that now afforded her a little peace of mind. No longer was she perpetually in angst about what had happened to Charles. She found herself gratefully acknowledging that she would finally let weeks go by without going over it again and again in her mind. Now at last she could accept it for what it was, one of life's 'things'. Sometimes there isn't a reason for it, it just is. It just happens.

Something else also had assuaged her wanderlust. She realised that it was the place itself, Lindos, one of the oldest inhabited villages in Europe. She'd been fascinated to learn that the Tomb of Kleoboulos was two and a half millennia old, going back as it did to the sixth century before Christ. She and Alyson had taken to wandering together out to the tomb on Sunday evenings, often returning in the dark by picking their way by moonlight among the stones along the narrow goat-path that wound its way along the edge of the bay to the North of the village back to the car park on the hill above the lane which led down to the far end of Lindos Beach. They'd evolved a kind of game that occupied them for hours. They'd think up questions to ask "old Kleo", as they called him. One of them would pose the question and the other would then have to answer as she'd assume that Kleoboulos would have. Of course, neither of them had any idea what the ancient village head, poet and sage would actually have thought, but that didn't matter. It usually ended up with both of them collapsing in tears of laughter as both questions and answers became sillier and sillier.

Alyson, too, had developed her own feeling about their potential plans. She also had come to the realisation that she'd rather not leave Lindos. They'd visited lots of islands in the three years during which they'd been travelling, sometimes staying for months. Yet here they were in Lindos, both thinking, even before they'd actually discussed it together, that they didn't really want to pack up their meagre belongings and head off to who knows where yet again. Lindos had the kind of "home" feeling about it. It made them feel like they'd seen enough of everywhere else and could happily stay here until something happened that perhaps would force their hand, yet both hoped that this wouldn't be any time soon.

Alyson, as she walked home through the ancient narrow streets from a good night's dancing at 4.00am during August of 2001, made a decision to talk to Claire the next day. She wanted to suggest that they hang up their 'moving on' boots for a while. She had another reason for this too. A Greek woman who ran a small wedding coordinating business in partnership with a British girl, had told her that they needed a hairdresser to do the hair of their wedding parties and guests as and when required. Alyson felt good about the potential of earning some cash for herself and paying her way with her and Claire's living expenses. Despite all of Claire's kindness during the past three years, the one thing that had bugged Alyson was that she wasn't contributing anywhere near as much as she wanted to from a financial point of view. Now she had the opportunity to change all of that.

3. Lindos – June 2005

This season had been going very well for Alyson. She'd been very busy doing the hair for brides, bridesmaids and guests galore and both Anthoula and Sally, who ran the wedding business, were very pleased with her. It was still only June, but it was looking like she'd be well occupied for all of the remainder of the season.

Even Alyson was amazed when she found out that British people wanting to get married abroad were booking weddings on-line - with websites like the one run by her two bosses - at a rate of knots. She found it amazing too that Lindos was more popular than many of the more long-haul locations, perhaps owing to the fact that the flights are much shorter, the weather more reliable and the prices more competitive than for such places as Florida, or the Maldives, where you also ran the risk of it raining on the big day.

So, when she got up and gathered her stuff to ram into the bag she used for work on the morning of Friday June 17th 2005 she was feeling good, she was feeling bright and ready to face another clutch of heads which were waiting to be transformed before the wedding that they'd be attending in a couple of days time. She first called into the modest office on the edge of the village, where Anthoula had confirmed her list of names and the hotel at which they'd be expecting her, although she'd already called the bride and spoken to her anyway. Then she was off, up through the winding whitewashed walls and arches of the village as she made her way to the hotel, which was up at Krana, the valley above and behind the village of Lindos itself.

Alyson would often go up to Krana via Lindos Reception, a café on a difficult bend in the road just up above St. Paul's Bay and just across from the Atmosphere Bar. It wasn't the most direct route from the village to Krana, but it was by far the less stressful, since the lane which led directly up from the main square to Krana Square was frenetic at the best of times, crammed as it was during the season with tourists walking in both directions, taxis weaving their way up and down, tourists in hire cars and riding scooters (badly) or even quad-bikes and the courtesy bus which ran every fifteen minutes ferrying yet more visitors to and from the village from Krana Square above, where often they'd spilled out of tour buses, freshly arrived from Rhodes Town.

Walking up from the office and past the Police Station she'd be able to cut through a couple of the more quiet, albeit steep, lanes and arrive up at Lindos Reception without having had to elbow too many tourists, or, what's worse, get stuck behind a group of three or four who were hell-bent on strolling so slowly that they almost went backwards, often insisting on taking a photograph every three feet or so. She also liked to go via Lindos Reception because she knew Sheena, who worked behind the bar there and could pick up a take-out frappe and have a little bit of a chat before walking up the pavement along the gentle hill which then led past the back of the village and then down a gentle slope towards Krana Square.

Having arrived at the hotel's reception she asked the Bulgarian girl who worked behind the desk how to find room 45, and then set off into the hotel complex as directed. According to Alyson's list she had seven girls and women to do in a period of several hours. The wedding was taking place in a few days, in the courtyard of the tiny church in St. Paul's Bay. 'Probably be one of about twenty weddings taking place there that day' thought Alyson, since she was by now quite used to seeing one wedding party walking up from the churchyard whilst the next waited at the top to walk down. Today was the trial run.

"What's involved exactly?" Asked Alyson just a few years earlier, as she sat with both Anthoula and Sally in a bar in the village; it was a kind of interview. The women explained that firstly they'd like to be sure of quite how good Alyson was and so asked if she'd be prepared to do both of their hair in order to show her ability. She agreed and so they fixed a time for the following day. Meantime, they proceeded to explain how it all worked.

"What happens is," said Sally, "we'll call you in advance, sometimes up to eight weeks before each wedding which you'll be doing. That way you can be sure to put it in your diary and there will be less chance of any last minute hiccups. After all, it's the big day for the bride. We have a system whereby we give each bride when she arrives a Greek mobile phone to use exclusively to contact or be contacted by us in the days leading up to the wedding. We will give you that number along with the bride's name. We'll also tell you the date when she'll be arriving on Rhodes and, usually, where she'll be staying. We'll also give you the date and time of the actual wedding. What you will then do is call the bride once you know she's on the island and in her accommodation, which will usually be in or near Lindos. Maybe Psaltos, maybe Pefkos, sometimes Vlicha, but not usually any further away than that. We have had a few staying at Haraki and even Kolumbia, but that's rare for weddings at St. Paul's Bay. Usually it'll be a hotel at Krana or a villa in Psaltos. Occasionally it may be an apartment or even a studio in Lindos village itself, but what matters is you calling and arranging to make your first visit for a trial run."

"A trial run?" Asked Alyson.

"Yes," continued Sally. "When you consider that these folk are coming out here in high summer from the UK, 90% of the time they're going to want their hair putting up, because of the heat. Usually you'll do the bride, the bridesmaids and perhaps the bride's mum. Now and again they'll include a few others, but usually you'll be doing about four or five women, very occasionally more. That will take a few hours anyway, as you'll know. The trial run is to enable you to do all their hair as they'd have it on the day, but it gives them the opportunity to make last minute decisions and perhaps change it before you do it on the morning of the wedding. Of course, what they pay us includes all this and the trial run and we'll pay you a fee per head, per wedding party. Does all of that make sense?"

Alyson indicated that it did indeed and that she was up for the job. In fact the whole prospect had made her quite excited at the challenge. She called her mother that very evening to tell her and received her warm congratulations on how her life was going in general. Christine was genuinely glad for her daughter. In a way, Alyson was living a life on behalf of her mother. It had been Christine who'd dreamed of a Greek idyll, of life on a Greek island where she'd sip Ouzo whilst watching the brilliant sun kiss the turquoise sea at the end of the day. Perhaps she'd actually have found her Adonis to make the scene perfect. She'd even allowed herself to imagine lounging on the deck of a luxury sailing yacht as they plied the seas from island to island. Christine wouldn't even have minded if this had been whilst working as a crewmember, as long as she was there, tasting life in the land of the Oracle, in the land where myths and legends had been forged so long ago. Although she still harboured her own ambitions to some day make it out there, she was almost as content to receive regular bulletins from Alyson about what she was getting up to, what she was experiencing.

4. Cardiff, UK – June 1998

After over a week with no word from Alyson, Dean was like a zombie. He was going through the motions of his normal routine, his mind entirely consumed with where she was, when she would be coming home, IF she would be coming home. He mentally went over and over again and again what had happened with his father. Ought he to call the man and make things right? It would take a good deal of consumption of humble pie, but perhaps it was for the best. But then, every time he almost made the decision to do so he'd feel terrified that the next moment Alyson would call. In the end he decided that he had to give her a fortnight before making a decision to do anything. After all, it was quite likely that she'd booked the holiday for two weeks and would be coming back in the middle of next week, all smiles and expectant of his having done what he had to do. There'd be a big kiss and hug as she exited the terminal building's Arrivals door and he'd remark on how brown she was. He'd tell her what had gone on and she'd be so proud of him. 'I have to give her until next Wednesday whatever' he resolved.

At work things were difficult. It soon became evident to his immediate boss, Marketing Manager Paul Burden, that Dean wasn't himself. He was snappy and wouldn't readily take to being told if there were changes to a piece of work that he'd produced. At the best of times it's hard for a designer to change something when he knows that the client is out of order design-wise. But the client pays the bills and so you just have to do it. Sometimes though, you can with tact get the client, or in this case the MD, to accept a compromise, but this takes diplomacy and Dean wasn't currently in a diplomatic mood. By the time the fortnight had elapsed and it became very likely that Alyson wasn't coming back, he'd become a disruptive influence in both the studio and the office in general. He couldn't help himself. He was angry at life, angry at himself for being a fool, angry at Alyson for not even getting in touch and livid with his father, who he now saw as the cause of his entire life having been de-railed. The girls he worked with, his two fellow designers Lorraine and Charlotte, complained to the boss that he was causing a bad atmosphere in the studio. Dean was lucky that Paul liked him. If he hadn't, things would have been much worse. Huw was up at the Golf Club most of the time anyway, so their paths didn't cross all that often.

The Marketing Manager popped his head into the studio at

8.45am on Friday, two days after Dean had rather hoped that Alyson would have come home, called him to tell him to pick her up from the airport, and things would have returned to almost normal. Yes, OK, he may have had to give his father the car back, yes he may have to find another place to live; but his soul-mate and lover would have been beside him and he was confident that they'd have sorted all this out. Cue happy little love nest and comfy life with the girl he adored.

But here he was still alone and moping into his first cup of coffee of the morning, shuffling A4 briefs around in the studio "in" tray to see which one would least irritate him to take to his desk and start work on. He always arrived at the studio at around 8.30am, a good half an hour before the two girls were expected in. In fact, they both normally got in to work a matter of minutes before nine and would throw themselves into their seats to make it look as if they'd been beavering away for ages when Paul Burden looked into the studio, which he'd always do after he'd arrived at his office at anything between 9 and 9.15am.

So it was with some surprise that Dean looked up to see Paul's face at a quarter to nine.

"When you've got five, Dean, pop into my office, will you?" Was all he said and the face was gone. Dean didn't have a clue what this was about. Probably something coming up in the near future for which his input was wanted. Maybe a word about the studio budget, or perhaps finally the green light for the studio to have a much-needed upgrade of the Apple Macintosh computers and software (the hot topic of conversation over lunchtime pints) from the company which supplied all the studio's materials. Now that would be good. Not for a moment did Dean think that it would have anything to do with him.

Five minutes later, as the two girl designers were hanging their coats up near the door and flicking their hair into place as they walked into the studio, Dean emerged, nodded to them and crossed the open-plan marketing department. He passed the other female staff pretending to work at their PC workstations whilst actually checking out the internet's gossip sites, not noticing the fact that they were casting knowing glances at each other at the sight of him making for the Manager's office, and walked through the glass door.

Paul Burden looked up and, gesturing to the leather-upholstered Captain's Chair across his desk, with a slight smile told Dean to sit down. Dean complied, folded his hands and began to spin his thumbs around each other, a habit he'd inherited from his father and which he hated. Each time he noticed himself doing it he'd stop and disengage his hands in disgust.

"Dean," began his boss, "is everything all right? I mean, if you don't mind my saying so, you've been rather tetchy of late. Not your usual sunny self. What's going on? Or is it something you don't want to share with me?"

Dean took a moment before responding. The mind works exceeding quickly in such circumstances and his thoughts ran through all that had occurred before Alyson had gone, then to his disastrous interview with his father at Limpley Stoke, to his turmoil over the first two weeks of Alyson's absence and then to how he was now feeling. He realised that he didn't even really understand himself how he was now feeling, except that it wasn't happy. Nothing was right and everything irritated him. Things that he would usually take in his stride, like tiny copy changes to a press ad, when there were five different sized versions to be sent and the copy date, indeed the copy hour, had been passed, now infuriated him and he let it show. When Lorraine, one of the other designers made sarcastic comments about a track that he liked when it was played on the radio in the studio, calling it a racket, he'd formerly have ignored her. When she'd done it yesterday he'd torn her off a strip for not appreciating good music from legendary bands. He hadn't even considered whether the track in question came from an era before her time. After all, he was into Led Zeppelin, even though he was only a toddler when they were in their heyday, but Lorraine was only eighteen and fresh out of sixth form. She hadn't gone down the college route like him and had secured her position in the company by the way she'd impressed Paul Burden in a hands-on test that he'd asked Dean to set for her to see what she was capable of, using the software on the Mac.

"Dean?" Are you still there? The lights are on..."

"What? Oh, yes, sorry Paul. What was it you wanted to talk about?"

"I was asking you if there was anything *you* wanted to talk about. Dean, the fact is, Lorraine and Charlotte have been in to see me and they both say you're impossible to work with lately. Now I know that's not the real Dean, so I'm asking you – what's up buddy?"

It began to sink in. Dean's behaviour was now threatening his position at work, his job in the studio, where he'd so impressed his future boss and the other directors over the eight months since they'd taken him on. Already he'd taken control of the fledgling studio's budget and managed to reduce spending on materials. Already he'd introduced some forms to streamline jobs as they come into studio and eliminated the possibility of work going to print without a signature from either Paul or a department manager, thus ensuring that it was very clear where the buck ought to stop in the event of a mistake. His design abilities had transformed the company's public corporate identity in a very short time and he was looking like a potential high-flyer. His father would have been proud of him, even though he hadn't initially approved of his son's choice of career. But now, here was the boss suggesting that he was causing problems.

Dean knew he had to pull his socks up. He had to reassure Paul Burden that he was going to return to the normal Dean and fast. He began:

"Well, there has been something..."

Paul Burden's desk phone rang. He picked it up, at the same time raising the other hand in a gesture of 'hold on. Got to take this call." Immediately he was into a conversation with some business associate or other. This could be a long one. Dean hated trying to talk to Burden at the best of times. Their conversations were always being punctuated by the boss picking up either his desk phone or his top-of-the-range mobile phone. It meant that Dean could hardly ever complete a sentence, or so it seemed to him. He sat there and tried not to twiddle his thumbs. At least this time he was getting a breathing space, which enabled him to think about how to phrase his explanation carefully. He really needed to keep this job. He needed to keep building on the progress he'd made to ensure that he'd be well thought of. If he were to leave under a cloud it wouldn't be the most auspicious start to a career. What kind of reference would he one day be leaving with from his very first real paying job out here in the grown-up world?

What seemed like half an hour passed, during which Dean had studied every corner of the Marketing Manager's office, from the self-congratulatory photographs on the wall behind the desk of PB shaking hands with various minor celebrities or rugby players, usually in their golfing kit out on the fairway somewhere, to the story-boards leaning against the wall near the door where he'd come in. He'd stared at the family snapshot in a stand-up frame on the desk in front of him. There was PB with his gorgeous wife and two sons. There was a family that hardly ever saw the dad and husband, since he was always at the beck and call of his MD along with the company's Sales and Marketing Director, who just happened to be the MD's son. How often was Dean leaving work at 5.30pm to see that PB was heading into a meeting in the MD's office. Or perhaps the MD and company owner Gerry Street would call PB and anyone else he'd need to bounce off and tell them they'd have to meet him in the Wheatsheaf, the pub nearby, where they'd probably sit for hours afterward, with no one having the guts to say, "I'm going home to my family now."

No, each of the pawns that Mr. G. Street played with was very malleable. Each would always be where he wanted them to be, no matter what hour, no matter what day. Sometimes, no, often, Street would want the directors in the boardroom on a Sunday morning. A group of five or six department managers, along with the hapless Huw, the designer whose work Dean was perpetually correcting, were in the intimate group (way out of Huw's spending depth) that habitually went straight from work to the squash courts every Friday evening. Their respective wives and children would always know not to expect their husband/father home before late on a Friday night. And most of them put in appearances at the office at least for a couple of hours on a Saturday morning too. No one wanted to be the one who appeared not to be pulling his weight. Mr. Street didn't look with favour on any man whom he'd put into a top of the range Audi or BMW not showing his worth by putting in a few extra hours, every week, every month, every year. Commitment, that's what he needed to see from his team, commitment. Gerry Street would approve of Dean's father.

Street was a driven man and he expected his department managers and lesser directors to be the same. There were already a few rocky marriages among the men in Mr. Street's inner circle. But then, when you're one of the richest men in Wales, you don't have to even wonder if someone's going to argue when you tell them they're 'working on' that evening. So? Your son's in the School play? What are you a wimp or what? Tell the kid where the money comes from for his new trainers, his hi-fi, his trip to Disneyland Florida every year.

Dean found himself coming to the realisation as to why he didn't like Gerry Street. This man was a carbon copy of his own father. Money was all that mattered. Sickeningly for Dean, at this point in his life and career, he wasn't in a position to tell the likes of Mr. Street where he could shove his outlook on life.

Finally, Paul Burden dropped the phone into its cradle. He smiled at Dean and said, "OK, Dean. A nod's as good as a wink, eh? I'm glad we've had this little chat. Look, I'm due in a meeting up at the leisure complex five minutes ago. But I hope you'll be back to normal from here on in, Dean. I don't want to lose you, but the atmosphere in the office and the studio needs to remain upbeat and sociable, I'm sure you agree." By now he was already snapping shut his attaché case and collecting his car keys from the desk as he rose from his chair, thus signalling to Dean that he too was expected to rise and exit the office.

Back at his desk, Dean summoned the courage to apologise to the two girls. "Sorry girls," he said with some considerable effort, "I ought to have come clean with you about what's happened with me and Alyson. That's why I've been a pain lately. I'll try and be nice, honest."

This was all it needed. Lorraine was at his side in seconds, "You and Alyson not getting on? Why didn't you tell us before? Charlotte, we're taking this boy up the pub lunchtime and we're gonna get him cheered up."

Dean signalled a weak thanks and pressed his index finger to his mouse.

5. Lindos – June 2005

"Well, I'll be a…!" Exclaimed Brian. He'd been sitting in the pool area of the hotel at Krana, having discussed playing at a wedding party and doubling up as DJ for the evening do too, when he saw the girl who'd been preoccupying him for a couple of weeks striding past carrying a large bag over her shoulder and just finishing off a take-out frappe. She even drew nearer as she searched for a bin into which to throw the spent plastic frappe cup and so he found himself calling out:

"Hi! Going somewhere important?"

Alyson looked over at this man who'd hailed her. In that instant Brian's heart leapt into his mouth, she was sooo like Christine.

She wasn't quite sure how to answer. Did she know this man? He must be old enough to be her father, yet he's actually very young for his age, she thought. I even like his taste in clothes. Wait a minute, the penny dropped, he's the guy who plays and sings in the bar down in the village a couple of nights a week. She cracked a smile.

"Hi! Yes, I've got a wedding." Seeing his face adopt a slightly puzzled expression, she added, "Not mine! I'm a hairdresser."

"Oh, yes, right, of course. Have you got a mo, just before you march off to make someone's head look stunning?"

Cheeky mongrel, Alyson thought. But then she replied, "OK. Sure." Throwing her bag down on the floor next to a seat, into which she then flopped, she looked expectantly at this man, wondering where this was going. Surely he didn't fancy his chances with her. Mind you, she thought, if I were to go for an older man, he'd be a definite possibility. Perhaps that's what I really need; someone old enough to be a father figure and steadying influence.

Slightly rising from his chair by way of showing a smidgen of chivalry, Brian continued, "Brian Worth, and you are?" At this point he tried hard to conceal his confused mixture of feelings. There was trepidation, there was anxiety, there was excitement and there was a hint of desire. He knew that the moment she told him her surname there could be no doubt. But then he realised that if she were indeed Christine Wright's daughter, Christine may well have married before producing her, or perhaps this girl herself was married, or had been.

"Alyson Wright, pleased to meet you. To what do I owe this pleasure? Was my slip showing?"

Brian's reaction was instant. That name – *Wright.* He knew right then and there that he was looking at Christine's daughter, however incredible that may seem. The world was not so big after all. It was very hard for him to reply. His mind told him that this was Christine, since the girl so closely resembled her mother that almost thirty years had disappeared down his stream of consciousness in a millisecond. He was instantly transported back to Porky's Bar in Bath. Those had been good times, albeit fairly brief. Odd moments flooded back in seconds. There'd been the time when Christine had wanted a bit of a heart-to-heart with him, a shoulder to cry on, and they'd gone up to the Salamander to eat a meal.

How that occasion had embarrassed Brian. He'd begun thinking that this would be his chance to declare his feelings. He was prepared to run the risk of rejection, but he felt that once they were seated at a table in the tiny first floor restaurant, subdued lighting and candles adding to the atmosphere of persuasion, he'd be able to make his move. OK, he was twenty-six and she was sixteen. But he felt younger and she looked older. Anyway, what do such things matter when you're smitten. And Brian had really been 'smote' big time. He'd never up until now allowed her to see how he felt, but here they were going up the stairs in the Salamander and he thought, 'I've got an hour or two of relative privacy with her here. Let's not blow it.'

He'd never eaten Indian, odd though that may have seemed for a man of his age. What made him select a Vindaloo? Christine went for a tuna salad and 'thicko here' (he mused) ordered the hottest curry on the planet. Of course, he was never going to be ready for quite how hot it would taste. He would never have believed that anything could be so spicy. He'd always persuaded himself too that he'd be able to handle anything. It's only food after all. Woo hoo!

Christine ordered a vodka and lime, the kind of drink that a sixteen-year-old could handle without too many problems. Of course, the waiter never dreamed for a moment that she was under eighteen, because she looked easily as though she were in her late teens and had done since she was fourteen. The only thing that Brian did right was to order a pint of draught lager. He was going to need it.

He waited until they'd ordered their food and the drinks were in front of them before asking Christine what it was she'd wanted to talk to him about. Here, now, sitting near a hotel pool in Lindos twenty-seven or more years on he couldn't rightly recall, apart from the fact that it had nothing to do with any feelings that she may have harboured for him. All that he did remember - and all too vividly, was the fact that as she talked, he spooned a huge mouthful of curry and rice into his mouth and thought that his head had caught fire. His face must have registered a degree of alarm because she then asked him whether it embarrassed him that she was telling him all this, whatever 'all this' had been.

Brian had been initially unable to answer. All he could do was take huge gulps of his lager until it ran down his chin either side of where the glass made contact with his lower lip. His mouth felt as though all the top layers of skin in there had been stripped away and his only thought was – maybe I need to go to the hospital! She'd laid her fork hand against the rim of her plate and asked, "Brian? Brian? What's the matter? I'm sorry, I..."

Brian found his voice, "No, NO! It's not you. I just suddenly felt unwell. It's nothing, it'll pass." He'd spent the remainder of the time in the Salamander picking at the mountain of hell-on-a-plate before him and swigging huge quantities of lager until Christine had finished her tuna salad, thanked him for being so understanding and told him that she felt much better and really ought to be going. It was all he could do to stand as she gathered her jacket from the back of her chair and whisper that he'd see her later as she left. The waiter had displayed a knowing smirk whilst clearing away an almost full plate from his place and he'd settled the bill as fast as he could and scuttled off down the stairs in total embarrassment.

"Are you OK? The slip comment, it was meant as a bit of a joke. Not a very good one I'll grant you. I don't wear slips, especially not with trousers!" Alyson's voice brought Brian back from his reflection.

"Sorry," he replied. "It's just that... well, where do I start?"

"Well, wherever it is, please make it fairly soon as I have an appointment with a few heads," replied Alyson.

"OK, OK. Look, you have a copy of Jean Paul Sartre's book '*Nausea*' don't you? I mean, I think I saw you with it the other night in the bar where I play."

"I do, yes. But what's..."

"Can I ask you, does it have a handwritten dedication in the front of it?" Noticing that she was now looking slightly uncomfortable, he hurriedly went on, "Don't worry, this will all come clear in a moment. Let me guess, it says something like:

'*To my little spiritual daughter Chris. I hope this won't depress you too much, but it certainly opened my eyes!*' And it's signed by someone called 'B'. Right?"

Alyson's eyes registered the fact that Brian had touched something deep down inside. Her face went pale and she stared at him. Her mouth opened, but nothing came out. Her mother had given her the book and explained that it had been given to her by this man that she'd worked with. When would this have been now? Before Alyson was born, probably 1976 or '77. What did her mum say when Alyson had asked her? Some guy who was a musician. A MUSICIAN! Here she was talking to this man who was certainly old enough, and he was a musician. He was a M-U-S-I-C-I-A-N. She allowed this thought to sink in whilst she racked her brain for more of what her mother had told her. That's right, she'd harboured feelings for the guy, even though he'd been a bit older. But she'd never told him and he'd eventually left to go in search of a career in London. That was the last that her mother had seen or heard of, …what was the man's name, now? B, Ba… Barry? No, Bartholomew? Give me a break. BRIAN!!! It was BRIAN. He worked in Porky's with my mum. All this came flooding through Alyson's mind as she stared at the man across the table.

"You're not, I mean you can't surely be …Brian? *THE* Brian who once worked with my mum in Porky's Bar in Bath a million years ago!?"

"The very same. And I'm sorry if I put you on edge. I have to tell you that the first time I saw you I almost died of a heart attack, you look so much like Christine. You move your head, your hands, your mouth and eyes exactly as she used to. Still does, hopefully. I *am* Brian and I have not passed one single day in the last twenty-seven years without thinking about your mother.

"Dare I ask, …how is she?"

"Look, Brian. We really must talk of course, but I have to run now. I'm sorry. Look, look… I'll come to the bar tonight and we'll arrange to have a proper talk. I'm sure my mum will be thrilled to know that I've bumped into you. She may take some persuading that it's actually you. But I'd say that the book clinches it."

6. Lindos – June 2005, Brian Reflects

"Now what are the chances of that happening, eh?" I recall some comedy show always using that phrase back in the mists of time. Who was it? Oh, yes, that bloke with the huge shirt collars and the line of pens in his jacket pocket. Harry Hill I think he was called. Funny guy, I liked him. Well, he'd have repeated that phrase today if he'd been there when I saw Alyson and we talked, briefly maybe, but we talked and she *IS* Christine's daughter.

It's a funny old world all right. Here I am in Lindos, two thousand miles and twenty-seven years away from a girl I once would have liked to get together with. Then her daughter ends up sitting in the bar where I'm playing a few times a week. Just turns up out of the blue and almost freaks me out. Mind you, now it's sinking in a bit I can't believe my luck. She's bound to be able to put me in touch with Christine. How *'katapliktiko'* - as the Greeks would say - is that?

I know, I know. Looking back I ought to have kept in touch. But then, at the time I didn't think I had a chance and so what would have been the point? I'd have probably made things difficult for her if she *had* found Mr. Right. Imagine me phoning up one evening and he answers the phone. Not a good scenario. Of course, if I had got signed and made a record or two, things might have been different. If I'd turned up with a pocketful of cash and a huge sports car maybe she'd have thought I was worth the risk. But then, if she came with me for those reasons I'd never have trusted her anyway, would I? Ah well, water under the bridge and all that. But where have all those years gone so quickly?

I suppose I ought to be grateful to be sitting here in Lindos, on the Greek island of Rhodes. How did I get here? How many years did I spend strumming my strings in the pubs and small venues in and around London? How many times did I play to a crowd who were to a man not paying the slightest attention to what I was doing? Yea, I had a small band for a while, during the eighties. Trouble was, pop music was horrendous then and unless you had enough mousse in your hair to make it stick up like the comb on a Roman helmet and you'd dyed it green and pink, oh, and wore enough eye make-up to keep Max Factor in profit for a decade or two, you just weren't going to get noticed. It's a bit galling that these days you've got the likes of Jack Johnson selling shed loads of CDs, and yet, when I wanted to do that kind of stuff in 1985 it was a non-starter. I didn't have a huge bank of synthesisers and some bloke standing next to me looking half-man half-woman. Couldn't have afforded a decent synth anyway.

Still, at least I met Spiro from Corfu when I was really down on my uppers and needing a gig. I can't say I ever really enjoyed playing all that Greek stuff in his taverna London N7. Don't get me wrong. After a while the music began to work some kind of magic in me. I didn't have a problem with it *per se*, no. It's just that it wasn't my music, it was someone else's. I really liked the rhythms and stuff. Playing along with the bouzouki and an electronic keyboard, we got into some great grooves. I used to love it when we did those numbers that went on for a quarter of an hour and I could improvise a bit. The bouzouki guy was generous in that area, he'd be happy to let me go for it now and again and the dancers! Well! They used to still smash a lot of plates then too. These days, health and safety and all that crap, they're not allowed to any more. So they chuck paper napkins and flowers. Very nice but you couldn't beat watching someone sweep a pile of broken crockery across the floor to make way for the next Zebekiko, when some bloke would whirl like a dervish all over the floor, throwing his legs over the heads of the other guys and some pretty tasty women, who'd crouch around him and clap and whoop and whistle. I tell you, the Greeks know how to let their hair down.

Must have been about then when I began to think about coming over here for a holiday. See if it was really like it seemed from my London N7 taverna experience. It was about then I think that I last saw my dad too.

I got my creative talent from my dad, Kenneth Thomas Worth, born Southampton, England 1926. I think it was what happened to him as a child that made me determine that, whatever happened and however badly I managed financially, I was going to be a musician and that was that. How he turned out like he did was a minor miracle.

He was born in March and within a few months his mother had been diagnosed as mentally too unstable to bring him up. Dad always told me that the doctors said that he'd 'bitten his mother's nipple' when feeding and that this had resulted in her contracting 'milk fever'. I have never been able to find out quite what that meant or what the medical experts of the day taught about such things. But that was what he always told me had happened. Anyway, the end result was that she was committed to an 'asylum', as they called mental hospitals in those days. Nice friendly, homely places they were not.

His father, my grandfather, took him when he was six months old to his own mother, a tiny woman already in her early sixties, and handed her his son. Dad once told me that his gran told him that she opened her front door to see her son Thom standing there with this little bundle in his arms, which he thrust at her and told her that she was going to bring Ken up. With that he'd turned and walked away.

Dad never saw his own father until he was fourteen years old. Even then he only came to meet him because a kindly older cousin had taken him on a train journey in 1940 and eventually they'd arrived at this strange front door in Southampton, where, when the householder opened it, his cousin had said, "Ken, kiss your father." Needless to say my dad refused.

I have vague memories of my parents taking me in their ancient Austin 10 to this place out on the Mendip Hills to visit my grandmother. I can still see her face now, but can't remember a lot more about those visits, apart, that is, from long echoey corridors painted bottle green and brown and dingy halls where we'd sit around the perimeter while I played with a toy cowboy and my parents tried to communicate with my grandmother, Dorothy.

Dad was raised by his gran and he always said that she did a grand job. At school it had soon become apparent that he was a whiz kid on the piano. In fact, when I was small, dad had an upright in the 'front room'. Everyone had a 'front room' in those days, the 1950's I mean. It was that room which was only used if we had important visitors, or perhaps the fire would be lit in there on Christmas Day and my dad would allow himself his only cigar or two of the entire year. We weren't very well off, but at least dad had a steady job in an engineering factory. He'd play that old upright sometimes and mesmerise me. There'd be a Dicky Valentine record which dad would put on the gramophone, or perhaps *'The Shifting, Whispering Sands'* by Eamonn Andrews, both of which were 78's. Mum would always put thrupenny bits into her Christmas puddings. There'd be port and lemon and if I was lucky I'd get a sip or two.

I asked my father once why he didn't pursue his piano playing as a career. He told me that he'd had to leave school at fourteen to become the breadwinner. His gran had become very old and riddled with arthritis and was bedridden. As a teenager my father repaid his grandmother's unselfishness without bitterness and with plenty of love. Him and my mum, once they'd met and begun 'courting', as it was called then, used to go out to the cinema, then come home to dad's place, which was only a flat of modest proportions, and give his gran a bed bath and sit with her until she fell asleep. Only when she died did they marry.

So, basically my dad sacrificed his artistic ability as a musician in order to serve an apprenticeship in engineering and provide for his gran, who'd raised and cared for him for nearly twenty years. This only had one good side to it. When I told dad that I wanted to play guitar when I was about ten, he bought me one. Well, to be strictly accurate, we sought out an appropriate acoustic for a young beginner and he made me save up half of the asking price, which was £15. "Son," he said, "You save up £7.50 and I'll match it. But one of the first lessons you'll learn in life is that nobody owes you anything. This world doesn't owe you a thing. So I want you to grow up appreciating everything you ever have because, Brian, I believe it's the best thing a father can ever give to his son."

I worked on a milk round with a nice bloke called Alan Brown, who'd always treat me to an iced bun when we passed the bakery on our Saturday morning round. I think I got something like five bob a week. But I can't be sure now, it's too long ago. I did get a few tips now and then as well. But after what seemed like an eternity I emptied out my tin with a slot in it on the dining room table and proudly presented the cash to my father, who went up to the attic and returned with my first guitar!! He'd only already gone and bought it, hadn't he. But he sure wasn't going to let *me* know that until I'd done what he asked of me.

I miss that man, I had as good a dad as anyone could have wished for. When I consider how he was brought up, I always thank God that he turned out to be a totally good man. He could so easily have been turned bitter by how his own father treated him, but he didn't. Instead he found a diamond of a girl to marry and they had me. They both always told me that they were going to give me the best childhood a kid could ask for. They did just that. When I was sixteen and wanted to form a band, dad could have said, "Get yourself a proper job." Instead he just advised, "Son, get a day job, sure. That way you'll always have something coming in. But if you want to go playing music I'll support you in any way I can. I only wish I had a few more of the readies. But what I can do for you, I'll do. If I couldn't be a musician, there's no reason why you shouldn't have a bash."

Anyway, I've spent most of my adult life scratching a few pennies from playing a guitar, so I can't really complain. There were a few occasions when I was in London when I thought I'd cracked it. I got a few pretty big gigs as support for a few bands or artists that did get a deal. I supported Dire Straits once, when they used to play the pubs. But somehow it never quite came together.

Ah, what the hell. I'm still alive and, when that bloke from Rhodes asked me if I'd fancy spending a summer over here a couple of years back I thought, why not?

Then I moved down here to Lindos, met Tzambikos, who offered me this "residency" and the second summer I play here this girl walks in. This dead ringer for the girl I lost because I was too stupid at the time. I wonder what she'll tell me about her mother. Seems odd to be calling Christine some grown-up girl's "mother." There we are, I suppose. Everyone has the same problem with the passing of time. If you haven't seen someone in ages you always kind of expect them to look the same.

Still, I'm taking comfort from something Alyson said, "I'm sure my mum will be thrilled," that was it. Will she be though? Or will she turn out to be married with a clutch of other kids to go with that boy she'd had before I met her? Maybe the best I can expect is a bit of memory-lane-ing and then a "so long and do keep in touch."

Expect nothing and you won't be disappointed. Must remember that. I always try to. After all, it's never failed in the case of my musical career so far.

7. Lindos – June 17th 2005, Brian and Alyson

Brian had placed the guitar on its stand and, taking a fresh bottle of Mythos beer with him, he walked to the table where Alyson was sitting, this time minus the friends.

"Hi, thanks for coming in tonight," He began, "I kind of thought that you wouldn't show up again. Don't ask me why. Maybe because you'd spoken to Christine and perhaps she didn't think it was a good idea to pursue this."

Piped music began to play, an old Santana album. It was Brian's intermission. It was about half past ten and impossibly warm. Alyson's bare shoulders made it hard for Brian to concentrate on her very beautiful face.

"I haven't talked to her yet. But I know she will want to hear from you. She never married, you know." Seeing a definite sign of optimism flash across the face of the man across the table, she deduced pretty quickly that he still held a torch for her mother. Now all kinds of other scenarios flashed through her mind. The first time he'd hailed her she'd thought that he might just be hoping to start something with her. Now she suddenly thought, 'maybe I'm looking at a future step-dad.' She found herself getting into a reverie about this now. He'd do OK as a step-dad, looking very youthful as he did for a man in his fifties. Not that she actually knew exactly how old he was. She always knew that her mother had wished that she'd declared her feelings to this man. Not having talked much with him herself, she knew that it was a bit early to speculate, yet she already believed that she knew what her mother had seen in him. Did he have kindly eyes, or was that just fanciful imagination? She realised that Brian was waiting for her to continue.

"Mum's had a few guys, sure. But none of them have lasted for long. I don't think she's been particularly difficult. I think it was more that she kept trying to find someone like the elusive Brian, who'd walked out of her life, just like that." Now she saw something else again in Brian's eyes. What was it? Something that showed that he was puzzled, perhaps.

"What?" Asked Alyson.

"Well," Answered Brian, "You just told me something that I wish I'd known nearly thirty years ago. You see, I always loved your mother. She was very young, I know. But we worked together for quite a while and I knew I loved the girl. She had a baby…"

"My older brother, George."

"Yes, but I didn't mind. She'd told me all about the father and that she'd just been a stupid girl and stuff. She seemed to me to be always trying to purge herself of something. I, I… forgive me. This is difficult. Alyson, how much do you know about your mother's lifestyle during the seventies?"

"Oh it's OK. I know that she had a lot of men. When I grew up to be, oh, it must have been about eight or nine, around eighty-six or eighty-seven, she kind of came clean and told me that she'd been trying to stay in a single relationship. Or, if we didn't happen to have an 'uncle' living with us for a while, she'd be sure not to have one-night stands and things. But I do know that she was very wild when she was a teenager. My grandmother wasn't exactly a paragon of virtue anyway. Mum told me that she'd been a pretty naughty girl too. My mum's very intelligent. But then you know that.

"Mum and I used to have a lot of heart-to-hearts. I know that she was living the low life because she kind of felt that it was all she deserved. Do you know what I mean? It's like a self-fulfilling prophecy. Because she had a low sense of self-worth, she thought she wasn't worth anything, so she lived the way that she felt she was destined to. It took her a long time to acquire a sense of self-respect, to realise that she didn't have to keep paying for the way she was brought up. She eventually realised that perhaps she did have a chance to do something with her life. The problem was, she'd already had four kids by then and she was only twenty-three, going on twenty-four. I couldn't have had a better mother though, even though to an outsider our family looks like the classic thick lower class dysfunctional prototype. She and I are like soul mates and, even though I've been away from the UK for quite a few years now, we're very close. I ring her every week and I send her letters.

"You know something? She always dreamt of coming to Greece."

"I do know that." Said Brian. "She and I worked together all through the summer of 1976, the only summer I can remember that made the UK feel like the Mediterranean for several months. It was extraordinary. Christine used to say that she dreamed of Greece, the land of the Gods."

"Well, I'm still hoping that she'll get out here some time. My youngest sister, Gemma, she's twenty-two now and still living with my mum. She needs to get herself sorted out. Mum's still strapped for cash, always has been. But I've been saving up and I'm going to buy her a ticket myself one day soon."

Brian realised that he was frightened. He was frightened of talking to Christine after all these years. Would she still look good? He knew that this shouldn't be the only thing to go by, but he couldn't help but look at the daughter he saw before him and wonder whether Christine would have "lost it" or whether she'd still wow him if he saw her. He was also scared of perhaps meeting Christine again and then finding that all the intervening years had put so much distance between them that they wouldn't hit it off. But then, he told himself, she's still single and so is he. What if they came together now and it all fell into place?

Then he also realised that he was frightened of this *not* happening. He so badly found himself wanting it. Alyson spoke,

"Tell you what. I'll be calling her tomorrow. Why don't I tell her about our chance meeting and our little chat tonight and see what she says. Then we can decide if I give you her number, or give her yours. How does that sound?"

Tsambikos was gesturing to Brian that it was time he was back at the mike.

"Sounds just perfect."

Part Four

Closer Than You'd Think

1. Dean, Cardiff – August 1998

I'm going to call my father. Well, perhaps I ought to re-phrase that. I must call my father. It's now more than six weeks since his ultimatum and Alyson hasn't come home. I can't even begin to describe how I'm feeling, how I've been feeling. I daren't open Alyson's wardrobe and see all her things still in there. There are still a couple of pairs of her shoes in the hallway. I haven't been able to move them. All right, so she took most of her toiletries with her, but there are still odd things like creams and nail varnish remover in her bedside cabinet. I haven't been able to touch any of it. I haven't been able to bring myself to accept what is becoming more and more likely, the probability that she's gone for good.

I'm still puzzled though. Having come to know her as I thought I did, I can't get my head around why she's done this. I mean I'd have sworn to anyone that she'd be the kind to tell me if she'd decided that I wasn't the guy for her. Apart from the issue about my father, we were so good together. I just know that there must be some weird explanation that I haven't thought of yet. There must be.

Alyson is so open. She says what she thinks. She told me that she loved me and, initial doubts aside, that she knew she'd done the right thing to throw her lot in with me. I know one thing. I've had girlfriends enough to be sure that she was the one for me. I'd settled into a false sense of security, or so it seems now, that she and I were set to stay together. I can't recall us ever arguing so badly that it reached the point of raised voices or fuming moods. She never stormed out in a huff. She knew that she only had to give me that certain look and I'd crumble anyway. I'd have given the earth for her, however trite that may sound. When it's the truth, it's the truth, after all.

I've even talked to her mother on the phone, while Alyson was still here. I was looking forward to meeting her some time soon.

Now there's a thought. Is Alyson's mum's number written down somewhere? Maybe I could ring her and see if she knows anything. Maybe something awful's happened and she doesn't know how to contact me. No, that's silly. I'm sure she has this number. Or has she? Maybe she only has Alyson's address and – yes – that's a thought, I think it was always Alyson who made the call when they talked, never the other way around.

Have I got the guts though? The thought of ringing Mrs. Wright fills me with fear. Why is that? What's wrong with you Dean? Pull yourself together, man. But no, I don't think I can do it. What if she doesn't know and then I go and put my stupid great foot in it? I think I'll have to face up to it. She's gone, pure and simple. I have to accept that, however galling it may seem, my father's right. Alyson's probably right now in the arms of some Greek charmer who's persuaded her that he's all she ever wanted and…

You're never going to convince yourself of that are you Dean?

Why, if she never intended to come back to me, did she leave so many of her belongings here? Her modest CD collection is still piled around the hi-fi in the lounge. Her herb teas still taunt me if I open a certain kitchen cupboard. There was some of her dirty washing in the washing bin, which I've even washed, ironed where necessary, folded and placed on top of the chest of drawers for her to put away when she comes home.

When she comes home. I'm finding it increasingly hard to say that now. It's been around two months. And I have to admit too, that she doesn't have very much materially anyway. She was never one for possessions. I haven't seen that book around the flat either, the one by Jean Paul Sartre that she told me her mother had given to her on a kind of indefinite loan. Now why would she have taken that with her? I mean it's not as if she hasn't read it, probably several times. Perhaps I ought to call the Police, or even Interpol. But then what a wally I'd look when they came back and told me that she didn't want to be found.

Face up to it boy, the probability is that she's gone and you have to get on with your life.

I sound like my father now.

At least Dean hadn't been experiencing any more problems at work. He'd knuckled down and made a gargantuan effort to be nice to people, especially Lorraine and Charlotte, the two other designers in the studio, after the Marketing Manager had flagged up his grouchiness. No way could he now be described as the happy outgoing guy he'd been before, but at least he was biting his tongue and getting on with his work in a cooperative manner. The girls, to be fair to them, had done as they'd promised on the day when he'd been summoned and taken him up to the nearby pub during the lunch break for a talking to. They'd done their best to persuade him that he was still very young and good-looking enough to find someone else. These kinds of things were a part of life and you had to square up to them and move on. They'd meant well and Dean had decided to humour them by accepting their counsel with grace. He knew that this would go a long way towards them coping with his moroseness anyway. In fact, during the succeeding weeks they'd gone out of their way to let him have his pick of the jobs coming into the studio's "in" tray and been quick to reassure Paul Burden that they were fine with him again and that they had no issues. Once or twice he'd been on the brink of snapping at one or the other of them, but he'd managed to check himself and redouble his efforts, so at least it seemed that his job was still safe. Why, he'd even told the MD, when they discussed a layout, that he'd change this or that as requested, instead of fighting his corner with a designer's passion.

So, eight weeks after Alyson had gone from his life in such an abrupt manner, he called his father on the phone.

"Hi Dad. Dean." He began.

"Hello Dean. It's a funny month this, son. Didn't I give you one month? More like two have now passed. Still, never mind. I'm assuming you have some news for me?"

"She's gone."

"Well, well. My son has a modicum of sense in his head after all. I must admit I'd underestimated you Dean. I was all prepared to wash my hands of you in the hope that it would be what was needed to bring you to your senses, but here you've gone and done the right thing after all."

"Dad, I didn't… I mean, it was she who…"

"Dean, my boy, I don't want to hear the details. You just told me that she's gone, am I right?"

"Yea Dad. I did, and she is. I'm on my own now."

"Well, then that's OK isn't it. All part of life's rich pattern my boy. Call it the steep part of the learning curve. Anyway, plenty more fish in the ocean Dean, most of them much better catches than a council house chancer, who…"

"DAD! Now you're talking in a way that I don't want to hear, all right? I just wanted you to know that you needn't take my car back and, if you're happy to go on doing so, I'd appreciate your help with the rent for a little while longer. I have complied with your ultimatum. I'm…"

"I wouldn't call it an ultimatum, Dean. Rather a father's way of getting his dear son to see sense. Let's move on, shall we? When are your mother and I going to see you? It's been a while. Even your sister's fed up with not having anyone to argue with. Why not get yourself over here this coming weekend. We'll have a cosy little family bonding session. How does that sound?"

"Great dad. Great."

"Well, you could inject just a little more enthusiasm. But never mind. No doubt you're still pining for this little minx, so I'll let it pass this ti…" The phone went dead.

Francis Waters didn't mind. He allowed himself a wry smile and, standing up in his office in readiness to leave, he spoke aloud, "Youth eh? Folly and fancy. Still, my boy's back in the land of the living.

"Thank you God."

2. Alyson, Lindos – June 2005

Alyson knocked on the door of the hotel room and waited for a response. Some sounds of excited giggles and girls laughing and stomping about came through the door. Eventually, after a couple of screams and a few more giggles, a young woman in nothing but a white bath towel opened the door and, before Alyson could introduce herself, said in the kind of accent which Alyson would have described as upper class,

"AhAAA! Girls, our coiffeur has ARRIVED!" She did this without breaking eye contact with Alyson and then stood to one side and beckoned her enter with a wave of her hand.

Inside the room, which would be better described as a suite, there was nothing short of pandemonium. Six young women in various stages of undress were sprawled across the beds, leaning against the door frame of the French doors onto the balcony or crouching in front of the mini-bar, one finger to the lips in contemplation as to which bottle or can would be next. Alyson, not fazed at all by the scene before her, having now done this work for a number of years, asked with some degree of volume added to her normal speaking voice,

"Hi ladies. Which one of you's the bride then?" at which a strikingly attractive blonde girl with wet hair who was standing in the bathroom doorway raised her hand and admitted to being the candidate. Alyson made eye contact and continued: "So you'll be Fiona Kyle, right? I rang you the day after you arrived on the island. Alyson Wright, hairdresser to the stars!"

The young woman known as Fiona replied, a giggle trying valiantly to defeat her attempt at stifling it, "YUP! That's ME all right. How do you want us then?"

"Well, I've got six of you according to my list and the actual wedding's at 4.30pm next Monday. Agreed?"

All six voices responded, more or less in unison, 'AGREED-Duh!"

Alyson was soon discussing with Fiona Kyle how she was going to have her hair arranged for the wedding and did likewise with the bridesmaids and maid of honour. Four of the former and one of the latter were present. Once the mood had become a little more contained, with a couple of girls out on the balcony slouched on sun-loungers and sipping wine and one more reading glossy magazines whilst stretched across one of the beds, the other two having disappeared into the bathroom where the sounds that emanated soon indicated that at least one of them was taking a bath, whilst both carried on a spirited conversation in loud raucous whispers, Alyson began the dry-run of the bride's hair.

"Where are you from, Fiona?"

"The West country. But I refuse to do an 'ooh arr, ooh arr!' Everyone I meet for the first time seems to think that if you're from anywhere west of Swindon you probably walk around all day with a piece of straw in your mouth and drink scrumpy cider. I'll admit to doing the latter because when we go to the young farmer's shindigs the scrumpy *is* rather good. Gets you smashed in double-quick time I can tell you."

"I'm actually from Bath myself. Not that I've been back for quite a few years though."

"Really? From Bath? How wonderful. Fellow yokels, thee and me girl. I'm actually from Castle Combe, not that far from your neck of the woods is it?"

"'Bout ten miles I'd say. I used to go there sometimes. Lovely high street."

"Yahh, rather. Rode my stallion down it once or twice, not naked though. Too ruddy cold! How long have you been living out here then? Sorry, what was your name again?"

"It's Alyson. I've lived on Rhodes since 2001, but before that I was sort of island hopping for a few years with a friend." Fiona went blnak just for a millisecond at the name Alyson. Then she shook her head ever so slightly and responded,

"Lummy. So how come you ended up here on Rhodes then?"

"It's odd, but I live in a small studio-cum-apartment up at the back of Lindos village, an area where quite a few Albanians and others also rent accommodation. We have a small terrace out the front and, after moving there from a "Captain's" House down in the village, Claire and I just decided independently of each other in fact, that we wanted to hang up our wandering boots. The view across the rooftops of the village to the Acropolis is quite beautiful."

"Soooo," answered Fiona, "You and Claire, you-ah, you…?"

"No, neither of us is gay if that's what you mean. I was actually kind of running from a relationship – with a man – when we met, and she suggested we team up to go travelling the islands. She's quite a bit better off than I am, but I didn't know that until we'd agreed to go travelling."

"Sounds soooo exciting. I kind of wish I'd been in your shoes now. Boring old life I live I'm afraid. All I do is manage daddy's racehorse stable. Spend all my time up to my knees is horse pooh. Talk about exotic, eh?"

"I can think of worse lives to be living." And she could too. Alyson's mental pictures flew back to the time before she'd met Dean. She pictured with extraordinary clarity her mother's modest run-down council house in Twerton. She thought of the various "Uncles" she'd known whilst growing up. She remembered having a "My Little Pony" and, as she'd entered her teens and gradually left off playing with it, had thought to herself: 'this is about as close as I'll ever get to owning a horse'. She remembered the scuffed second-hand shoes that she'd worn for school when she was just entering her teens. Police cars were perpetually visiting the local pubs near her mother's home on weekend evenings, as a result of some disturbance or other. She felt that the life she'd led before meeting Dean had been about as far from this girl's life as one could possibly get. Yet they looked like they were of similar ages. How strange to think that a mere ten miles away there had been this little plum-in-the-mouth silver-spoon girl growing up in such disparate circumstances.

"So," continued Alyson, dragging her thoughts back to the here and now, "How did you meet Mr. Right?"

"Oh, you know, at some 'do' or other. I rather think that daddy sort of set us up, our two 'daddies' in fact. Mind you, I'd have pretty soon told the chap to get on his bike if I hadn't fancied him. It's not like he swept me off my feet like in some fairy tale. But I'd say he's the genuine article, my 'Mr. Right' if there ever was such a thing. I was always a bit susceptible to a guy with long hair. Perhaps it reminds me of a horse's mane!" She said this with a slight chuckle, as if to invite Alyson to laugh along with her, which the young hairdresser made a half-hearted attempt to do.

Alyson decided to change the tack of the conversation a little. "Is this your first time on Rhodes?"

"No, I've have been once before. Been to other parts of Greece though, too."

"And, do you like it here? Or perhaps I ought to ask where else you've been."

"Lindos is a dream, isn't it? Santorini's amazing, but Thira's too high up for me. Great sunsets, but not a very nice colour to the beaches. Mykonos I loved, but too many gays everywhere. Have you been?"

"No, but I have been to Santorini, plus a few other places." The conversation continued with the various heads that she had to beautify and Alyson soon found herself saying goodbye to the excited wedding party and closing the hotel door behind her.

3. Alyson – Lindos, January 17th 2007

Hello, Kleo. Me again. But then, you knew that didn't you. You still haven't revealed the secret of the pair of trainers. Sadistic sod aren't you. Ah well, maybe it's for the best. Maybe I'm better off leaving things as they are. Sleeping dogs and such.

But if only it hadn't gone the way it did. I mean, if you lose something, …some*one*, it's probably better if you can't ever have them that they stay lost. It's a cruel torture to be given another dose of hope and have that dashed too. Of all the places to choose to have their wedding. Life's full of coincidences I suppose. That's why so many people try and attach meaning to them, but I can't do that. It doesn't make any sense to me to do that. So many innocent people in this world are suffering while we in the more affluent countries keep thinking that God or fate or whatever is planning things out for us, is doing things 'for a reason'. Dean taught me that.

Just under two years ago, Kleo, my whole life turned upside down – again.

4. "Going off on one" Claire – Lindos 2005

So often one's life turns on one brief moment. One moment, when we could have been somewhere else, but we weren't. We were at a particular spot where something happened that changed the course of our life completely. Had Alyson not gone out with Nicky on that particular Saturday night in October of 1997, she wouldn't be in Lindos now. Had she not decided to sacrifice Dean for the sake of his career and family, she'd also not be here. She'd probably be working in a salon in South Wales and Dean would be struggling without the backup and security of his family to make a kind of career for himself and probably learning to resent Alyson in the process. At least, that was how she persuaded herself to see things.

A lot of water had gone under the bridge for both Dean and Alyson since she'd walked out in June of 1998 to take a trip to Kefallonia. How different Claire's past few years would have panned out, how differently Brian's life would be going to turn out had he not seen Alyson across a sweaty bar terrace on a hot June evening in Lindos in 2005.

Since they'd settled at Lindos, Claire and Alyson had begun to see less and less of each other. They had no problems with their friendship, it was simply that Alyson was young and soon became absorbed in a social group of her own age, all of whom liked to go out until the small hours a couple of times each week to places where Greek music played and they danced incessantly, as did the Greeks of their generation. Claire, on the other hand, would read late into the evening, glass of red wine at her side, then retire before midnight and sleep until it was light. Before long she'd read Thomas Hardy's entire output of novels and most of George Eliot as well. She admired Eliot especially, because he was a 'she' of course. Mary Anne Evans, born in 1819, had decided to write under a male pen-name in order to be taken seriously, such was the social view of women at the time. Claire admired her as a pioneer of feminism, a closet feminist perhaps, but nevertheless she had proved something. She proved that women weren't just an accessory for their men to have around in order to produce their heirs and make their dinner tables look prettier during soirées with guests.

Claire had begun, since she'd been living in Lindos for about four years now, to consider moving on. She didn't have much in the way of family back in the UK, but she did have a cousin or two and an aunt who'd been recently widowed. She also had one or two friends from the days when she and Charles had pursued a very active social life in the UK. She'd never told Alyson that she had been an artist. She simply hadn't been able to pick up a brush ever since losing Charles. Now, however, she felt the need returning to begin creating again and all her equipment was back in Bristol, locked and gathering dust in her studio in Clifton, awaiting the return of her hands to be lain once again upon brush, palette and canvas. She was also experiencing a kind of emotional and spiritual crisis. Born in 1951, she was becoming ever more conscious of her mortality, approaching as she now was her "autumn" years. The year was 2005 and Claire had turned fifty-four. She was grateful that she'd always enjoyed good health. She'd never been fanatical about exercise, but had always made herself walk several miles briskly at least two or three times a week. She was a self-trained nutritionist and knew all about a healthy diet. She was never one to over-indulge, but would have a couple of extra drinks just now and again, if the occasion demanded it.

But what she found herself doing more and more, as she moved into the high summer of 2005, was reflecting on the brevity and apparent pointlessness of it all. She'd had a marvellous partner in Charles. They'd both married when quite mature in years, in their early forties in fact, and had enjoyed just a few short years together before Charles died. What no one ever discovered, including the police, was the fact that he hadn't killed himself at all. He'd been murdered by some people that he'd become involved with and from whom he'd tried to extricate himself, unsuccessfully. But the fact that he died in the way in which he apparently did was one of the building blocks of Claire's state of mind later.

Most of us in the "civilised" world are brainwashed by evolutionary teaching into believing that there is no purpose to anything. There is no real point, apart from perhaps reproducing our kind and leaving the next generation to get on with it. But such an outlook didn't sit well with Claire, who was one to see beauty in everything. She would ponder as she sat atop the Lindos Acropolis on summer evenings, watching the sun drop toward the horizon, on why we humans even perceived such a thing as beauty. 'I mean,' she would tell herself, 'I'm supposed to believe that everything evolved out of necessity. But where is the necessity in beauty, the arts, especially music? Why, indeed, do we feel love at all?'

She would research on her newly acquired laptop all about the capacity of the human brain and, as a result, became perplexed by the fact that, during an average human's lifespan, he or she only uses something less than one percent of the brain's capacity. If our brains had evolved out of necessity, why weren't they considerably more simple? She'd thought about perhaps investigating religion, but that only left her even more confused, largely because of the total absurdity of what most religious people do or believe. Here in Greece she'd been along to some festivals and watched people kissing icons. She'd studied the priests of the Orthodox Church and wondered what precisely all their paraphernalia had to do with the man they claimed to follow. The funny tubular hats, the robes, the gold they wore or crammed their churches with. And the beards really got her going. OK, so perhaps it's meant to display a man's maturity of years, but she couldn't fail to be repelled by these men and their general sense of superiority. Wasn't Christ meant to have been a humble man? Didn't he say once that he had nowhere to lay his head? Then there was the perennial problem of how religions supported war and conflict. It seemed to Claire that every nation has its own version of Christianity. This seemed to apply to many non-Christian nations too. Evidently the creator was being called upon to give the victory or his blessing to this nation or that one, as against all the others on this planet.

No, although she decided that there was just cause for being 'spiritual' in some way or other, there wasn't anything to be gained by joining any of the religions. How often had a "Born Again" Christian told her to let Jesus into her life? The problem was, when she asked them to explain quite how or why and what Jesus was going to do for her they usually floundered. Their religion seemed to her to be emotion-based and not logic or knowledge-based. It was like a kind of comfort blanket. As long as they could convince themselves that they personally were saved, that they themselves were OK with God, then they slept nights. "Faith is a gift", one such believer had told her once. To which she'd replied, "Well, you'll never get me to worship a god who gives it to some whilst withholding it from others. Doesn't sound like a very fair or unbiased god to me."

She'd begun to lay awake in the small hours thinking, "I'm not going to be here some day. Will anything exist when I'm gone? Or is it all, the entire universe, inside my brain anyway?" What was it that Joni Mitchell had sung in that song on the album *"Court and Spark"*? *"Everything comes and goes"*. Yes, much as George Harrison had been trying to express a similar idea with his album *"All Things Must Pass"*. Even in the movie *"The Sound of Music"* she remembered hearing a fundamental truth, which Julie Andrews and Christopher Plummer sang about in the summer house one romantic evening, *"Nothing comes from nothing, nothing ever could"*. At least that left Claire with the abiding belief that there had to be some kind of intelligent first cause, otherwise, why would anything exist at all?

After months of such deliberations Claire was of the mind that she wanted to return to Bristol and take up painting. At least becoming absorbed in her art would be an anaesthetic. It would keep the pain of not understanding anything about existence from consuming her for a while.

5. The Ikon Bar – Lindos Sat June 18th 2005

Lindos is a very beguiling place. There have been people living in a village on the site for three thousand years. Prior to Rhodes Town being established and growing in the fifth century before Christ, it was even the island's capital of sorts. The history of the place oozes out of every wall, every street corner, as one walks in the village. It's an easy place in which to become disoriented, even temporarily lost. Walking through the village following what the locals and regular visitors call the "main drag", one glimpses every few seconds a side street so narrow that you could touch both walls simply by stretching out your arms. And everywhere the buildings are painted white.

Today the lanes echo to the sounds of radios and TVs burning in the residential house, of which there are many. Women call their small children in to eat or prepare for bed and men still sit in several kafeneions dotted about the village that stay open during wintertime. Although thousands of dusty feet in flip-flops and sandals tread these streets every summer, many of the owners of those feet don't realise that Lindos is a living, breathing village. It has banks, stores, a school, a local Post Office and a Police Station. It's not simply a playground for holidaymakers. Many of the one thousand or so permanent inhabitants work in the tourist industry and of course appreciate the visitors coming. Yet still, as the season draws to a close at the end of October each year, the locals find themselves feeling relief that they now have few months in which to recover from the long working hours and the constant hubbub which a huge influx of visitors inevitably involves.

As was her habit, Alyson was flopped into a low padded seat near the street in the front of the Ikon Bar as the light faded. It was Saturday evening, June 18th. Sipping at a frosted bottle of Mythos Beer, she idly watched the tourists as they passed by in both directions. Families struggling up and down the inclines with baby-buggies, parents trying to contain excited or fractious children, people bumping into others out of frustration at having their progress impeded by those not needing or wanting to get through the village anything like as quickly as them. Voices drifted into and out of her consciousness…

"But we ate there last night, Let's try somewhere else tonight."

"What time did the man say we had to be ready for the coach in the morning?"

"Still haven't got anything for Beryl. I must get something for Beryl."

"Yes, please! You want to look at the menu, we have roof terrace!"

"Will you shut up!! You're NOT having an ice cream, we're going out to eat and you'll spoil your meal!"

"We came up this street just now. Told you we were lost."

"Alyson, Alyson!" The voice was unmistakably Claire's. Alyson looked up to see Claire standing in the narrow street and looking at her with a smile. "Where've YOU been recently? I don't seem to have seen much of you. How're things?"

"Claire!! Sit!! Sit!! I'll stand you a drink, red wine?"

"No, I think I'll have a Campari and Sprite. Nice aperitif."

Having ordered Claire's drink from the girl who was passing with a tray-full of glasses, Alyson responded with her amazing news.

"You're not going to believe this, Claire, but I bumped into a man yesterday. Well, actually I've seen him a few times in the past few weeks, but he actually collared me yesterday and told me he recognised me."

"Recognised you? From where?"

"Well, to be honest, he didn't exactly recognise me. He said he saw my mother in me and asked if I, …no wait. It was Jean Paul Sartre. The book."

"*Nausea?* The one your mum gave you and you always have in your shoulder bag."

"Yea, that's it. Well, he called me over while I was going to do a wedding trial run up at the Lindos View and told me he'd seen the book and almost collapsed with surprise. He told me that I looked so much like my mother that he'd done a double take. Then, when he saw me with the book, he said he knew I had to be Christine's daughter. It was spooky at first because he asked me if there was a dedication in the book, which there is, and then he told me what it said. Claire, he only worked in a bar with my mum back in Bath in the seventies! Amazing coincidence or what?"

"Amazing indeed. What's he doing here in Lindos then?"

"Oddly enough, I'd seen him several times already, because he plays guitar in that bar where the guys from the firm hang out. He looks like he's probably older than mum, but he's not 'old' in his ways. He's a fab guitarist and it seems that he used to have a crush on mum. This is what's so sad really."

"Mum? It's Alyson. How's things? Everything OK?"

"Fine love, just fine. What about you? Met a rich Greek bloke yet?"

"No, mum. Told you before. I'm not going to rush into anything unless I'm absolutely sure."

"Alyson, love, it's got to be five or six years since Dean. Surely you're not going to punish yourself until you're an old maid."

"It's seven years this month, actually, Mum. Anyway, I've got something to tell you and I hope you're sitting down."

"Had I better do that, then?"

"Maybe you should. I've run into Brian."

A pause, then, "…Brian. Brian who?"

"What do you mean, 'Brian who?' You've told me all about him enough times and I've got the book that he gave you in my bag. That Jean Paul Sartre story that's so depressing."

"You can't mean *THE* Brian. I haven't seen or heard of him since, what, must be well over twenty years. He left Bath when I was pregnant with you! Went off to London to get signed. Never did see him on The Old Grey Whistle Test though. You've bumped into Brian? Are you sure? I mean really sure?"

"Mum, he told me what was written in the front of the book. Said it was him that wrote it. Told me too that he'd always wished that you and he had become an item. Didn't you tell me that you'd hoped the same but you thought that he'd only ever seen you as a daughter or something?"

Silence from the other end of the telephone. Then Alyson was aware that her mother was crying. "Mum, mum! He wants to see you. What do you think?"

"Sad? Why?"

"Well, talk about misunderstandings. Brian worked with my mum in a bar called Porky's back in Bath from about 1976 to 1978. She told me once that she'd always wished that she could have got together with him but, because he was quite a bit older than her, she felt that he'd never agree to go out with her in a romantic way. She said that he was a close friend and confidant. He used to try and advise her when he saw her going off from the bar with different guys when they finished work, but she never dreamed that it might have been because he had feelings for her. She was very young then. My mum had to grow up fast. My older brother was born when she was still sixteen. Anyway, I phoned her today and told her I'd just run into him."

"I assume that was a rather large bolt from the blue for your poor mother."

"Yea, well, yes it was. But, see, Claire, here's the thing. I reckon he still carries a torch for her and I know she still feels for him. Maybe it's not too late."

"So, what did your mother say?"

"When she'd got over the shock she said that she wants to see him. Isn't that great?"

"It is Alyson, it really is. Talking of shocks, I've got one for you."

"You have? Don't tell me, you've hooked up with a Greek professor?"

"Don't be silly!"

"OK, so not a professor. You're going to cruise off into the sunset with a sailor?"

"No, nothing as romantic or adventurous, sweetie. I'm going home."

"Oh, don't be a bore, Claire! The night is young and we haven't seen each other for ages, why don't we…"

"No, I don't mean home here in Lindos. I'm going back to the UK, Alyson. You don't need me any more and I'm not making any sense of my life."

Her younger friend's face adopted an expression of total disbelief. Then changed to one of sadness. She made as if to speak, but Claire continued:

"Alyson, we've had a blast, a whale of a time. You've been a good friend and travelling companion to me. I couldn't have asked for anyone better. How glad I am that I took you under my wing back then in Kefallonia, when you were looking like a little girl lost and about to burst into tears when we got off that plane. As far as I'm concerned, we shall always be close friends and I'll always be pleased to see you any time. But you've begun to make a life for yourself here and mine is approaching closing time. I need to decide what I want to do with my life. You're still so young, but I'm fifty-four and nothing's making any sense to me at the moment. At least if I open up my studio in Bristol I can immerse myself in painting again and dull the pain somewhat. I still know some galleries and agents. I'm sure I'll be able to show some work quite soon after I get working again. Alyson, you do understand, don't you?"

Alyson had been listening intently. But for the last few seconds her face had adopted an expression that Claire couldn't read. She was no longer looking at Claire either. She was gazing into the nearby narrow Lindos street, where the sky had begun to darken and the lights were now on as the sun was soon to set. People were reading restaurant menus as the smell of suntan cream gave way to that of insect repellent and cologne.

Claire didn't say any more, rather she followed Alyson's gaze into the street and saw a young man standing there, also transfixed. He appeared to be alone. He was probably in his late twenties and had shoulder-length mousy hair, tied back in a ponytail. His facial features were such that he could have posed for a portrait of the original Adonis. Claire gazed at his piercing eyes and thought how she wished she'd have been twenty years younger. His physique was well developed although not to the point of ugliness. How she hated those bodybuilders who developed their muscles until that grotesque 'lumpy" stage. They seemingly didn't know when to stop. No, this young man was simply gorgeous. There was no other word for it. But he wasn't looking at

Claire, sadly.

He was returning Alyson's gaze as though not quite believing what he was seeing.

In fact, that's precisely what Dean Waters was thinking too. He most certainly didn't believe what he was seeing.

6. Bath – September 2000 - April 2005

In the UK, the autumn of the year 2000 was the wettest since records began in 1766. Dean was, however, no longer depressed. It was over two years since Alyson had destroyed his faith in women and up until the previous June he'd still not been able to start a lasting relationship with anyone. He would usually meet a girl, arrange to see her again, then spend the intervening time until they were to meet for a second date persuading himself that he'd not be able to trust this girl. He'd also compare her looks and body to that of Alyson and invariably find her wanting.

Back in June, Bath Racecourse had held a "Ladies' Day" and his father had rather deftly left him alone with the daughter of an eminent resident of Castle Combe, One Charles Kyle, barrister. Charles had on a pretext told his rather willowy daughter Fiona to take something insignificant over to Julia Waters, wife of his good friend and financial adviser Francis. He knew full well, of course, that Julia had gone off with her daughter Aimi on some errand or other and that her son Dean was "holding the fort" while his mother was away. He was brushing down one of his mother's mares when his father called Charles on his mobile and suggested that this may be their chance to get their two offspring together, apparently by accident.

From the other side of the horse's flank, Dean heard a female voice.

"My, she's handsome. I wonder if the person behind her is too."

'Dean stopped brushing and peeped over the horse's back to see the rather attractive form of Fiona Kyle admiring the mare. She was holding a small piece of tackle, what it was he couldn't rightly recall now, as it was three months later, but he did recall that, on first impressions, this girl compared rather favourably with Alyson.

Unaware of the fact that they'd been set-up, he found himself chatting rather freely with this girl and, before he knew what was happening, he'd been invited over to her father's place for dinner the following Sunday evening. He went.

Now, three months later, he was depressed over the weather, yes, but rather disconcerted over the fact that he'd now been seeing Fiona since June and rather liked the girl. So far, she'd proved to be intelligent, witty and extremely easy on the eye. He found himself ruminating on the fact that this was the first time since Alyson had disappeared that he actually enjoyed the company of one girl continuously. Of course, he still lived in Cardiff and, although Fiona had been over to stay a few times, he was exercising extreme caution about how fast he dived into this relationship. Fiona didn't seem to mind. She seemed to be happy to progress at whatever speed Dean felt comfortable with. It hadn't been long after their first meeting over the back of one of his mother's horses, that he'd come clean and explained what had happened with Alyson and why this had made him ambivalent about any new relationship. She was patient all right.

She didn't actually have a real job. Managing her parents' stables gave her something to put on a CV, but she was a silver spoon girl and yet still didn't mind that Dean was hell bent on making his own career as a graphic designer, starting at the bottom. She didn't know how much help Dean's father had given his son and Dean didn't tell her, because he dreamed of total independence from his father one day, hopefully fairly soon. Fiona gave Dean the distinct impression that, well off though her parents may be, she didn't measure everything in her life against its financial value.

Fiona may have had it all, but she appeared also to have her feet on the ground. She doted on Dean and pretty soon it became apparent to Dean too that he had developed feelings for Fiona. Could this be the relationship that finally acted as a catharsis for his relationship with Alyson? Could Fiona finally bring him relief from the torture, often self-inflicted it had to be admitted, which he'd endured since losing Alyson in June 1998? Could he finally be coming out of the moribund state that had plagued him for so long?

The weather in September may have been awful, but Dean finally came to feel a little more positive. He found himself looking forward to every minute spent with Fiona and had finally begun to drive out the demons of his preoccupation with Alyson. He'd begun to think that perhaps his memory of Alyson had become enhanced with fancy and that, ultimately, this had proved destructive. It had made him put his life on hold for too long. Thinking along these lines, though, confused him for a while. He found himself feeling guilty that he'd finally be prepared to wash all hankering after Alyson from his mind and heart. What if she turned up again as soon as he'd perhaps made the decision to stay with Fiona permanently, maybe even asking her to marry him?

But then, was there any justification in continuing to string Fiona along when he clearly did believe that he may even love her? So what, because if Alyson turned up again, would she deserve to have Dean back after all the time that had passed? Wasn't it she that had destroyed his life? Wasn't it she who had walked out on him? He'd had every reason to expect her home after a couple of weeks and yet she'd not come back and hadn't even had the decency to contact him to explain. No, Dean had finally begun to clarify his mind.

Fiona answered her mobile.

"Hi beautiful," It was Dean. He never failed to call her beautiful and it made her feel special.

"What do YOU want, sexual favours?" She replied.

"Are you busy a week Wednesday?"

"Why, ought I to be?"

"Well, if you're gonna be like that, I'll just have to go to Greece on my own."

"GREECE? What are you on about, Dean?"

"I've booked us a week in Lindos. This weather's getting me down. Fancy a bit of sunshine?"

"Do I!!"

So they'd flown off to Rhodes and spent a week stretched out on the beach during most days and dining in a different taverna every evening. They took a trip to Rhodes Town and hired a car to drive through the hinterland and gasp at the whitewashed villages scattered across the mountainsides in the south of the island. They walked along the sandy strand out to the island at Prassonissi and laughed as Dean pretended to be a ghoul whilst walking through the tunnel at Epta Piges. By the time they were queuing to check in for the return flight Dean had made his decision. Fiona was the girl for him. Fiona Kyle would hopefully drive the demons of his past hang-ups away and he would find happiness.

By the summer of 2004 they'd become engaged, to the delight of both sets of parents. Dean's father had tried to make a gift of a rather fast Italian car to his son, but Dean had respectfully refused, telling his father instead that the couple would be grateful to receive gifts for their new home once they'd decided where it may eventually prove to be.

In the autumn of 2004 they'd begun making plans for a June wedding in Lindos, the place that had captured their hearts during their brief visit to Rhodes a few years before. Dean's fledgling Graphic design partnership with Adam Hastings, a freelancer whom he'd met through the job at Streets a few years before, was showing signs of making some headway and their smart offices in Cardiff Bay gave off all the right signals. The name Waters-Hastings sounded good and was creating ripples in all the right places in the city. They'd already landed a couple of good regular clients and Dean and Fiona were house-hunting out in the Vale of Glamorgan.

One day in early 2005 Fiona asked Dean, "Why did you pick Lindos back in 2000?"

"Well, you know I'd been to Greece years before on a yachting holiday with my parents?"

"Yes, you told me once, I think."

"I suppose I'd always wanted to go back to Greece, but I'd been a bit nervous about it, because of the fact that it was where Alyson had gone when she left me. Then I finally thought, what's the furthest spot in Greece from Kefallonia? Rhodes, right? Well, all right, one could argue that it's Kastellorizo, but it's splitting hairs a bit. Plus I'd heard about the wedding thing and I suppose even then I was starting to think, 'why not do a reccy?'"

"You're continually surprising me, darling, you know that? You're such a sweetie, to think that you already had such thoughts way back then. I do so love you."

Dean had also decided, back in the autumn of 2000, that it would be a good test of his mettle. He'd worried that Alyson having gone to Greece would perhaps stop him from ever going back there, yet he had loved the place when he'd been before and was hoping that the first Rhodes visit would set his mind at rest, which it had done. After all, the fact that she hadn't come home to him didn't mean to implicate that she'd stayed in Greece necessarily, did it? She probably, he thought, came back to the UK and made other plans. Perhaps she'd met someone on that holiday whom she'd fallen for. This thought, though, still stuck in his throat. He thought that he'd known her well enough for such a thing not to have happened. Why, hadn't she even shown him a ring that she'd planned on wearing for the duration of the visit so as to scare other guys off? Had all their months together meant so little to her? Still, he'd long since given up speculating about what may have happened, what may have gone on in her mind. The only thing that still aroused his curiosity was what may have transpired, had he had the courage to telephone her mother. No, he didn't know the number, but with a little digging he knew that he could have found it out somehow. The fact was, though, that he hadn't done it and now he had Fiona.

It was still only quite recently that he'd finally cleared all of Alyson's belongings from the flat and taken them to Tenovus, his favourite charity, which had a chain of second hand shops raising money for cancer research across South Wales. He and Fiona were finally looking for a house in which they were going to live as husband and wife and it was a fitting time to finally purge Alyson from his life, however painful it still might be to do so.

Up until the moment when he'd walked out of the Tenovus shop in Albany Road, he still kind of kidded himself that he could savour the possibility of a reunion with Alyson, whilst also starting a life with Fiona. But then, he was no Utah Mormon after all. No, he'd finally felt more focused. Walking along that street in Cardiff he'd felt, quite without having planned it this way, that a huge weight had lifted itself from his shoulders. He could now actually begin to focus on his life with Fiona. After all, he was a lucky man. Fiona turned heads in much the same way as had Alyson. A lot of his friends and acquaintances had made it very clear that they'd love to have a girl like her on their arm. Why, even Adam, his business partner had once said, "Dean, mate. I don't care if it means she'll be second hand, chuck her my way if you chuck her at all, won't you!"

Things were settling into a kind of life plan after all. No, he wasn't particularly happy with this world. He felt that, almost imperceptibly, he'd slotted into a groove of normalcy that he'd not ever wanted to slot into. He never wanted to become Mr. Average, with a nice little home, a nice little income and 2.4 kids. But it now seemed that, without even trying, this was what was happening. The young idealistic Dean, the Dean who was going to change the world, was giving way to Mr. Pragmatic. When you're still a teenager you think that you're going to flag up all the injustice in the world, make your voice heard, be the next Bono. But in reality everyone needs an income. Everyone has to provide a roof under which to live and bring home food for the table. No one is exempt from the basic human needs for companionship, food, security and a warm family environment to cushion oneself from the knocks. Dean was coming to realise that, if he wanted to change the world, he'd first have to settle into a way of life that gave him the opportunity to save some cash, in fact get into a position where he'd be able to put something back. First, though, it involved a few years of graft, of learning, of becoming a responsible adult member of society. Sitting around in scruffy bars wearing beads and growing one's hair seemed a statement of intent when he was nineteen. Now that he was almost twenty-nine the real world was knocking, telling him that he was no different from all the others who'd gone before, all those hippies who'd bathed in the mud at Woodstock in 1969, those that had lived the hippy dream, so temporarily, in San Francisco back in the late sixties. It was all just so much naivety.

Time to be a grown-up. He and Fiona it would be, thick or thin, good times or bad. Plus, he could always call his dad if the situation demanded it.

Part Five

Crash, Bang, Wallop

1. Lindos, June 18th 2005, evening

Claire was nothing if not intuitive. She knew that the beautiful young Adonis in the narrow street outside of the Ikon Bar was Dean. She could tell both from Alyson's reaction and that of the young man. Burning with curiosity though she was, she decided that perhaps she ought to beat a retreat. However slim the chances were of such a meeting taking place, she knew it had to be Dean. There was no point in asking why such coincidences happen, they just do.

So often people say things are 'meant to be'. But they simply haven't the courage to accept the fact that life is full of such weird coincidences. Taking hold of the strap from her bag, Claire rose and spoke.

"I'd better be going. We'll talk maybe tomorrow, yeah?"

Alyson didn't take her stare from the young man, who was still standing there. It was as though he were auditioning for one of those statues that people do at, for example, the entry to old Rhodes Town, the kind of thing where someone whites their face up and perhaps dresses up like an ancient Greek and stands completely still with a cap on the ground in front of them for contributions. She slowly became conscious of the fact that her friend had risen and replied, almost absently,

"What? Oh, sure. Yes. Sorry Claire." Without saying anything else, she held out a hand to squeeze Claire's forearm and let her go, without looking in her direction.

Still she stared unflinchingly at the face that she had walked out on almost exactly seven years before. Why was he still so beautiful, so handsome, so downright 'Dean' as she'd remembered him? What was he doing here, now, in Lindos and still with those eyes, hundreds of miles from Kefallonia and a couple of thousand from the UK? How could this be? She closed her eyes and waited for a few seconds. Opening them again she saw that, not only was he still there, but that he had tears running down his cheeks. He'd taken a couple of steps towards her. People were knocking his shoulders as they passed, not wilfully, but simply because the street was a buzz with holidaymakers all intent on enjoying a warm summer evening in a beautiful Greek village on a shimmering Greek island.

There were a lot of aging hippy types about too, their numbers having increased rapidly with the UK flights bringing Pink Floyd fans to Rhodes for the inaugural Lindos FloydFest, which was due to get into full swing during the coming week, culminating in two live shows out at the far end of St. Paul's Bay from a Pink Floyd tribute band, Think Floyd, on the evenings of the 24th and 25th, that coming Friday and Saturday.

How perfect a location was this, Brian had thought, when he'd first learned that there was going to be a festival of Pink Floyd music here in Lindos. Having grown up listening to the band, he well knew about the Lindos Pink Floyd connection. Richard Wright, the band's keyboard player, had owned a villa in Pefkos for many years, which had in more recent times become a bit of a place of pilgrimage for Floyd "anoraks". David Gilmour who, for Brian, was just about one of the greatest exponents of the guitar of his era, still owned a house in the village itself and it was rumoured that he'd perhaps be around for the first ever FloydFest (turns out he was too). A lot of people in the village knew him, as he still quite often spent time here during the summer. Brian had heard many a raucous tale from Socrates, the larger than life character who owned the bar named after him, usually called by all who frequented it "Sox" bar. The bar was situated in a sixteenth century "Captain's" House on the main "drag" through the village and was a favourite for rock fans. Socrates himself was a huge bear of a man who sported dreadlocks of a kind and rode a Harley. If you caught him at the right moment he'd regale you with his stories of times spent with the members of Pink Floyd, all of whom had frequented the village regularly throughout most of the seventies, when the band was at the height of its popularity, with albums like *Dark Side of the Moon*, *Wish You Were Here* and *Animals* selling by the shed-load worldwide.

Yes, Brian was well pleased that the FloydFest was coming up fast and couldn't wait to see just how good this band "Think Floyd" were. He entertained the hope that, once the concert was under way, appropriately as it would be beneath a clear black, starlit Greek sky, with the acropolis of Lindos as a dramatic backdrop for the whole thing, he'd be able to close his eyes and pretend that he was listening to the real thing. He still had vivid memories of the Bath Festival of Blues and Progressive Rock, held at Shepton Mallet showground in the summer of 1970. Pink Floyd had come on-stage at some time well after midnight and, although there had been some bad weather, by now it was a starlit, albeit chilly, night and people lit little flames all across the huge dark crowd of 150,000. It had been a "cosmic" experience as the

Floyd had played *"A Saucerful of Secrets"*, with its really "spacey" bits, along with *"Set the Controls for the Heart of the Sun"*, which Brian, as a young 20-year-old had played over and over again from his copy of the double vinyl album *"Ummagumma"* for weeks afterwards. Aaah, those were the idealistic days, thought Brian, who was nowhere near the Ikon Bar at this pivotal moment in the lives of both Alyson and Dean.

Dean stared at Alyson and couldn't quite get himself to move. It was as though someone had thrown the magic boomerang and only he was affected by its ability to make time stand still.

Alyson, too, felt paralysed. What was she supposed to do? An enormous urge to rush to him and throw her arms around his chest overwhelmed her. Yet, she also heard her inner voice saying, "No. You can't. He'll probably not want to even talk to you. He has every reason to be furious. You never explained why you did what you did. He'll snap out of this momentary paralysis any moment. Let him go. It'll be for the best."

Yet still she stared, the expression on her face trying to tell Dean that she still yearned for him. It was as though she hoped that he'd read her mind and find in there something to tell him that there was still an explanation. Maybe now, the fact that he'd suddenly appeared out of nowhere was an opportunity to throw caution to the wind and re-start where they'd left off back in 1998. What would he do?

The answer came soon enough. After what had seemed like an hour, but was probably about thirty seconds, he tore his gaze from hers, turned and marched off to the left, in the direction of the main square. Alyson didn't think, she grabbed her bag, flew out of her seat and began to chase after him. A few yards away, she cursed, turned, ripped open her purse and threw the first banknote she could tear out of the pocket on to the table with her half-finished beer. Already tears were beginning to blind her but she didn't give herself time to think about the rights and wrongs, the whys and wherefores, she was in automatic pilot and she needed to navigate to that man's side, fast.

Dean wasn't running, but he was striding with great, determined steps, bumping into and barging tourists every few feet, to the cries of "Oy!! What's your game?!!" and "Watch where you're going, will you!!" plus some even more colourful responses. He didn't hear any of these, but simply strode on. With one part of his mind he was telling himself that he had to get away as far and as fast as he could. With the other he was deliberately not breaking into a run in the hope that she would indeed catch him. What would happen if she did he hadn't even begun to work out. As did Alyson, Dean also found his vision blurred by tears, which he swept from his face with the backs of both hands in turn. Where was he going? He didn't know. He was just 'going'.

How could this be? How could he be walking through a place as magical as Lindos on a June evening, just two days away from his wedding to Fiona, and yet spot the girl he'd spent years trying to get over just sitting there, only feet away, looking every bit as beautiful as she had the last time he'd seen her, back in Cardiff in June 1998. Why had he decided to go out for an early evening stroll? The mates who'd come out here with him, even including his father, were going to be waiting for him at Yanni's Bar at nine. This now occupied not one single tiny fragment of his brain. All he could think about was Alyson's face, their past together, his rage over the way in which she'd abandoned him and his strange elation at having just seen her again.

He reached the t-junction by the church and turned left, up the brief slope and then right toward the square. Why he went this way he didn't know. All he knew was that his mind was in turmoil and nothing made sense. Nothing would focus beyond Alyson's face and his irrational desire, so he tried to convince himself, to welcome her into his arms and kiss her and smell her hair and feel seven years dissolve in minutes.

But he was engaged to be married. His fiancée was just a few hundred metres away up the hill and they were to be married the day after tomorrow. Everything was arranged, everything in place. The photographer was booked and the wedding company had the entire itinerary for the day printed out for everyone. The reception was due to take place at the hotel in Vlicha Bay. There was a live band and a DJ all lined up. Everything was arranged and most of it paid for. A hairdresser had been booked to call at the hotel where the girls were staying to make all their heads pretty for the big occasion. He and Fiona were then going to board a cruise boat at the harbour in Rhodes Town to spend a few days cruising on a short honeymoon. Later in the year they were also booked to go to the West Indies as a later, longer honeymoon. His father had paid for that one as a wedding present. Well, that along with a new Audi TT. Fiona's parents were going to pay for an extension to the new house they'd bought in the village of St. Mary Church in the Vale. Dean's life was all mapped out for the foreseeable future and yet, somehow, nothing mattered now except this terrifying urge to stop and let Alyson catch him.

He stumbled on, past the donkey 'garage' to his left and along the last few metres leading to the square, all the while struggling with himself. He wanted to get away, to pretend that he hadn't seen Alyson. Yet, too, he wanted so desperately for her to catch up with him. He wanted to rant and rail at her for deserting him. People were turning to stare at this young man who seemed to be crying uncontrollably and walking unsteadily, all the while brushing against others.

He stumbled over a souvenir display outside a shop. Tacky Rhodean souvenirs made in China flew across the lane. "Bloody druggies," someone muttered, "they're everywhere these days. This time of the evening and he's already out of his skull. Good-looking boy like that. I dunno, tch."

Alyson tried to run to catch up with Dean. She too was in mental turmoil. 'Shouldn't I just leave him be? What's it going to accomplish if I do catch him? I'll just wreck his life just as I would have all those years ago.' Yet she couldn't help herself. She kept going, trying to navigate around groups of people who were in no mood to hurry to step aside for her. It was the height of rudeness to barge through people who were enjoying a relaxed evening on their holidays. People whose lives were all on track, who were enjoying their fourteen days of bliss before flying home to begin saving up for the next one. She tried to run, but too often was brought to a halt as she had to allow someone or several people in a group to pass the frequent obstacles whilst coming in the opposite direction. Her mind was full to bursting with emotion and she couldn't get it to function rationally. Automatic pilot had kicked in and she couldn't hit 'override". She kept going. Very soon she descended to the t-junction by the church and then stopped dead. Panic threatened to take control as she looked first left, then right, then left again. Which way? Which way did he go? If he'd gone right then she had very little chance of catching him. He could have gone deeper into the maze or followed the path up to the acropolis. He could have taken another turn and found his way down toward the beach.

Which way? Inside she heard herself scream. No, it was outside. She found herself shouting "AAAHH!! Which way? Which way did he GO?"

The old man who kept the tiny supermarket on the corner tapped her heaving shoulder.

"You follow the man? The man who cry?" he asked. Seemed that he had a pretty good grasp of the situation. He pointed up the slope toward the right-angled turn in the lane that led back to the square.

"Thank you!! Thank you!!" Alyson said and, tears covering her cheeks and her nose running, she made off up the slope, once again dodging and ducking to get past the other people who moved impossibly slowly.

Dean found himself in the square, staring up at the huge tree in its middle, around which there was a constant flow of vehicles. There were tourists in hire cars, realising that it wasn't the shrewdest of moves to try and drive down here, there were taxis, tooting their horns impatiently at such tourists in their brightly coloured little boxes. There was the courtesy bus, which ferried visitors up and down to the square from Krana several hundred metres up the hill. There were the municipal police, whistles perpetually hanging from their lips, looking for any excuse to blow them. And everywhere people. People in the tiniest of articles of clothing, owing to the oppressive heat of a late June evening in Lindos.

Where to go now? Should he simply stop and hope that Alyson caught up with him? Why did he run? Perhaps it would have been better to approach her and see what she had to say for herself. He began to realise that the reason he'd retreated was that he wasn't ready for the confrontation yet. He needed a little space to get his mind and heart sorted out before handling the emotion of it all. But, on balance, he wanted desperately to talk to her. He knew now, after seeing her, that he'd never rest until at least he'd heard her out. Perhaps it was all his fault after all. Of course it was. If he'd been more of a man back in 1998, talked to his father, told him what was what, she'd never have felt the need to get away like that. He'd driven her to it. Who knows what kind of life she'd had to live following her leaving. Perhaps things had been really tough for her. He racked his brain to remember the last thing she'd said to him. "Don't worry, darling, I'm not in the market. If it'll help, look…" and she'd shown him the ring that she'd placed on the third finger of her left hand.

Yes, it was becoming clearer now. If he'd not driven her to it, she'd never have gone. But, why, oh why didn't she come home? He found himself walking again, but this time at a normal pace. Skirting the right hand side of the square, which looks out over an orange grove down to the beach below, he reached the other side and began the short climb around the Mavrikos Taverna to the right fork, which was the beach road.

Alyson tried desperately to go faster. Finally, after what seemed like an age, she reached the square and found herself staring at a mass of bodies. People were everywhere. Some were sitting on the white steps around the tree, others looking at the menus of the tavernas at either end of the square. There were people getting into and out of taxis and people standing around in knots talking excitedly. How could she ever hope to find Dean now?

Just as she was almost deciding, however reluctantly, to give it up as a bad job, she saw someone disappear around the corner by the Mavrikos at the far end of the square. Walking up toward the beach road. She knew it was Dean. He was dressed all in white, his sleeveless cotton t-shirt almost luminous in the light conditions.

Alyson ran. She reached the Mavrikos and then the right fork on to the beach road. Dean was probably only fifty yards ahead and appeared not to be hurrying. Now Alyson's doubts began to creep in. Would be turn and rant at her? Would he berate her for the way in which she'd deserted him? She could only hope that he'd come to realise that what she did was out of her love for him, that she couldn't bear to be the reason for his possibly permanent exile from his family, the kind of family that she'd never had. Maybe he'd simply ignore her and just keep walking until she stopped pursuing him.

Whatever thoughts seared through her mind, her body seemed to have a will of its own as she half-ran, half 'power-walked' after him, still occasionally finding the need to clear the water from her eyes. There was no getting away from it, whatever would transpire from this, she was going to catch him and grab hold of him and look him in the face. She was going to talk to him, if only to apologise, if only to try and explain. Now that she'd been given this opportunity to do so, there was no way she was going to let it slip out of her grasp. He could go his way afterwards if he wanted to, but he'd go away knowing that she'd always loved him, that she'd not simply been little miss fickle. He'd always understand that she left because she couldn't be the wedge that drove him away from his family, his future, his loved ones.

Dean reached the parked cars on the right hand side of the descending hill and finally his legs became stone. He stopped and felt himself surrendering to the inevitable. Perhaps there was indeed some explanation that would help him understand. He must hear her out. He still couldn't bring himself to turn around, yet there he stood, breathless and disoriented. He became aware of a presence behind him. Keeping quite still, his arms at his sides, he waited, his chest heaving from his laboured breathing.

For the first time in seven years, he heard that familiar voice.

"Dean. Dean, I…" He so wanted to turn around and yet couldn't move. His mind fought itself. 'No! This can't be.' It told him, and then immediately said, 'She's here. She wants to talk to you. Look at her'.

"I'm sorry." These words came out from Alyson's lips in a desperate breath. A breath that almost threw them at Dean's back with the hope that he'd feel the desolation that she felt. "Dean," she struggled with the huge obstruction in her throat to speak, "I know that no words are enough, …will ever be enough. But I had to give you up. Don't you see?"

Still he didn't turn around, yet his head fell to his chest and she could see that he was weeping. With gargantuan effort she took a few more steps and walked around to face him. Standing inches apart, face to face, although he still looked at his feet, she raised a hand to his cheek. Gently she stroked that cheek for a few seconds, then brought her fingers to beneath his chin and raised his face to look at hers. Nothing around them mattered. Everything else, the tourists, the cars creeping up and down the slope, the shimmering waters of the bay below, on which twinkled the reflection of a waxing moon, just four days from being full, it all kind of became a cotton wool cradle, the centre of which was this couple.

"Why?" He whispered, "Why, Alyson?" He was milliseconds away from erupting into a bellow. A hair's breadth from shouting at the top of his lungs, "HOW COULD YOU HAVE DONE THIS? I THOUGHT WE WERE TOGETHER FOR LIFE!!!" Yet he didn't. He gazed at this beautiful face and saw the yearning still in those eyes. Whatever she'd done and why ever she'd done it, he knew he had to hear her out. Without conscious thought, his own hand lifted from his side and brushed some hair from her wet cheek. He tucked it behind her ear and the vaguest hint of a smile crept over his lips. How could he not do so, when faced with this beautiful, disconsolate person who was oozing need, the need to set things right with him.

"Oh, Dean. How come you're here? How did you find me?"

"You really don't know? You didn't know I was here …*why* I'm here?"

"No. Unless it was to find out what happened to me. But then," reality sank in, "I suppose you can't be looking for me after all this time. You'd have had no idea as to where I was, would you, my love?"

"What time is it?" Dean asked, but before she could answer he could see for himself. Lifting his left arm and glancing at his watch he saw that it was around 9.30pm and the sky was dark, His friends would be supping their drinks at Yanni's Bar, wondering what the hell had happened to him. It wasn't like Dean to be late. Stuff them. Stuff everything. "Let's walk." He said.

"OK. Can I lead the way?" She asked. He nodded.

"Come," she said and took his hand. She led him further down the hill. At the tight bend in the road she crossed the hot asphalt and led him up the steep ramp on to the path that led out along the bay to the headland where stands the Tomb of Kleoboulos. Leaving the stone wall, which surrounds an area that's now used as an overflow car park, behind them to their right, they walked past the needle-shaped memorial to some politician or other who'd hailed from Lindos. They were now quite alone, with only the moonlight and the sound of nearby goat bells to accompany them.

"It's hard, Dean. I know you have every reason to hate and despise me, but I do want to explain. If I'd never caught sight of you this evening, if you'd come and gone without me ever knowing, then that would have been that. But I did see you, and you saw me. Now I'm sure I have to take this opportunity to explain. I'm not even going to pretend that I'm entitled to come back into your life again, but at least when you walk away you'll think better of me, maybe even still love me just a little. Will you listen to my story, Dean, *will you?*"

2. Bath, June 18th 2005, Christine

I don't know how to react, my lovely girl bumping into Brian like that. How do we, any of us, deal with events that hit us out of the blue as we go through life and all of a sudden change everything? How many times I've wished that Brian hadn't waved goodbye in January 1978. How many times I've wished that I'd told him that I wanted him. Still, spilt milk and all that. No use going back over all the 'what ifs', it never gains you anything, does it. How can I have ended up with a life like this though? I'm still struggling with where all the years have gone. I keep thinking that I'm going to get into gear and then I look around and another ten years have got behind me. No one told me when to run, I missed the starting gun. Who sang that?

I'm definitely the kind who has the tendency to always pick the wrong type of man. I must be. How many times have I taken some bloke in to live here in this house and then seen it all go sour? Too many, I'm ashamed to admit. Now, here I am, forty-five years old, starting to go through 'the change' and with four kids to worry about.

George, well, at least he's kind of settled now. I'm quite glad he's playing in a reggae band. He's a bit of a Bob Marley himself really, I suppose. His parents were one of each too. George passes for black like Bob used to. He may be a bit too fond of the weed, but he's a good boy and very talented, least I like to think so. That bass amp he bought through e-bay is the business. It's made him feel like he's well part of the band, even though the guitar was second-hand.

How did I ever end up having Shirley? When was it now, 1980, when I was the ripe old age of twenty? My third child and me only twenty. Where did my youth go? She's all white, like Alyson, but no way is she as good-looking as her older sister, though. Still, at twenty-five she's off my hands and her partner seems a straight-up kind of guy. Just hope she can stay with him and not start a chain reaction, like her mother.

Gemma's still with me of course. Twenty-two and still not sure what she wants to do with her life. Thank goodness for supermarkets and the constant need for checkout staff. She dreams too much that girl, like Winston, her father.

That reminds me, I still haven't told Alyson that I kicked Winston out four years ago. Is it really that long since she left? 1998 she said. I could have sworn it wasn't as long as that. Now here she is talking to Brian in a bar in Greece and there's me not having seen him since she was here in my belly. Strange or what?

She asked me if I wanted to talk to him again. What would I say if I did? Last time he saw me it was 1978, when I was only eighteen and already had one child and another on the way. He was well out of it. Least, that's what I told myself he was thinking when he left Bath. Now she goes and tells me that he actually did want to be my man, to have a relationship that was more than just 'friends'. I can't believe that we both thought that and neither of us was brave enough to own up. How different would my life had been if we'd got it on? But then, with my luck he'd probably have left me with another baby on the way and then gone off to become the next Cat Stevens.

I had to tell Alyson I needed time to think. I can't make decisions like that quickly. Am I really brave enough to meet up with this man and have all those images from so many years ago come flooding back? How often did he give me that look when I'd leave Porky's with yet another bloke? Probably worried that I'd end up beaten and dead in some countryside ditch or something. Fact is, there were one or two occasions when I came close. What a stupid little idiot I really was. Now I'm just a stupid older idiot. Have I really learned anything from this life? If so, what?

Oh, Brian. What do you look like now? Alyson seems to think that you've worn well. Have I though? Well, I suppose you'd be the one to decide that, if I decided to let you see me again. Shall I? That's the sixty-four thousand dollar question. Would it be too much of a risk, or would it simply be another reunion of old friends. Another one of those occasions where people who knew each other years ago got together, had a drink and reminisced, before going their separate ways again, promising to keep in touch but with no real intention of doing so? What if I hoped that it would be just such a reunion, only to find that I fell for you big time and you didn't fall for me, or the other way around. Who am I kidding? We're not young kids any more either of us.

Where's that mirror? Hmm, yes, I suppose I don't look too bad. Least I've still got my figure. Thank God for whole foods and exercise. Oh, and Harvest, the really wicked organic food store in Walcot Street. They've been there since as long as I can remember. Henna too, has helped. I suppose I could still pass for thirty-something.

So, what am I going to do? Does Brian really *know* that he wants to see me? Maybe it was a bit of a knee-jerk after spotting Alyson like that. Oh, come on girl. No use second-guessing him is it. Eenie meenie, myney mo… OH, what the hell. Why not. But then, he's a long way away and can I really expect Alyson to buy me a ticket?

But I'll tell her it's on and we'll see what can be arranged. Who knows? Maybe, just maybe, it'll turn out good and my life will finally get sorted out.

Not very likely, knowing my luck. But damn well worth a try.

3. Brian, Lindos - June 18th 2005

'I suppose I'd better be off. Got to get to work for about 9.15 tonight. I wonder if Alyson will come back to me about Christine. I so hope that she does. She seemed pretty straight up. I reckon I can trust her.

'I'll grab the guitar and be off through the village. Yea, I know, at this time of year it gets pretty crowded in Lindos during the evening, but I really love the vibe. I love the smells of cooking from the tavernas and the buzz from the bars. I get the feeling that it's going to go well tonight. I'm up for it. Got a couple of new songs in the set. This time of year the bar's usually crowded by half-ten, once most of the "grockles'" have eaten and want to get down to the serious business of bar-crawling.'

Brian was soon ambling through the village, letting the tourists thronging the narrow streets dictate his pace. Waving to a few people he knew and feeling happy enough to whistle, he was soon approaching Yanni's Bar, in the heart of the village. Glancing in as he walked past, he saw the usual scene, all the tables occupied with people at various stages of sun-exposure and alcohol saturation. There were those looking nicely browned off from having been here for almost two weeks and having gone easy on the sunbathing, with liberal use of a high-factor cream. Trouble is, they just start to think that they look "assimilated" when they find themselves with their cases up at Lindos Reception at some hideous time of the night, waiting for the transfer coach back to the airport. There were the others too, those who'd just arrived and overdone it on the first day. These glowed pink in the bar's lights and looked like they'd be tossing and turning once they got to bed, trying to find relief from the stinging and itching sensation which you get from burned skin. 'They'll never learn' he told himself. He liked to think that he was a bit of an expert now on how long someone had been out here. He could read skin by its shade of red-stroke-brown and guess pretty accurately how long the subject under examination had to go before flying home.

Something made him do a double-take. Having just passed

Yanni's, he stopped short, which resulted in an American woman bumping into his back. He turned and offered her his profuse apologies, which she accepted gracefully before continuing on her way, and asked himself something. 'What did I just see?' Walking the few feet back to the point where he could see into the bar again, he noticed a group of men, most of them half his age, but one of them, dressed in an obviously expensive cotton polo shirt, bearing a prominent designer logo, and a pair of sharply creased navy chinos, hair immaculately coiffured, was much older. 'Looks about my age', thought Brian. What was it about this man?

Brian walked on toward his place of work, all the while turning the older man's face over in his brain. He knew that man, he was sure. But from where, exactly? He'd spent a long time in London after leaving Bath and had played in so many clubs, bars and dives that he tried to convince himself that it was just some bloke he'd seen somewhere. Yet, that face. It was too familiar. Granted, the man seemed older than he'd have been at the time when Brian had come across him the first time around, but come across him he certainly had, probably many years ago.

And he knew that he didn't like him, but he couldn't put a finger on the reason.

4. Claire, Lindos - June 18th 2005

Claire found herself walking aimlessly through the streets of Lindos. She almost went into several bars, but each time checked herself. She began to feel hungry, yet she didn't want to eat amongst crowds of happy people, all with company. What she'd seen at the Ikon Bar had unsettled her somewhat.

'Why do I feel unsettled?' She asked herself. Was it because it was the first time she'd ever seen Alyson focused on something so much that she'd ceased to engage with her friend when conversing? Did Claire feel a sense of jealousy? How could she, when she'd already decided that she was going to return to the UK anyway? Maybe it was simply the fact that she felt that, when that young man, who simply had to have been Dean, the person Alyson had been trying desperately to get over for the past seven years, had happened by, it was a defining moment, a watershed in their friendship. An era in Claire's life was coming to a close, *had* come to a close in those few seconds when he'd appeared in the street.

'I think it's all to do with the fact that I'm lost,' thought Claire, who'd now begun to walk away from the hubbub of the centre of the village. She found herself walking in the direction of the path down to Pallas Beach. Within a few minutes she felt better. She'd almost absentmindedly been aiming for the Rainbird Bar, which boasts possibly one of the best views in the Aegean, looking out as it does from a vantage point way above Lindos bay and affording beautiful views along the beach from above. The turquoise waters of Lindos sleep beneath you and the Tomb of Kleoboulos dominates the headland on the other side of the bay. Tonight was a good time to sit here, with the moon approaching full in just a few days more. Its pale glow shimmered on the waters as Claire took a seat and ordered another Campari and Sprite. The light was fading and she perused the menu. She hadn't eaten and she now felt the pangs telling her that she'd do well to order something while she sat and mused.

'Maybe those two are simply destined for eachother after all.' She thought. Then she checked herself for using such a term as "destined".

'Oh hell, whatever', she thought. 'What I think I mean is that it looked to me from their expressions that they're neither of them going to be any good with anyone else, so they may as well accept the fact that they're going to have to work through the consequences and have done with it. I just wish I had someone like her young man to give me some solace now, at my stage of life. Why, Charles, why?'

Claire had ordered a superb looking tuna salad and was now on a second gin and tonic, accompanied of course by a bottle of mineral water to dilute its effects. She'd nodded to one or two Lindos residents and chatted for a while with the British girl who, with her Greek husband, ran the bar. It was now becoming quite dark. But, by the light from the moon, she was drawn to some movement on the far side of the bay. She'd been fortunate enough to secure the corner seat at the edge of the balcony and soon became quite sure of what she was seeing. Two human shapes were making their way past the monument behind the parking area above the far side of the beach. Claire could tell it was them from the white top that Dean was wearing, which showed up well in the moonlight.

Alyson and her young man were walking in the semidarkness out toward Kleoboulos.

"I hope old Kleo helps you make some sense of things my darlings." She muttered aloud, gently raising her glass in their direction.

4. Yanni's Bar, Lindos - June 18th 2005

Francis Waters had begun the evening in ebullient mood. His son was getting married the day after next and it was going to be to a girl of whom he heartily approved. He it was, in fact, who'd set up the meeting between Dean and Fiona, along with Fiona's rather well heeled father, at Bath Racecourse back in 2000.

Now, though, it was 9.30pm and the group of men who'd arranged to meet Dean for a bit of a stag night was getting ever so slightly miffed. Yes, the wedding was on Monday, but they'd decided that the stag night should be Saturday so that all would be totally compos mentis and no one would be able to complain of a hangover at the wedding. Plus, they fully expected it to be another 'session' at the reception and so didn't want to spend a whole 48 hours smashed.

Dean had gone out for a walk alone in the village some hours earlier and had arranged to arrive at Yanni's at 9.00pm. Francis Waters didn't like to be kept waiting. There were six other men with him, among them Deans' best man for the wedding, Malcolm, who had been with Dean on the night when they'd first met Alyson and her friend Nicky. Malcolm and Nicky had actually gone out with eachother for over a year, but the relationship had petered out, whereas Dean and Alyson, well, Malcolm had been flabbergasted at how quickly they got 'into' eachother, but after a while had come to the conclusion that they were indeed made for one another. When Dean had phoned home from Cardiff the following summer to tell him that he'd been left in the lurch it had been difficult to believe. But then Dean had found Fiona and everything had begun to finally look rosy again. Until now that is. This wasn't Dean's usual behaviour pattern.

Dean's business partner Adam Hastings was also in the group. Adam was a rugby-playing graphic designer from Bridgend who'd hit it off with Dean right from the first time they'd met, when Adam was doing a little freelance work for Streets to take some of the pressure from the overloaded in-house studio at the time.

The men had been carrying on an animated conversation for over an hour when things began to become rather subdued as each one began glancing at his watch with more frequency and wondering what was keeping the bridegroom-to-be.

"He'd better turn up pretty sharpish or he stands the chance of seriously damaging the evening's potential," declared Dean's father, who tended to have the kind of effect on this group of his junior companions that resembled that of a Sergeant Major on a group of square-bashing soldiers. They all deferred to him with a mixture of awe and downright intimidation. Looking once more at his Tag-Heuer watch, his mood was fast turning from mild irritation into one of full-blown anger. His son had been living up to his expectations for a few years now and Francis Waters didn't want any last-minute hitches marring the joining together of these two families. Think of how much face he'd lose, not to mention kudos or, even more importantly, income from prospective clients.

"Look chaps, I think it's time we hatched a plan to find this recalcitrant son of mine, am I right?" The rank and file agreed. "What say we split up and do a tour of the village, meeting back here in – say – half an hour? Hopefully one of us will find the imp haggling over some flashy piece of jewellery or other, or trying to escape some tourist who's asked him for help because they're lost or something. I think one of us had better stay put here in case he arrives in the interim. That may as well be me. Agreed?"

The lads agreed and, whilst Francis Waters ordered another malt whiskey, he waved his son's young peers off and settled in to scan the passers-by in the hope that one of them would bear the familiar face of his son, tail between legs, entering the bar with a huge look of apology on his face.

Dean's father whipped out his Motorola 'QWERTY" Phone and dialled his son's number for the third time in half an hour.

6. Lindos, June 18th 2005, evening

Dean nodded. "I'll listen." He answered. So she turned and continued walking by the light of the pale moon. He followed. Both remained silent as Alyson picked her way along the northern rim of Lindos Bay, carefully navigating the rocky areas and trying to stick to the goat tracks as she made for the point, where stood the silhouette of Kleoboulos' tomb, black against the shimmering sea. Occasionally something scuttled away in the undergrowth. Now and then a few goats were freaked and leapt and jumped as they endeavoured to put more distance between themselves and the two interlopers. They were not used to two humans coming out here at this time of night.

After more than half an hour had passed, during which time Dean had wondered quite how much longer they would walk, Alyson finally led them up the rocky slope to the tomb. Dean had never been here before and was surprised by the size of the thing. The ancient stones looked inky black where they were in shadow, but as they reached the structure's vertical wall and used their hands to steady themselves as they walked around its circumference until they'd reached the side which was bathed in the moonlight, Dean could make out the fact that the stones were huge and carved in a curve, to give the structure its circular shape. The walls were higher than his head for most of the way around. Finally, Alyson sat down on some bare rock, facing the sea, which lapped silently many feet below, with her back to the wall of the tomb.

Dean sat beside her, although they didn't touch. It was as though he was telling her that the jury was still out, not all the evidence having been heard. She didn't look at him and allowed perhaps several minutes to pass, during which time he became aware that she was gently weeping. He was very tempted to reach out and pull her to him, but something stopped him doing so. Perhaps it was the image of Fiona in the back of his mind, or the thought that there was so much hanging on his shoulders back across the bay in the village of Lindos itself. Several times his mobile had rung, but he'd now switched it to silent mode. He'd done this as they walked. He had a pretty good idea about how his father would be feeling now and it made him feel sick in the stomach.

At least Fiona and her entourage would be none the wiser for a few hours yet. They'd taken themselves off to have a hen night in Old Rhodes Town, even having booked into a hotel for the night. They planned to get back to Lindos late on Sunday afternoon.

Finally, Alyson spoke. Her words were so soft that he had to strain to catch them at first. She stared out at the thousands of jewels of moonlight dancing on the surface of the flat, black sea. There was a small fishing boat bobbing gently as its occupant tried to catch something for his family's table tomorrow. It appeared as a black shape out on the water some half a mile or so from the spot where they sat. Stars blinked as though in expectation of Alyson's words.

"I went always intending to come home at the end of the fortnight. But when I was away I saw things more clearly. I went over our situation again and again and, whichever way I looked at it, I was the biggest fly in the ointment of your life.

"You'd told me that day, when we went for the drink in the Huntsman, that it was all rather rash to invite me into your life like that. But I felt like you did. It seemed as if we'd known eachother for much longer. What was it that sparked between us? I'll never know. I only know that it was the right thing at that moment and our subsequent time in Cardiff had proved it. But Dean," Her words came with difficulty as she struggled to control her emotions, "Dean, You were going to lose your family over me. I know it. I knew it. And when you did, you'd only have come to hate me eventually. You'd have reached some point in your life, whether it was a need for financial help from your dad, or just to talk to your mum, even fight with Aimi, when you'd have known that the reason for your no longer having that wonderful family of yours was me."

Dean made as if to interject, but she raised her right hand from her lap just enough to tell him she hadn't finished.

"Dean, I never had a normal family. Oh, all right, my mum loved me and I didn't want for anything really. Things were always tight, but I was fed and clothed so I shouldn't complain. But to have had a mum and a dad, to have lived in a 'normal' family as I was growing up, with outings on the weekends and Sunday dinner in the oven; all that stuff, I could only dream what that would have been like. My mother spent the early part of her adult life doing penance for her upbringing. I almost did the same. I didn't, thank God. But it was close for a while. My mum saved me and you saved me too. I'll always be grateful for that. But the fact still remains that I could never live with myself, even if you claimed that you could live with me, if I'd come between someone else and their birthright, the right to have and keep a real family, a family that gets together on Sunday evenings, a family that's there for one another when times demand it, the whole cosy thing that makes a family what it is.

"Can't you see, Dean? Whatever you say, however much you may remonstrate with me, the fact is you would have come to resent me in the very least, even if you didn't actually come to hate or despise me. You *know* you would. And what would we have been like with eachother once we'd reached that stage?

"So I had to let you go. There was no way I could even communicate with you because I knew what you'd have done. You'd have talked me out of it and so that whole nightmare scenario would have begun. I had to deal with my grief over losing you too, Dean. I'm sure you must have cursed me and ranted at me over what I did. But it was for the best. It was Dean, don't you see?"

Dean Waters cried. He sat with his back to the Tomb of Kleoboulos, gazing out at a serenely peaceful ocean view, and let the tears roll down his cheeks. "What is this place?" he asked.

Alyson was at first bemused. She'd just tried to make him understand what had happened between them seven years ago and here he was asking about the ancient building behind their backs. Then she realised. She understood. He needed more time to assimilate his thoughts, for her words to filter through all of the emotion and the inner turmoil that he was feeling. She still didn't know what he was doing here in Greece, on Rhodes, in Lindos. In less than forty-eight hours he was due to take Fiona as his lawful wedded wife. He was struggling to understand his state of mind. Could he still go through with it? Did he have the courage to explain things to Alyson?

"It's known as the Tomb of Kleoboulos. He was the ruler of the village of Lindos something like five hundred years before Christ. Apparently he was a bit of a bard though, too. There were seven ancient sages of Greece and he was one of them. Quite an erudite man, by all accounts. Of course, there are several ways to spell his name in English. If you've seen the statue up near Krana square, it's him. Do you know, Dean, that one of the sayings reputed to be his is: '*Be fond of hearing, rather than of talking.*' If only more of us humans would follow that rule. Perhaps we wouldn't jump to conclusions about others so readily, like your father did about me.

"So. Are you going to tear me off a strip now Dean? You have every right. I can't imagine what I put you through, but I've been trying to for seven years. I've never had another relationship in all that time, you know. Even now I can't bring myself to take an interest in another man. Perhaps I'm going to end up an old maid.

"Dean? Talk to me, please."

Another few minutes passed, during which Alyson tried to fathom what this young man was thinking, how he was going to react, what he was going to say. Finally, after heaving his chest in a big breath, he began.

"You're too good for me Alyson. I can't even bear the thought that you did what you did out of love for me, out of consideration for me. I had it all when I was growing up. You didn't. I so wanted to make that up to you. I had work, …have work, I could have supported us." He let out a long sigh, "But I know what you're saying. I understand how you reasoned on the situation. I too took a long time to come to the realisation that you weren't coming back. I left all of your belongings, the ones you left behind, exactly where they were for a couple of years. I almost lost my job over being such a git at work. I was told that I had to pull my socks up or be shown the door. That was so hard. I didn't feel like being nice, but I had to try.

"It was the not knowing. So many possible scenarios went through my head. It was like when some parents lose their child and the police tell them that they're going to scale down the search. You know, they eventually decide that the child is dead, but the parents can't move on with their lives because they want 'closure'. Well I never had 'closure', Alyson."

A pause. Neither spoke. Then Dean continued, "I talked to my dad you know, just like I'd promised I would." Alyson turned and looked at Dean, her eyes wide. For the first time since she'd caught up with him on the beach road, their gazes met.

"He gave me an ultimatum. Give you up or he'd cut me off. I told him to get stuffed." Alyson started, her body turned toward Dean and her hand rested on his knee. "I was given a month to get you out of my life or I'd lose the car, the help with the rent on the flat, everything. My wonderful father told me that he'd wash his hands of me and I told him that it was fine by me. I loved YOU Alyson. I was going to do it for *you.*"

She began to cry again. "I really didn't think you'd do it." She whispered.

They sat studying the small fishing boat for a while and then Dean spoke again.

"I'm out here for my wedding."

7. Yanni's Bar, Lindos - June 18th 2005

It was now after ten o'clock and Dean's would-be stag party was re-gathered at Yanni's Bar in the centre of the village. The mood, though, had subtly changed. The anger of just a short while ago had given way to a growing concern about Dean's wellbeing. Malcolm spoke up,

"This is very odd. Dean's not this kind of bloke. He doesn't do this kind of thing. But what on earth can have happened to him in a place like Lindos? Rhodes isn't big on crime is it? Do people get mugged or something out here? I wouldn't have thought so."

"Look, chaps, I'm getting jittery. Dean's my son and this is completely out of character, as you so rightly say Malcolm. What's really odd is the fact that he's not answering his mobile. What if he'd done something stupid, like going for a swim after dark on his own. Who would even know where he was? What's difficult is that, if we go to the police, they'll probably tell us that it has to be at least twenty-four hours or something like that before they'll take it seriously. But he's getting married the day after tomorrow. Thank God the girls have gone to town. At least we can keep them out of this until we get some idea as to what's going on."

"Has he been behaving oddly at all lately?" Asked Geoff, another of the party, to no one in particular.

"Not that I've noticed," answered Adam Hastings. "He's been rather elated recently to be honest. Said he'd finally got his life on some sort of even keel. He was really looking forward to this whole thing. It doesn't make any sense to me."

"If I were the one marrying Fiona, I'd definitely not do a disappearing act. If it weren't so perplexing, I'd offer to step in as bridegroom" said Alan, but instantly regretted having said that.

And so the conversation continued. They went down every possible avenue of thought as to what could have happened. Eventually, though, since Dean wasn't answering his mobile phone, they had little recourse but to start looking on foot once again. Two went up to his hotel room, two to the beach at the far end of St. Paul's Bay, which was Dean's favourite beach for swimming. Another two decided to check out the few tavernas where Dean had eaten since coming out to Rhodes. Dean's father just decided to walk the streets and lanes of Lindos in the hope that he'd run into Dean, who'd be able to offer a completely innocent explanation and all would be well.

By two thirty on Sunday morning, everyone was beside himself with worry. They'd found nothing. They had no clues. They had no news. And the wedding was now just over a day away. Reluctantly, they agreed to retire to bed and meet again over breakfast in the morning.

Hopefully, Dean would turn up with his bowl of breakfast cereal and tell them he'd just experienced last-minute nerves. But somehow, no one believed that this would happen.

8. Kleo's Tomb - June 18th 2005

"Dean," said Alyson, "That's not funny. After all I've just told you, it's not the moment to say things like that."

"I'm not joking Ally," replied Dean, using his pet name for Alyson for the first time in seven years. "I only wish, I *sooo* wish I was. But I'm not sure now that I can go through with it. I don't know what to do, to tell you the truth."

Alyson stared at Dean's face with an expression of shock, amazement, disappointment and disbelief. Neither of them spoke for a few moments. Dean found the words to carry on,

"Ally, I kept my torch burning for you for over two years. But what was I to do? Did I really expect to ever see you again? I met Fiona in 2000, at Bath Races. It was Ladies' Day or something. Looking back on it I'm pretty sure that our two fathers set it up. But, well, she's a beautiful girl both inside and out, Ally. She's had it easy, granted. Her dad's a barrister and she's only ever known life in the Pimms set. But she does have her feet on the ground.

"Ally, I know how horrible this is for you. But I have to tell you my story now. Isn't that only fair?"

Alyson nodded. She couldn't speak even if she wanted to. Tears flowed even more freely from her eyes as Dean went on.

"If I'd had even the slightest sign that you may come back into my life I swear I'd have waited. I *would* have waited, Ally. Fiona's wonderful, but she's not you. If we hadn't seen eachother a few hours ago I could have been very happy with her. I do love her. I have to admit that to you. I can only be completely honest with you, Ally. You know that.

"But now? What do I do? I'm a prize idiot for thinking that Greece was the place to come for our wedding. But then, I've found you again and that's set my mind racing. After what you've just told me, I don't know what to think or what to do. I'm in an impossible situation. The day after tomorrow we're supposed to be going through the happiest experience of our lives just the other side of that headland, that Acropolis up there. We're getting married outside that little church in St. Paul's Bay. It's a civil wedding, of course. The only reason it's taking place there is because it's such a photogenic place. You know all of that, of course.

"But Alyson, I don't want to go through with it now. At this precise moment I only want you and I to walk off into the blue and stay together for good. But I have seven men, including my father, over there in that village right now going ape about the fact that I didn't turn up for my stag night. Fiona's got a bunch of girls with her and …

"What is it? What have I said? Ally, that look on your face. What's the matter?"

"Fiona. You said your fiancée's called Fiona. Fiona Kyle, am I right?"

"What?! Yes, but, how, I mean…"

"Dean, you know what I've been doing for a living for the past few years here?"

"Well, I know you're a brilliant hairdresser, so I suppose it has to be something to do with that. Why, what?"

"Dean. I do weddings. I work for Flight of Fancy, the internet wedding service. Ring any bells?" Dean's face betrayed his feelings. He knew that the wedding had all been arranged through Flight of Fancy. He began to think he understood what had happened. But still wasn't sure.

"Dean," continued Alyson, who had now gathered herself and was staring into his eyes, in which she saw the reflection of the moon above, they were that close. "I went up to her hotel the other day and we did a trial run. I've met your fiancée, Dean. I've met Fiona. I've done her hair, …AND all the other girls. I'm due back there on Monday to do their hair for the wedding. I had no idea it was you she was marrying. How could I have?"

Dean was completely exhausted emotionally. What else could life now hit him with? He stared at Alyson and felt as though he couldn't take any more. Why, why, why? Where to go from here? Everything went around and around in his head and he felt as though it would explode. Could anything he'd ever have believed have prepared him for such a situation as this?

It's odd what the brain will do when it's in meltdown. For a few moments Dean's mind was back in Bath in that bar in October of 1997. He saw Alyson's face among the crowd of those drinking there that night and thought, 'Wow! What a beauty. I must meet her.' And he had. He had spent several hours talking to her and had been so happy that Malcolm had paired up with Nicky. He hadn't fancied Nicky at all. Loads of moments from their time in Cardiff flew through his mind. These were some of the most happy times of his entire life so far. Everything was great. He had a new job, a partner with whom he saw eye to eye about almost everything and the envy of most of his friends. He was going to change the world. He and Alyson were a team and nothing the world would throw at them would shake their relationship.

There was just the small matter of his father.

Alyson looked at him and perhaps understood what he was musing about.

"She's very beautiful, Dean. She's like a model. You're a lucky man."

This charitable angle was something that Dean couldn't take.

"NO! Alyson, NO. I mean, yes, she is beautiful, but she deserves something better. She doesn't deserve to be a second choice. She doesn't deserve someone whose devotion isn't one hundred percent. She deserves better. I can't give her what she deserves, Ally. I can't. Not NOW."

"But Dean, I'm glad that I've had this chance to explain to you, of course. But if I'd thought when we first locked eyes in the village earlier this evening that I'd be putting you into this quandary, then I have to wish now that we hadn't seen eachother.

"Once, I stood between you and your family, but now it seems I'm doing the same again, only this time with much more serious consequences. How can I cause that girl all this heartbreak? How can I?" She stood up and made as if to walk away. But Dean, not stopping to think about anything, not the potential consequences, not the tangle which he'd have to unravel for not only himself, but for all those people who'd made the journey out here to see him safely hitched and settled with a gorgeous girl who had it all, stood too and grabbed Alyson's arm. He spun her around and before either of them knew it, they were kissing. They kissed with a passion that attempted to exorcise all the problems that now confronted them, a passion that tried to purge their hearts of all of the potential consequences of their actions.

But it wasn't going to work. Dean held her so tightly that it hurt her. She didn't protest because she felt it was only what she deserved. Alyson Wright, wrecker of other peoples' lives. Perhaps it would be best if he squeezed all the life out of her. Perhaps she should break free and throw herself off of this promontory into the inky liquid far below. Only if she ended it all would she be free of the torment that followed her. How could she even think that she may have finally found a degree of happiness? Yes, she was lucky enough to have come to live in this evocative place, this jewel of the Aegean where the sun shone for more than three hundred days every year. But what was sunshine? What was anything if you don't have peace of mind, if you don't have happiness?

Part Six

Consequences

1. Lindos, June 19th 2005, small hours.

The view from Kleoboulos' Tomb is breathtaking. It isn't as high as the Lindos Acropolis, true, but it has a magnificent vista of Lindos Bay, and it's arguably better to have the Acropolis as part of your panorama, than to be situated up on top if it, looking down. A huge plus point is that to enjoy the view out there you have to have walked for the best part of forty-five minutes over rough ground in order to experience it. For this reason, it's a solitary place. It's not often that more than a handful of people are out there at any one time. Many visitors to Lindos stare out at it and wonder what it would be like to stand atop that ancient structure, but very few have the motivation to make the trek. Often the nearest they'll get to it is when they take an excursion that involves a day spent cruising the East coast of the island onboard a boat, during which the vessel perhaps passes beneath the headland on which stands the tomb and the guide onboard will give the guests a little basic information about the place and its intriguing history.

Looking north from the tomb one gets a stunning view of the Bay of Kalathos, all the way up to Haraki, with Feraklos Castle standing above it and, further away again, the mountain behind which is the village of Arhangelos. Vlicha Bay is mainly hidden behind an outcrop of land, but the village of Kalathos shines white against the hillside on which it sits, way across the deep blue bay. At night the lights of Haraki twinkle appealingly in the distance and the yellow lights, which illuminate the castle above, are clearly visible. The old windmill, which the path to the tomb passes a few hundred metres back toward Lindos Bay, is also of interest. The door has long since disappeared, but one can climb the stairs within and examine the huge components, still in position, like the gearing and wooden cogs which used to creak and moan as the mill ground the grain which was placed under the great sectioned mill stone, which is still in place and one can only guess at how heavy it is.

Time teases us humans. How many years has this old mill stood sentry before old Kleoboulos' Tomb, as if to warn all those approaching, as if to remind them of how transient they all are. How many lives have come and gone while this mill has stood silent, let alone while the Tomb has stood sentinel on the headland. Jesus Christ walked the earth, the apostle Paul passed nearby on his third missionary trip. William the Conqueror came and went, as did Henry V111, Nostra Damus, Galileo and Adolf Hitler. Old Kleo has lain there and seen them all come and go.

OK, so there are those who refute the idea that this building is actually old Kleo's tomb. It doesn't matter. The fact remains that it has stood here for millennia and continues to remind all those who come to touch it and contemplate that there are greater things in this universe than their little lives.

Dean and Alyson stood as if soldered together for a long time, without words passing between them. Dean drank in the smell of Alyson's hair and she, her head buried into his upper chest, found comfort in the familiar smell of his cologne. She recognised it instantly as Kouros, by Yves Saint Laurent. It was the only male fragrance he'd ever used and she found comfort in the fact that he still used it today. She too was mentally wandering through their past times together. Was it too late to recover what they'd lost? Was it right to wreck a whole bunch of other peoples' lives in order to reunite as a couple and declare to all and sundry that they were going to stay together this time, come what may?

Alyson could also very easily have convinced herself that she ought to end it all, or at the very least, embark on another odyssey which would take her to who-knows-where in order for her not to be the cause of so many other people's problems or heartbreaks. What would the remainder of her life have in store for her if she did that? But then, was she really so wicked that she herself didn't deserve to take what happiness life offered when it came her way? Does anyone deserve anything at all when you bring it all down to basics? Is anyone more entitled to happiness than the person next to them? The whole question of destiny reared its head and again she found herself thinking about conversations she'd had with Dean during happier times. He always spoke with such common sense. Dean was Mr. Logic. He could have written the script for Spock's part in Star Trek. Nothing happened for a reason, everything was coincidence. But every cloud has a silver lining too.

Who cared if their meeting the previous evening was planned, meant to be, or whatever? The fact was that it had happened. What it did possibly tell Alyson was that maybe, just maybe, Dean had come to Greece, albeit to the opposite end of the country from Kefallonia, to see if he couldn't indeed catch a glimpse of her again, however remote the possibility. 'We humans are great at self delusion, aren't we', she thought. We always hope beyond hope that something extremely unlikely will nevertheless happen. Well this time it did. So why shouldn't I grab this moment and run with it? To hell with the consequences. But then, she also had a conscience that, annoyingly, kept interjecting. Could she live with herself if this poor girl Fiona was going to have to fly home heartbroken? What about Dean's parents? OK, so his father was a bit mercenary in fiscal matters, but still and all he was Dean's dad and wanted what he thought was best for his son. The more she stood glued to Dean in the grey light of the moon, the more confused she became.

"Alyson," Dean said, almost as a question. It was as if to say, 'do you hear me?' She raised her head to look at him again and nodded. 'Yes,' this implicated, 'go on.'

"Alyson, I can't go ahead with this wedding. It may cause all kinds of repercussions. It may finally kill off my relationship with my father. It may lose me a few friends and it may break Fiona's heart. But I can't do it. Anyway, what's worse, to go ahead and marry her when it's you I love most, or to set her free with the chance that she'll get over me and find the man she really deserves some day?

"No, Ally. It doesn't matter that it may never have happened. The fact is, I saw you in that bar. You saw me too. At that moment I knew that it was still you I wanted, still you I loved. That's why I sort of half-heartedly bolted. It was only because, for a moment, I believed that if I got away from you things would be OK. But they wouldn't have been. That moment taught me something vital. It taught me that I must have *you*. Seven years, huh. Seems like a few seconds. We're still young. You're still as beautiful as ever. And I must be with you. Call it naïve, but I still feel that maybe we can change the world if we're together. What do you say?"

How could she reply that it was going to be even harder on her than it would be on him? He would lose a lot, true, but she would gain the seething hatred of his family and ex-fiancée. This time it would be for good, she couldn't see it any other way. Could she do this to him?

"Dean I… How can I do this? How can I be the cause of so much disruption, anger and disappointment and…"

"Alyson. Listen. I have made my choice. Now are you going to stand by me? I will not let them blame you."

"How can you stop them? You're daddy's golden boy, he's always going to say it was me, not you."

"Then let him. If he thinks that I am just an easily led, weak-willed wuss, then fine. But I'll tell him, I'll tell them all, that I have made my decision and that it's ultimately for the best. I'll change my flight back so that I'm not on the same plane as Fiona and I'll go back to Cardiff, see Adam and start making arrangements for you and I to marry. I do want this Alyson. I do. After the past few hours of absolute pandemonium in this head of mine I now see things crystal clearly.

"See, it has to all boil down to something very simple. Some people, a lot of people, can live a lie all their lives. I'm not one of them. You are the truth to me and I want to live honestly, not as a shadow of the man I ought to be. The past seven years have gone and we are back together. If I have you, and you have me, what is there to worry about really? What do you say?"

Alyson thought for a while, she bit her lip, she shook her head slightly, but then nodded confidently. If her head didn't quite feel as confident on the inside, she'd sent Dean the external signal that they were in this together. Whatever was to be would be.

They talked on as the constellations turned above them. Dean found himself telling Alyson about how he'd finally cleared out her things when he finally decided that he was going to be with Fiona. Alyson approved of the fact that he'd taken many of them to a charity shop. She told him about her travels around Greece after the chance meeting with Claire on her arrival in Kefallonia. They had a great deal to discuss, to catch up on from their seven years apart, and both wanted to know all the details from the other. The sky had begun to lighten rapidly as 6.00am approached and the sun was about to rise over the ocean beneath them. They stood to watch the spectacle before realising that they'd spent the night out there in the open and both were hungry and tired. Despite the problems that lay immediately ahead of them, they felt better that they'd resolved what they were going to do. There would be no going back. There would be no disappearing acts this time. They were going to risk everything, at least Dean was.

They walked back into a deserted village, the only life in the streets to greet them being the feral cats, that sat eyes half-closed on the rims of the rubbish bins and lazily regarded them with little interest as they passed. Alyson had agreed to show Dean where she was living, so that he could come there once he'd done what he planned to do in a few hours time. Chances were, he'd by then have nowhere else to go.

Creeping into the hotel and up to his room, Dean wondered with some degree of trepidation what kind of fallout there was going to be about his having stood up his own stag night group the previous evening. He undressed and slid into the bed, having taken a few gulps from the bottle of water that he'd nicked from the deserted bar and brought up to the room with him. He'd rummaged around and found a foil-wrapped chocolate croissant in the room and chewed that to assuage the hunger and soon fell into a restless sleep.

Just a couple of hours later, still before 9.00am, he was awoken by a tapping on his door. A voice, which he recognised as Malcolm's, said in loud whisper,

"Dean? Are you in there? Dean?" There was nothing for it, so Dean replied,

"Hold on! I'm coming." He slid out of bed, threw on a robe and opened the door, beckoning his old friend into the room. Malcolm sat on the side of the bed while Dean stood, awkwardly, waiting for what was to come.

"So? What have you been up to buddy? Where *were* you last night? You had the lot of us traipsing all over Lindos looking for you. Your dad was livid that you weren't answering his calls. What's happening, Dean, cold feet or something? I hope it's going to be good, for your sake. Just as well the women were up in town, or it may have been a lot worse."

Dean stared at his friend of many years and wondered where to start. How much should he tell Malcolm now, at this minute? Should he perhaps keep it to something simple and wait until he could announce to everyone himself what he'd been up to and what he was going to do? Malcolm just stared, expectantly.

"It's complicated, Malc. I think I'm gonna have to tell everyone all together what's been going on. I can't tell you everything right now."

Malcolm couldn't even begin to understand what had been going on. To him this all seemed very out of order and he decided to push Dean for a little more.

"Come on mate. How long have we known eachother? I can't for the life of me think what you might have been up to, but I'm going to be your best man tomorrow. Don't you owe it to me to let me in on the act? I mean, where were you?"

Dean sighed and reconsidered. "Oh well. I may as well start with you. But Malcolm," he always used his friend's full name when being deadly serious, "You must promise right here and now that you won't tell anyone else what I'm going to tell you. I need to be the one to tell everyone else, OK?"

"OK, OK, just cut to the chase. What happened? I'm all ears."

Malcolm's body language concurred, as he sat forward, hands on his knees, head tilted toward his standing friend in anticipation.

Dean went on, "You're not going to like it Malcolm, but, well, here goes. I'm not going to marry Fiona."

Malcolm shot up and stood face to face with Dean, incredulity plastered all over his face. "You're WHAT? You ARE having me on here, aren't you? AREN'T YOU?" Malcolm could already tell from Dean's face that he was deadly serious. But what the reason could be was still beyond him. By no stretch of the imagination would he have guessed who Dean had run into the previous evening.

"Malc, look, please keep your voice down. These rooms aren't very sound proof. Look, if I married Fiona, who deserves the best, as I'm sure you'll agree, then she wouldn't be getting what she deserved because I can't give her my best. I do love her, don't misunderstand me, but it's not the same love as I have for Alyson."

"Alyson? What do you mean Alyson? She disappeared ages ago, what, seven or eight years it must be. You told me you were finally over her. God, man, what are you on about? Have you lost it or something? Is it cold feet? If it is then I'm sure I can talk some sense into you. But you haven't talked about Alyson for years now, Dean. 'My life's finally on track' again you told me. 'Fiona's the one I'm going to grow old with' you said. She's a bloody marvellous girl, Dean. The rest of us would give our eye teeth to be in your shoes and well you know it."

"Malcolm, I ran into her."

"You what? You're not making any sense, Dean."

"When I went out for an early evening walk through the village last night I saw her."

"Look, Dean. No, you didn't. You saw someone who looks like her. Prob'ly freaked you out for a moment. Got you feeling all nostalgic or something. What chance is there of you actually meeting the real

Alyson here? Must be a million to one, higher, probably. Dean, you're just getting a bit emotionally jumpy, that's all. Look, get some breakfast inside you and a drink too probably would be a good idea. You'll steady those nerves and everything will be fine. Trust me."

"Malcolm, I didn't just see someone who looked like her. We actually talked. We talked for hours. That's why I didn't show up at Yanni's. I was with Alyson and we were trying to make some sense of things. Malc, we cleared seven years worth of air. She explained what happened when she walked out before. She did it for ME Malc, for ME."

Malcolm made as if to interrupt, but Dean held out both hands, palms toward him and continued, "She knew what my father was like. She KNEW that he'd never accept her. She knew that he thought she was a low-life freeloader. She also knew, Malc, that if I stayed with her, married her, that my dad would cut me off without a penny. He'd disown me because he only thinks with his wallet. His values are entirely monetary and how he likes to boast about the fact. 'You can keep all your "love" talk', he told me, 'in this world it's all about getting real, and "real" means getting yourself on a secure financial footing', that's my father's mantra Malcolm. You know that.

"Alyson believed that she had to make the ultimate sacrifice because she loved me and didn't want to come between me and my wonderful family. She left me because she couldn't bring herself to drive a wedge into my family. She never had a decent family life, Malc, and she didn't want me to lose mine over her."

"Isn't this all a bit, I don't know, melodramatic? Your dad would have come around once he saw her, once he'd met her. No one could have spent long with that girl and not be wrapped around her finger. All us men are the same Dean; we're all suckers for a beautiful woman. But isn't this all a bit 'water under the bridge'? You have a beautiful woman and she's madly in love with you. You're getting married tomorrow Dean. All the arrangements have been made. There are people depending on it. A lot of money's been shelled out on this too. You couldn't just have a nice traditional wedding back home like most other poor mortals. You had to do something exotic and bring a bunch of people over here. Not than I'm complaining mind you, we're all having a blast. Correction! We WERE all having a blast until last night. What are we supposed to make of this? Dean, think about it for a moment. Alyson's been history for years now, why not just tell her that it's too late? She'll understand. Don't forget, it was HER who walked out on you, boy. Who's to say that she won't do that again? Eh? Have you thought of that?

"Are you REALLY prepared to throw away all that you've now got, the kind of prospects that most of us only dream about, for a whim about some girl you used to be with half a lifetime ago? Dean, am I making sense?"

"Yes, Malcolm. You're making perfect sense."

"Right then, so, no harm done. We'll concoct an alibi for last night and say no more about it. You'll get married to Fiona and we'll all live happily ever after, right? OK?"

"I didn't say I was going to change my mind. I only said you're making sense. But the thing is, I don't bloody care. I don't want to go on making sense, to go on doing what everyone around me wants me to do. I've been doing that all my miserable life. I seem to be always pleasing others and never myself. Well, no more! I'm going to do what I want to do from now on.

"Malcolm, if I'd had the courage to stand up to my bully of a father seven years ago I wouldn't be in this position now. I'd have told him what he could do with his stupid values and, you're right, by now he'd have come around and we'd be getting on again, only he'd probably be giving me a lot more respect that he does now. It's my fault that

Alyson left, Malc, *my* fault. She'd been on at me for months to confront dad. She even wanted the two of us to drive over there and talk to him face to face. It's because I kept stalling, kept saying, 'yea, OK. Soon. But not yet,' that she eventually went. She went because my own actions had told her that I was still putting my family above her. She had no reason to think I'd ever change, however good we were together when we were alone. If you like, she was forced into leaving me because I didn't show enough spine."

"Things are beginning to look a bit bleak mate. Can't begin to imagine what's gonna hit the fan when you break this to the others. You sure about this? Can't I still maybe talk you out of it?"

Dean answered with his face and Malcolm knew it was a lost cause.

"Well, what do you want me to do now? I was just about to go down for breakfast. Not sure I can be bouncy and flippant with the other guys after all this."

"Malcolm, I'm sorry to do this to you, ...to do it to anyone. There's no way I'm ever going to expect everyone to understand, or even forgive me. But I've got to do what I've got to do. All I ask is that, however you do it, try and keep this to yourself until I've spoken to Fiona. I owe it to her to talk to her first. Can you do that for me, keep schtum a while longer?"

"I'll do my best, Dean. Good luck mate. You're gonna need it." Malcolm moved towards the door and grabbed the handle. Before turning it, however, he turned back to his friend of many years and said, "For what it's worth. I'll stand by you Dean. We've been friends a long, long time. Even though it looks like you're depriving me of my first ever gig as best man." This half-hearted attempt at injecting a little lightness raised a tiny smile from the corners of Dean's mouth and Malcolm was gone, leaving Dean staring at the door of his hotel room.

2. Alyson – Lindos, January 20th 2007.

That night, Kleo, that night when we talked here. All night long we talked. It was almost too much to take in. The moment I caught sight of him in that tiny street at the Ikon, if I could only have imagined where it would lead us.

Happiness, what really is it? Maybe it's just a fleeting moment here and there. Those times when you get this overwhelming sense of euphoria. But they don't last for long, not nearly long enough. The rest of it's all just, I don't know, nothingness. Why did I ever let mum give me that Jean Paul Sartre book, Kleo? I had some kind of hope before reading that. All that existentialism, it's no good for anyone. If ever there was a more appropriate title for a book I haven't come across it yet.

I was stupid enough for that fleeting moment, when we stood right here on that night, to have thought that things might just work out. I just might end up really happy with life after all.

Now I've half a mind to…

No, I'm too cowardly for that. But what has life still got tucked away to throw at me? I bet you know Kleo, but you're not telling, are you.

3. Dean – Lindos, June 19th 2005.

"Come on Fiona, answer it." Dean had tapped the keys of his mobile phone to call Fiona, who would be probably checking out of the hotel in Rhodes Town in preparation for the drive back to Lindos. He hadn't left his room all morning and no one had knocked. He didn't rightly know why no one had come to the room, but he put it down to Malcolm's inventiveness. Perhaps he told the rest of the gang that Dean was sleeping off a hangover, or perhaps not feeling well. It didn't matter, whatever he'd told the others, it had done the trick.

"Hello, sweetie. Missing me?" The almost unbearable optimism in Fiona's voice knocked him off his guard completely. For a moment he was dumbstruck with thoughts as to how to break the news. "You there, baby?" she continued, "What's up?"

"Oh, nothing. How did the hen night go? Wild and wicked?"

"Knockout. But you'd have been proud of me. We did get propositioned by our fair share of handsome Greek men, some of which were very tasty I might add, but I resisted. Only have eyes for you sweetie. You know that, don't you?"

"Yea, I reckon. What time will you be back in Lindos then?"

"We're in the car now. I'd say by two o'clock we'll be at the hotel. Why, you going to be waiting outside reception? That'd be nice. Especially if you had a single red rose clutched in your sweaty palm just for me. Even better, between your teeth!"

"Well, Fiona, I've got something…"

"Something contagious? Hope not! Silly boy."

"No, something I…"

"Found under your pillow? Have you been waiting for the tooth fairy?" A slight chuckle ensued at the other end of the phone.

"NO. Look, Fiona, we need…"

"Can't it wait, hun? We're whizzing past Faliraki right now. Look, I'll be there in forty-five minutes at most. You can surprise me then sweetie, OK? Got to go. Love you immensely."

She hung up.

Dean sat in his room a while longer before deciding that he'd need to check with Malcolm what he'd told the others before venturing out. Just when he was going to call his friend, there was a knock on the door.

"Dean, mate. It's me, Malcolm." Dean let him in and waited to hear what he had to say. "You owe me big time, mate. I managed to persuade them that you'd had a drink or two and got waylaid by a couple of Greek blokes who insisted you share a celebratory tipple with them. Before you knew it you'd realised that you'd left your phone in the room and by the time you finally extricated yourself you went to Yanni's to find no one there. Even I don't know what time your dad left there, but that's down to you now. You then came back here, probably getting here before the rest of us, came up to the room to get your mobile and fell asleep on the bed. I came to see you this morning and you said you weren't feeling so good and would be down when you felt better. They probably believed me, but whether they think what you told me holds water, I haven't the faintest.

"So, you coming down to face the music now, then?"

"Where is everyone?"

"They're all round the pool, chilling and awaiting the girls' return. Apparently your mum phoned your dad just now to tell him that they were coming past Kalathos and would be here in another ten minutes. Best I could have done Dean."

"Malcolm, you're a solid gold guy. Thanks so much. Dean placed his hand on his friend's shoulder. I'll pick up the baton then, shall I?"

"It's too hot for me to hold any more."

The two friends made their way along the balcony and down the steps, through the hotel gardens to the pool area, all the while Dean was feeling anxious beyond belief. His perspiration was due to much more than a Greek June day's weather conditions. 'Here goes,' he thought as they came around the side of the building to the pool terrace. The guys were doing various things. A few were at the bar, supping on draft lagers, one or two were in the pool. But the only figure Dean wanted to check out was his father's. Sure enough, there he was under a parasol, gold chain around his neck glinting in the bright light and his Ray Bans were just visible over the copy of the Times he was reading. Espadrilles parked ever so neatly along with a bottle of Piz Buin beside the sun bed, he looked every inch the homme nouveau riche.

Francis had already spotted his son, but wasn't going to let on. 'He can sweat a little more while he comes over' he thought, and carried on pretending to be interested in the paper. Dean sat on the hot tiles beside his father.

"Hi Dad."

"Son."

"Look, I'm sorry about last ni…"

"Listen to me boy, and listen good." He spoke through his teeth in a strong whisper, just strong enough to be sure that his son got the message, but not so that the others would get any idea about what was going on. "I don't care a monkey's toss about what happened last night. What I do care about now, is that everything goes without a hitch from this very second until tomorrow afternoon, when you and Fiona will be man and wife. After that, go to blazes for all I care. But you're not going to ruin everything for your mother and I now, do you hear? Charles and I have an understanding, we've become fast friends since you took up with his daughter and that's exactly how it's going to stay.

"You have a damn good life, Dean, am I right?" He wasn't going to wait for Dean's reply, a fact of which Dean was well aware. Shaking his newspaper a little, he went on, "A lot of young men would give up everything to be in your shoes. Whatever you did last night, and I don't care if you had sex with half the women in Lindos, has no relevance from here on in. You could have run through the village stark naked shouting 'All Greeks are wankers!!' and I wouldn't care one jot.

"Just get this straight, son. You carry on as planned, or else you won't set foot anywhere near my house from now until the day you fall down dead. Now, that's all I'm going to say on the subject. Why not run along and have a swim or something."

Dean had heard enough to help him with his decision. Had his father assumed any other stance but that of the big bully, as usual, Dean may well have wavered. But this was just what he needed to firm up his resolve. Without allowing himself to think about it too much, he rose a little, on to his haunches, in readiness to stand up and walk away, and said quietly to the back page of the Times,

"I don't simply hate you. I despise you and everything you stand for. I feel desperately sorry for mother, having to stare at you every morning when she wakes up. You can take all your values and shove them. I don't need to be told that you don't have a son any longer. I don't have a father and I'd prefer to be an orphan than to have *you* in that rôle in my life. ...Bye then." This last sign-off was uttered with casual offhandedness, as one would say it to a friend whom one had just bumped into and had a brief chat with in the street. Dean then sprang to his feet, waved a hand at his friends, and went off to the hotel gate to greet the women.

He had a mission to fulfil and he was now well prepared to see it through.

Francis Waters fumed behind his copy of the Times, but didn't allow himself to show any reaction that others around him could detect.

Arriving at the hotel's front gate Dean saw that the women had already parked. No doubt they had gone to their rooms first to change and get themselves prettied up before coming to find the men.

Dean marched to the block where Fiona's room was located, climbed the external stairs and walked along the balcony to her door. Hearing voices within, he identified the other voice as Fiona's mother. He knocked three times with his knuckles.

Fiona's mother opened the door. "Oh, Dean. Can't wait to see her eh? Tell you what. I'm off down to the pool side. Did you see Charles there by any chance?"

"Sorry, no, Mrs. Kyle. But I'm sure he's about somewhere."

"Dean, it'll have to stop being 'Mrs. Kyle' before long you know!!" She pecked him on the cheek and made off along the balcony and down the stairs. Fiona's hand came out from the door, as Dean was still looking at the now empty walkway where her mother had just passed, and pulled him into the room by his polo shirt collar.

She sought out his mouth and planted a lingering promissory kiss on his lips. Pulling away, she registered slight surprise that he hadn't responded in the way he usually did.

"You OK? Not getting last minute cold feet are we?" she asked him.

Dean sighed and looked her in the eyes. He took a deep breath and began.

4. Alyson – Lindos, June 19th 2005, late afternoon.

Alyson sat outside the front door of her modest little flat in the rabbit warren of tiny streets up on the steep hillside in the part of the village that was perched beneath the ridge, above which was Krana Square. Her place was one of six, all of which surrounded a common courtyard, which had a superb view of the Lindos Acropolis and the great blue Mediterranean Sea beyond. Inside they were all very similar, the only variant being the exact dimensions of the rooms. There was a tiny kitchenette just inside the front door, which consisted of a small area of worktop, a modest under the counter fridge, two electric hobs, a combi-microwave and a small sink and draining board. Further in there was the dining area-cum-bedroom and off that was the cupboard-sized shower room, which was actually a wet-room, as so many Greek studios or village rooms are equipped with. There was no shower basin, but rather a chrome drain in the room's tiled floor. Wet-rooms were all very well, but so often one had to remember to take the toilet roll and place it outside when taking a shower, or risk it being reduced to a soggy pulp, since there was rarely a shower curtain to keep the water contained. The back of the building was actually built into the solid rock of the sheer hillside behind.

Out front, the landlord had provided for each dwelling a small white PVC patio table and two chairs, all of which had seen better days. The PVC had reached that stage which anyone living in such a climate was familiar with, it was the stage where the plastic had lost its sheen and had become almost powdery. You could scratch into the surface with a fingernail and white dust would come away. As a result, the chair-arms were criss-crossed with channels where the outer layer of PVC was gone and what remained would frequently leave white dusty marks on your clothes.

Alyson was very happy living here. All the other tenants were Albanian and – without exception – courteous, friendly and hardworking. Several were young couples with small children. She could trust each one of them too and never locked her front door. One couple, Elena and Mondi, had told her about the house they owned back in their home country. It sounded beautiful. They so longed to be back there, but with no work and no state aid, they had little choice but to remain here in Greece. Like just about every one of their compatriots, they'd learned to speak Greek within months of moving here.

She'd purchased a length of flower-patterned oilcloth and made covers for both the table outside on the terrace and the modest Formica-topped rectangular one inside. The outside table didn't ever lose its cover in the breeze because Alyson had also attached those steel clips at various stages around the circumference that are usually to be seen holding the tablecloths in place at a taverna.

She sat at the table, a tumbler of cheap white wine on the surface beside her, alongside a large bottle of mineral water. She also had a book open on her lap, something by Robert Goddard that she'd borrowed from Sheila at the laundry-cum-library in the village, but she wasn't reading. She couldn't concentrate to read. It was late afternoon and her thoughts were consumed by what Dean was possibly going through at the hotel just a few hundred yards above and behind where she was sitting.

How long would she wait here for his arrival? Would he come at all? She told herself that she'd be failing him to even doubt that he would, but when she considered the pressure that would probably be brought to bear on him, she felt that she couldn't even be too hard on him if he caved in. After all, there were two sets of parents, a bunch of friends, the registrar, the wedding people – the company that she herself even worked for, and the caterers at the reception. There were the gifts that had been prepared for the couple and the honeymoon later in the year, out in the West Indies. That was already booked, he'd told her. His father had given him the keys to a new car, which he was to collect from his parents' driveway on their return from Lindos. They were to drive over to Wales in it the morning after their return, after passing one night at Limpley Stoke.

Could anyone be expected to tell all those people, let alone his bride-to-be, that he wasn't going to go through with it? Alyson was in mental anguish, one moment telling herself that within a few hours she and Dean would be back together after seven years apart, the next convincing herself that he'd not turn up and she'd only be getting what she deserved anyway.

'Here I go again,' she thought, 'talking about what I deserve. What does *anyone* deserve, when you come down to it? If someone lives a really virtuous life, does that then mean that they deserve to be happy? Isn't it all rather really a total lottery? Some very nasty, wicked people have lived long and prosperous lives, whereas some absolute saints have died with nothing.

'"Only the good die young", that's a common idea. Yet I'm quite convinced that a lot of very good people live to ripe old ages and a lot of villains die relatively young. How old was Hitler, for example? Wasn't he only in his fifties? The good guy he certainly wasn't.'

So she mused on as the evening drew near. Still she sat there whilst some of her neighbours came in or went out, usually coming from or going to their work in some hotel or other. She sipped at her wine and stared at the seemingly timeless Acropolis, towering over the village beneath.

Finally, at around 6.00pm, when she'd tilted her head back against the wall of the house to allow the sun to warm her face, since from this time of day onwards she allowed herself a little exposure to sunlight and had closed her modest little umbrella a few moments before, a shadow came over her, causing her to open her eyes.

"Dean!" she started and sat bolt upright.

"Sorry. Expecting someone else?" Brian smiled down at her. "Managed to find out where you live. Hope you don't mind, the girls at the Flight of Fancy office told me, but I really do need to know what happened when you talked to your mum, to Christine."

5. Dean – Lindos, June 19th 2005, late afternoon.

Feeling browbeaten and thoroughly wretched, Dean threw what he could find of his belongings in his room into his suitcase and flight bag, whilst searching for them through a film of tears which wouldn't stop pouring. The sooner he could get away from there the better.

Fiona had ranted, screamed, struck him with fists, collapsed into his arms and then just thrown herself on to the bed to sob uncontrollably. He'd tried so hard to explain that he couldn't give her the love and devotion that she so deserved, that she'd be better off without someone such as he, that with time she'd get over him and find someone more worthy of her, but it hadn't made much difference. What had started out as a dream-wedding trip in an idyllic setting had turned into a disappointment, an embarrassment, a debacle, and a nightmare for everyone involved. After well over an hour of hysterics, during which he'd made a gargantuan effort to remain calm, even though he knew that one of his eyes would have turned black by morning, he'd finally told her that it was best if he left and did.

The fury that had been vented in that hotel room must have been heard from some considerable distance away. Mercifully, though, for Dean, the entire main building of the hotel stood between this room and the pool area, so it was less likely that the rest of their party would have heard it. At one stage though, there had been a ginger knock on the door and a voice had enquired, 'Is everything in there OK?' to which Dean had answered, "Yes, sorry. Just had some bad news. We'll be OK in a moment,' something which he very much doubted.

Having finally stuffed what he could into his suitcase and bag, he stumbled out of his room and, suitcase wheels drumming on the ceramic tiles beneath them, walked along the balcony and down the steps to the hotel gardens below. He'd decided that he'd call Adam from a safe distance, but that the rest of it could all go to blazes. He didn't have the mettle to go and confront everyone and knew anyway that they'd soon get the whole story from his ex-fiancée, once she'd calmed down enough to become coherent again. The house in the Vale, west of Cardiff, the new car, in fact the whole shooting match, he'd let the two families deal with. He'd write telling them the name of his solicitor and let it all be resolved through her.

But he would have to call Adam. He'd have to decide the best time to do it. Hopefully when there wouldn't be others there to ask who he was talking to. But he desperately needed to talk it through with his friend and business partner, so as to hopefully get him onside in all of this. He didn't need to lose his business now, with the certainty of already having lost his family for the foreseeable future.

Dean had to be circumspect regarding in which direction to walk once he'd left the hotel. The most direct route to Alyson's would take him right along the pavement outside the hotel's pool area. Not a good route in the circumstances. Yet this was the way he'd come back to the hotel after Alyson had shown him where she lived. No, he'd have to walk along to Krana Square and take the courtesy bus down to Lindos village. The quicker the better, in case any of his wedding party were to come out either to go the Flora supermarket or even to find him and give him a good hiding.

The problem with this route was that he'd be entering the village from a totally different direction from the one he'd hoped to follow in order to find Alyson's flat again. This wasn't a place where you could find your way around easily. Streets were extremely narrow, often steep or stepped into the bargain, not the ideal territory for someone towing a wheeled suitcase. All the package tourists that stay in the village itself, when they arrive, get their cases delivered from Lindos Reception to their rooms by a local with a tiny three-wheeled pickup, a bit like an Ape without the cab. All they had to do was to follow their rep on foot as he or she walked them around the village, depositing each party of new arrivals at their respective "digs" for the week or two until reaching their own.

Arriving at the courtesy bus stop at the busiest part of Krana, Dean was dismayed to see a huge horde of people waiting for its next visit. He couldn't face the idea of getting into a scrum to climb aboard. The largest thing any of these people was carrying was a shoulder bag, when here he was with a flight bag and a suitcase. No, he'd just have to cross the very wide road, on which coaches were coming and going continually, some reversing into parking bays, others exiting to begin the journey back to the north of the island, dodge the taxis and other cars whizzing this way and that, then walk down the long twisting lane to the village.

All the way down the lane he had to keep stopping for people walking in the opposite direction. The entire route down the hill there's a small area to the right as you descend which is painted with stripes to designate the pedestrian area on the hot tarmac, but it's quite inadequate at this time of year, plus the taxis which ply the lane don't worry about the occasional grazed walker as they zip up and down going about their business. It was a fraught walk for several reasons.

After what seemed like an hour, but was probably only about fifteen minutes, Dean arrived at the square and stopped to take stock. Before disappearing into the mêlée of the lane which enters the village from the far top side of the square, he had to do a quick GPS in his brain to try and work out which way he'd have to walk in order to find Alyson's place. One thing he hadn't done is to ask her for her mobile number. There had been too much emotion pulsing through both of their minds earlier that same day to remember such practicalities. Was it really only that very same morning that he'd walked back into the village, passing this very spot, after a night out at that tomb with the funny name, re-acquainting himself with the girl he'd never really got over, in an all night conversation?

Having thought for a few moments which way would be best to take him towards Alyson's place, he set off across the square and along the lane leading into the heart of the village. One certainty was that he'd have to go towards the right and climb the slope. He knew that she lived on the opposite side of the "basin" in which the village sat from the imposing hilltop on which stood the Acropolis. Reaching the open-sided "garage" in which the donkeys that ferried tourists through the narrow streets and lanes and eventually up the steep path to the Acropolis itself were kept, he turned right and was immediately faced with the need to retract the handle of his case and lift it, since before him were the first of innumerable steps that he'd have to negotiate if he were to arrive at Alyson's place at all.

After a few more twists and turns in the lanes, during which he'd encountered numerous junctions which afforded him views of only a few feet before the various options he was faced with turned right-angled bends beneath the ever vigilant gaze of small shuttered windows punctuating the never-ending whiteness of the walls of small houses, he felt the panic setting in. The further he climbed, the less people he encountered as he drew further away from the main tourist thoroughfares. Those whom he did encounter walked past excitedly, usually going downhill, engaged in animated unintelligible conversations, or bawling into their ever-present mobile telephones. Local women sat on steps outside of arched doorways leading into courtyards of various sizes, often with floors made of thousands of tiny pebbles, skilfully laid to create traditional Greek key-patterns of black and white, or to depict dolphins or flowers beneath the feet of those traversing them. Now and then, as he passed beneath an open window, set in the wall just above head-height, he'd hear through the chintz or lace the sound of a TV burning as the Greek newsreader informed the nation of the latest grocery price hikes in the supermarkets of Athens and Thessalonika. Occasionally the insistent thud of bass from a hi-fi told him that those within were younger and were listening to the kind of music that Dean detested; that noise which just thumps on incessantly while the kids hop up and down in a frenzy. 'No soul that stuff', he told himself in thought. Such moments led him briefly down a chain of thought that was almost a relief from what was consuming his conscious mind. He'd find himself mentally discussing why the kind of music that didn't exude the audible proof of real fingers striking real keys, or strumming strings, wasn't music at all. But all too soon he'd reach another junction, proffering him a choice of two ways to go, and he'd be brought back to the present with a jolt.

Should he go up to the right, or carry on along the level slightly to his left? Sometimes, in order to gain height and thus hopefully bring him closer to his target, he realised that he had to go back downhill a while and then double back. After probably twenty minutes of this, he was exhausted. His case was getting heavier by the minute, as he hardly had the opportunity any more to extract the handle and use its wheels, and his shoulder was tiring from lugging his flight bag. Changing shoulders didn't help. He always found that if he threw a strap over his right shoulder rather than his left, within seconds it would be slipping off and he'd be lugging it back up again with his other hand. Also, he found that he couldn't tug his case along so well with his other hand. He cursed his lack of ambidexterity. 'Does that apply to shoulders as well as to hands?' he wondered.

He sat on his case for a while at the foot of an impossibly steep set of stone steps, probably numbering at least a dozen, at the top of which was yet more whiteness. A dog barked incessantly. He found himself once more doubting his own sanity. What on earth was he doing? Just twenty-four hours or so ago, give or take an hour, he'd been happily strolling the enchanting village of Lindos, enjoying the warmth of a June evening in the southern Dodecanese, musing over the prospect of marrying a gorgeous girl who doted on him. All his close friends were just a few metres away and were soon to meet him for his stag night. He had even established a kind of peace with his dad and they'd been quite civil to eachother for several years now, a fact that had so pleased his mother. He was running a pretty successful graphic design business with his friend and partner Adam Hastings and they had exciting new clients coming onboard with encouraging regularity.

In short, his life was the kind, as he grudgingly had to acknowledge, that his father had pointed out up at the hotel pool just a few hours ago, that others would give their proverbial eye-teeth for. What had his father told him, albeit through clenched teeth?

"You have a damn good life, Dean, am I right?" Am I right. Am I right. How that phrase with which his father so loved to end his sentences resounded around Dean's raging brain. '*Now* look,' he thought, self-pity rising in him like an irresistible torrent, 'you're sitting here on your suitcase probably having cooked your goose with everyone you love, everyone you hold dear. You can't even find your way to Alyson's flat and she's the only lifeline you have. Didn't she even say that she felt that she was almost destined to be the person to bring only trouble and disruption? Didn't she say that she felt as though she ought to not to try and pursue a relationship with anyone for fear she'd bring them disaster?

'Hold on, stop this,' he told himself. 'There's no such thing as anyone being "destined" for such things. We all make our own decisions and we all carry the can for them. Life throws a random series of missiles at us and it's up to us how we dodge them. Allowing herself to think that way was liable to make Alyson repeat the mistakes her mother had made when she was younger. How we all pay in later life for being the victims of how we grew up.' He couldn't let her develop that line of thinking. At the very bottom of all of this was one thing: he and Alyson. They now knew after their chance meeting that they'd really only been waiting for eachother. What else mattered? All the mess and confusion that he'd now caused would eventually be cleared up. People move on. All right, so perhaps he had sacrificed his family for his love. It wouldn't be the first time anyone had done that. It wouldn't be the last.

"Boy, am I thirsty," he found himself saying aloud.

Just then he heard the sound of footsteps behind him. Someone was coming down the steep steps that he'd been contemplating a few minutes ago. A man brushed past him, obviously not a Greek, probably a tourist. As his leg made brief contact with Dean's shoulder he briefly looked down at him, said "Sorry mate," grinned and was gone around the next corner.

He looked about fifty, or maybe just over, but was in good shape.

He had wavy hair and clothes which screamed "artist, musician," or something creative. Dean was a skilled people-watcher from way back when he and Alyson used to sit in coffee bars in Cardiff and practice the sport. Oh, and he was obviously British.

How Dean found himself wishing they could have exchanged places for a moment. Probably that bloke hadn't a care in the world. Just out here enjoying his life and having a great time.

"I wish," thought Dean.

6. Brian – Lindos, June 19th 2005, early evening.

"Would you like a drink?" asked Alyson, tugging on her only other white PVC chair, to bring it out from the table for Brian to sit down. "Haven't got much I'm afraid. There are a couple of beers in the fridge, or else it's cheap white wine. Oh, and in a small tumbler, if that'll do?"

"Looks a lot like water to me," replied Brian, eyeing the bottle on Alyson's table. But that would do fine."

"No, silly. The wine's in the fridge. Can't leave a carton of white out in these temperatures, it'd soon be too warm to drink. I'll get it. Hold on."

She rose and entered the cracked brown-painted doorway immediately next to her chair and went to fetch the carton of wine and a tumbler, whilst Brian parked himself and threw one foot over the other knee. Alyson re-emerged a few moments later, a carton of supermarket wine in one hand and a small glass tumbler in the other. She sat down again and, as she poured, Brian studied her perfect features and deep brown eyes. He struggled again with his memories of times spent in the bar with this girl's mother. Alyson brought him back to the present.

"She was very surprised, to say the least," she began. "But I think she'll say yes."

"You think she'll say yes. Like, she didn't actually give you an answer then and there?"

"Look, Brian, it's a lot of years and a lot of water under the bridge. She was genuinely affected emotionally when I told her that it was really you. In fact, she didn't really believe it was you until I told her about what you'd written in the book, *Nausea*. Then I knew she realised because she started crying over the phone."

"She cried? That's good isn't it?" he realised that this didn't sound very caring, and so added, "I mean, good in the sense that she must still have feelings about me."

"It's all right. I knew what you meant. How many years is it since you two actually saw eachother?"

"Well, I left Bath in January 1978, so it's now twenty seven years and counting. I really can't believe that it's been that long. It might sound strange to you, I mean, how old are you? – You must be twenty-seven, since you were born not long after I left, but I still feel like I'm trying to get the hang of life. All the while though, as Leonard Cohen said a few years ago, *"Summer's almost gone and winter's tuning up"*, do you know that song?"

"I do. In fact that CD's in the flat behind me right now. My mum made sure I acquired good taste in music. And poetry I suppose, since I'd call Leonard Cohen more of a poet than a singer, or songwriter. This'll impress you: how does it go now? *'Now my friends have gone and my hair is grey, I ache in the places where I used to play…'* Tower of Song on the album '*I'm Your Man*', right?"

"Wow. I am impressed. Me to a 'T', sadly. But, going back to Christine, is there maybe a 'when' in there somewhere? I mean, 'when' as in when I may be able to meet up with her, or at least talk? Is she still in Bath?"

"Yes, she is. She has a council house. She's been in it since the year dot it seems. She's not in a relationship now, least I don't think so." Alyson thought about this and realised that Winston might still be around. But why hurt Brian's feelings? Anyway, if he was, he was probably headed for the door. If her mum had still wanted him she'd have talked about him a lot more during their recent conversations over the phone than she had done. Alyson couldn't remember the last time her mother had referred to him in the present tense. So it was probably accurate to tell Brian that Christine was single again.

"My gut feeling is that she will tell me that she does want to get in touch. But I'm afraid that's all I can give you right now. I'll be talking to her again in a few days and I've no doubt that she'll be wanting to know more about you, whether I've talked to you again, how you're doing and so on.

"I'm afraid the old expression 'patience is a virtue' applies here, Brian. But, for what it's worth, can I tell you something? I mean something a bit personal, not meaning to embarrass you, although I'll probably embarrass myself?"

Brian looked at her with a little perplexity on his face, then nodded, "Of course," he said, "fire away."

"I like you. I think mum was probably quite mad to have let you disappear like that without telling you what she felt. But if you and her do get together, then it would have my blessing, one hundred percent."

Brian's face flushed, but then, so did his sense of pride. He was somewhat taken aback by this girl's directness but, nonetheless, very pleased to hear her estimation of him. They talked on for a while longer and, when Brian's wine was all gone, he stood, bent to kiss Alyson on the head and told her he'd try his best to wait until she had more news. This time he gave her his mobile phone number and took hers in exchange. She promised to call him once she'd talked again with Christine and he replied,

"Alyson. Seems slightly insane to me, since you're all grown up and exceedingly beautiful, like your mother I should add. But to have you as a prospective stepdaughter would be simply wonderful!!

"Yea, I know, a bit early to talk in such terms, but, what the hell, I'm fifty-five and there isn't any time to lose! If your mum agrees to see me I may just propose there and then. Mind you, I still feel eighteen anyway!"

With that he bade her good evening and bounded off out of the courtyard and down the steps into the heart of Lindos village. On the way down some further steps he was surprised to come across a young man, a very good-looking young man with quite long hair, sitting on a suitcase in one of the tiny nooks created by the narrow Lindos lanes. In fact Brian very nearly fell over him and apologised as he swept away around the next corner.

Was there something vaguely familiar about this young man? Surely not.

Part Seven

Reconstruction

1. Alyson – Lindos, January 25th 2007.

The view from Kleoboulos is good for many things. It puts everything into perspective. It reminds me how small I am. It also reminds me of the best things about life. I know the old expression "the best things in life are free" is a bit over-used, but it's still true nevertheless. I once thought that it would all work out OK, that I'd finally be happy and no longer convinced that my life was doomed to be a failure from the start and there was nothing that I could do about it.

When we re-kick-started our relationship I was immature enough to think that it was all going to be downhill from then on. Just as Claire was leaving my life, after seven years during which we'd forged a true friendship, Dean came along again and another chapter seemed to be under way.

Brian.

Brian, it wasn't your fault. In fact, you had to say and do what any one of us would have done in the circumstances.

If only, though, you'd known what that would lead to.

Still, I have to heave a sigh of resignation as I gaze out at the blue sea. It's cold today, must be only the lower teens Celsius. But it's very clear and everything's vivid. A feast for the eyes. If only everything in my life were as clear.

What now, eh? Can there me any more twists and, if there are, will my poor little heart be able to bear them?

Sleep tight Kleo. One of these days I must try and find out if any of your writings are still available. I reckon they might just give me some solace.

2. Dean and Alyson – Lindos, June 19th 2005, early evening.

'Right,' thought Dean, 'onward and upward. I'm going to climb these steps and see where they take me. I must be near by now. The view, when I do get a fleeting glimpse of it, looks right. I can see the Acropolis through the gaps between the buildings in these narrow streets. Come on man, you can do it.'

"Dean?!" Dean!"

He could hardly believe his ears, as if it were a miracle, but it was Alyson's voice. It came from above those steps. Looking up he saw her. She was standing there a few metres above him.

"Dean!! I thought it had all gone wrong. Where have you been? Don't tell me you're not… No sorry, sorry!"

She ran down the steps to him and threw her arms around him in palpable relief. She'd realised that he may have been having problems finding her and so decided to walk just a few metres in each direction away from her flat to see if he was on his way. For a brief moment she'd thought that perhaps he'd come to tell her that he'd changed his mind; that he was going to marry Fiona after all. But seeing his case and bag, she knew that he'd done it. She knew that he'd thrown his old life away while she sat outside her front door biting her nails and waiting. Thank goodness she didn't have to work today, she'd never have been able to concentrate on a series of heads. She'd have messed up and she knew it, probably lost her job or something.

But now it was all alright. Here was her Dean, bearing ample evidence of having kept his resolve. His arms flew up to encircle her and his flight bag fell to the ground. He buried his head in her hair and felt her break into heavy sobs.

"It's OK, Ally. It's OK. I've come. Whatever happens now, it's definitely you and me against the world."

After a few minutes, during which she couldn't stop crying, she finally gathered herself and looked up at him. Through wet eyes and wet cheeks, she told him, "You silly thing!! You got lost didn't you!! I thought, I mean, I began to think…"

"Ally, Ally. It's OK. I've come. I'm here. We've got some planning and thinking to do. I think I've created one unholy stink up at that hotel. I don't think you'll be working tomorrow afternoon."

Dean picked up his case and Alyson collected his flight bag from the floor and they climbed the steps together.

Next day, they decided that Dean couldn't risk going into the village to buy bread or supplies, just in case anyone from his wedding party were to run into him. He'd probably be the first murder victim in Lindos since who-knows-when. Alyson wasn't known to any of them and so told him to hang around while she went out for some groceries.

"I won't be long," she said, "why not make yourself a peppermint tea and maybe think about when it would be best to phone Malcolm and Adam. I'll be back before you know it."

She grabbed a linen shoulder bag and was gone. Walking through the village to one of the tiny "supermarkets" she was feeling elated. Yes, she knew that there were huge problems yet to be surmounted, the fact that Dean had a business in South Wales and that she still had work and a place to live here in Lindos for one, but she now told herself that finally things were looking positive. Whatever else went on, if you have your true soul mate, the person you love more than all others, beside you, then surely you can cope, you can survive one way or another.

Dean's party were due to fly back to the UK on Wednesday, which would be June 22nd. He could use an internet café to go on-line and book another flight after that. Then they'd have to make plans as to where they were going to live. It made sense for her to go to Wales and live with him in the apartment that he still retained in Cardiff. Even though he and Fiona were due to move into their new home in the Vale, they'd have been staying in the apartment while the extension was being built, if the marriage had gone ahead. Dean had foreseen this and so kept the apartment on. Who knows, perhaps they could then make plans of their own for a Lindos wedding, one that would actually go ahead this time.

Eventually she found herself up at Krana, where she needed some things from the Flora supermarket. Browsing around among the aisles and red bodies of the under-dressed, over-tattooed great British multi-earringed, sunburnt sojourners she was suddenly brought up with a jolt. Picking up a packet or something-or-other, she was aware of a group of girls who were drifting towards her. The conversation told her all she needed to know.

"Bloody disgusting I call it. Ought to be hung, drawn and quartered."

"Doesn't deserve you, Fiona. I know it's tough, but you'll be glad about this after your emotions have simmered down. You're better than him anyway, always said so."

"Oh yea? Grace, I seem to recall you telling me that you'd have him if I didn't want him. What did you say? 'Drop dead gorgeous boy like that' or something. Now suddenly he's not good enough for me!"

"Alright, lovey, don't take it out on me. I was only trying to make you feel better."

And so it went on. Alyson knew right away that there was no way of avoiding them seeing her. They'd been certain to know her too, after all it was only three days ago that she'd done their hair in the trial run for the wedding. Before she had any more time to gather her thoughts, she came face to face with one of the girls.

"Hello there, how are you babe? Hey, you aren't going to believe this, but..."

Just at that moment, Alyson's mobile phone chirped from within her bag. She rummaged around for it, hoping that her audience wouldn't spot her embarrassment. She was so aware that she was the cause of the commotion and she found it hard to conceal the fact. Surely they'd guess. Surely they'd put two and two together. She so desperately wanted to get out of there.

"Hello Sally, what's up?" said Alyson, seeing one of her bosses' names on the phone's display and trying to sound upbeat. She was sure that the girls, who seemed to want to hang around until she'd completed her call, would suss. They'd see her face turning red and feel the way her skin was beginning to glow from perspiration. "Really? Oh, how sad. OK. Yes, OK. No problem, thanks Sally, thanks." She closed the phone and slipped it back into her bag. There was no escape, the girls wanted to spill the gossip about their friend's aborted wedding plans. Fiona herself seemed to want to tell her too. 'That was it,' she thought, 'they're going to go for me. They're just waiting, turning the screw. Oh God what am I going to do?'

The girl who'd spoken continued, "I don't think you'll be needed this afternoon darling. Fiona's not getting spliced after all." She waited for Alyson's response, 'obviously closing in for the kill' thought Alyson. She felt she'd better answer, so she told the girl what she'd just heard from her boss on the phone.

"I think I already know. That was the office. They said that I needn't go as the wedding was off at the last minute. They didn't elaborate," [she lied], "I'm so sorry. What happened?"

"The bastard's walked out on dear Fiona. Can you believe it? I mean, look at the poor darling, even with her face a mess from crying all night, isn't she the most divine catch any guy could wish for? But you know what he said? Talk about the lowest of the low, uh, …what was your name again?"

Panic rose to a micrometer beneath the surface. Had Dean told Fiona the name of his old flame? He must have, since he'd told Fiona some years ago all about what had happened. At least that's what she thought from what he'd told her during their all-night talk at Kleo's tomb the night before last. She stumbled over her answer, as if she'd forgotten her own name, but just as she was about to conjure up some name from the air, in the hope that Fiona wouldn't remember having asked her when they'd talked during the trial run, Fiona interrupted,

"Look, I'm so sorry. I do hope you won't lose any pay over this, but he's walked out on me." It was evident that she was fighting to keep control. Tears were ever ready to drop from the corners of her eyes and her voice wavered. But she clearly wanted to be the one to explain. She went on, "Seems he's bumped into his old girlfriend from years ago. I mean, what are the chances, hmm? The same old tart who walked out on him way back when has been living here in Lindos, it seems, for a few years and they bumped into eachother and she's sunk her claws in yet again. What am I supposed to do? I thought he loved me. I really thought he'd put that all behind him, I'm, I'm…" She couldn't go on. The others fought to be the first to throw arms around her or shove a tissue in front of her face whilst turning her away from Alyson. Did she throw a knowing glance over her shoulder just as they were hussling her away? The one who'd first spoken again turned to Alyson,

"Sorry darling. You can see how awful the whole thing is. If you catch sight of a tall handsome toad with impossibly lovely hair, …I do *sooo* love long hair on a man, don't you?" she added conspiratorially, "I suggest you kick him where it'll send his voice into another octave and don't have anything to do with him."

Alyson attempted a tiny smile of acknowledgement of the advice. The girl continued,

"Mind you, judging from what poor Fiona says, he only has eyes for the vixen from the past. Nice to have met you anyway, darling. How simply fab to live out here. Such a romantic place, ...well, for some anyway. TTFN." And she walked away toward the store's cash register.

Alyson remained rooted to the spot for several more minutes. She had to be sure that the party of women had indeed left and begun walking back to their hotel. How could they not have known? How could they not have seen her alarm? Perhaps they had indeed noticed and simply wanted to see her squirm. Maybe they had some other idea about how to wreak their revenge on her? The degree of distress exhibited by Fiona also had an affect on her. Could she deal with the fact that she'd now caused this huge emotional disaster in the life of another? Did Fiona really deserve to have this happen to her? This was meant to be the happiest day of her life. Now look how it's turned out.

But then she found relief in the thought that at least this had happened now, before Fiona and Dean had tied the knot. Imagine if they'd married and then Dean had seen her. To have run out on his brand new wife would not only have been far worse, it would have taken even more time and expense to sort out. Poor Fiona would have been married and then divorced quicker than anyone ever. No, in the long term it was for the best. Fiona would indeed find someone who really could give her his whole self, one hundred percent. She'd one day look back on this day and be grateful.

With this thought, Alyson rallied, went to pay for her groceries and walked home as quickly as she could. She just hoped that no one was following her. She didn't dare look over her shoulder to check if they were.

3. Dean and Alyson – Cardiff, February 2006.

When Alyson had said her goodbyes to Claire it had been a difficult parting. Even though they'd not seen quite as much of eachother in the closing months of their sojourn at Lindos, they'd developed an affinity that would last a lifetime. They resolved to telephone eachother weekly, and kept to it.

For Alyson, leaving Lindos had been difficult. So much so that she had to promise herself that she'd be back there to live again some day. She'd preferred the winters to the summers. During a Lindos summer it can get so hot in the village that you simply don't know what to do with yourself. Apart from the days on which she worked, Alyson would pass the majority of the daylight hours in her flat with the shutters closed up tight against the relentless, merciless sun. Residents found the endless succession of bright blue days, when clouds were a distant memory, a chore to endure. Everyone who wasn't actually working would try and sleep during the afternoon. This was made less easy by the noise of the tourists in the village, but at least most of them would find it so hot, with the contrast in temperature from the UK summer to that in Lindos being so much, that they couldn't cope by and large without either frequent dips in their swimming pool or the sea. So during the afternoon hours the vast majority would either be on the hotel or villa's pool terrace, or on the beach, rendering the village quite devoid of pedestrian traffic for a few hours before it woke up again during the early evening.

The winter months, however, were so beautiful that Alyson would often feel quite exhilarated. Yes it could be cold. Without some form of heating during the months of December through March one could feel very miserable in old Greek houses with no cavity walls. The inner surfaces would sweat and a black mould would grow. This was something that the locals simply lived with. Each spring they'd clean it off and apply a fresh coat of white emulsion or masonry paint, safe in the knowledge that they were in for seven or eight months during which they'd be lucky to see clouds, leave alone enjoy some decent rainfall. On bright winter days, however, when the sun shone, and these were many and often, she'd go walking far and wide and enjoy the sharp, crisp, clear sunlight, which she could allow on her face without feeling it ageing her by the second. Yes, she still needed to apply some protection, since the winter sun in Lindos still feels hot on the skin, but it didn't make you feel like you were being slowly turned on a barbecue spit like it did during July and August. She'd often walk all the way to Haraki on a Sunday. It would take her a couple of hours, but as long as she started back before 3.00 pm she knew she'd be back in Lindos before it got dark, which it never did before 5.00 pm, even in the depths of late December.

Dean had found a flight for the weekend following the

Wednesday on which the rest of his betrayed wedding party had flown home. He'd not been in touch with any of his family since, apart from the fact that he'd received a letter or two from his mother, suggesting a clandestine meeting at Cribbs Causeway in Bristol some time. She couldn't cast off her son as easily as could her husband, who had begun to lose her respect and love in a steady decline since the debacle out on Rhodes. Dean had replied by calling her on her mobile at times when he knew she'd be on her own. A Saturday morning was always a safe bet, because his father would either be playing golf or putting in some extra time at the office. In all the time he'd been growing up, Dean couldn't remember tinkering around with some DIY job or other with his father on a Saturday morning. His father was never at home at such a time. He used to envy his school friends the fact that they'd be fixing the family car or helping their dads plant vegetables or even learning how to service their bicycles. If he wanted to spend any time with his dad, he'd have to volunteer to either sit and kick his heels on an office chair on Saturday morning, or caddy for his father as he strode the links.

He'd told his mother that he would indeed meet her some time, but just not yet a while. She'd have to be patient a while longer. The only other communications had been carried out through his solicitor.

Dean had called Adam the day after they'd all flown home, to be sure that he wasn't in the company of any of the family. Adam was fine about it and assured Dean that it wasn't anything to do with him anyway. As long as Dean played fair as his business partner, he was keeping out of it and was perfectly happy to carry on as before, something which, when expressed, left Dean with a huge sense of relief. At least he could be reasonably assured of a healthy income for the foreseeable future, enabling he and Alyson to make some plans. He also called Malcolm, who'd been a little cooler, but also told Dean that he kind of understood and that he had to agree that it was better that Dean had called it off, rather than possibly having met Alyson after he'd been married to Fiona. They agreed to meet for a drink some time soon after Dean had returned to the UK and caught up with work a little.

Alyson had found a flight and come over at the end of September, since she'd had work commitments with Flight of Fancy that she didn't want to abandon and leave them in the lurch. They'd been very good to her for several years and even assured her that, should she relocate to Lindos again any time soon, she'd have a job as a wedding hairdresser like before. Her first British winter for seven years took its toll and she found it difficult to deal with the really cold spells and the grey skies, which so often seemed to hang above her for weeks. In Rhodes such skies never lasted long. Following periods of rain, which, although heavy, would also not last very long, the sun always shone again and she found herself able to wear a light t-shirt even in the depths of winter. She also grew slightly depressed by how low the sun was in the sky during a UK December and January, plus the fact that, even on sunny days, the sun had no power to warm her, only to give bright well-defined light, making frosty days pleasant to go outside and walk in. All the foregoing notwithstanding though, she and Dean truly fell in love all over again. They found themselves both thinking alike on so many subjects. They rarely argued and, despite Dean's isolation from his family, found a happiness that both had once believed would forever elude them. Alyson took Dean to meet her mother and also told him all about Brian. This seemed to catch Dean's imagination and he suggested that Christine go out to Lindos with them for their wedding, which they began planning for Friday July 14th, 2006.

They'd gone hunting for a new property to rent in October 2005 and come across a new house, which they really loved, out at Rhoose Point, very near Cardiff airport. Alyson found work in a local hair salon and so didn't need transport, as Dean would drive her the short distance to the village in the mornings before he went on into Cardiff to the office. She'd walk home using the shortcut over the railway line during mid-afternoon and would really delight in regularly preparing Dean an evening meal of something wholesome and organic.

Their lives were coming together in such a way that they felt very upbeat about going out to Lindos again, albeit this time with a smaller entourage than had gone with Dean the last time around. Malcolm was a definite and was honoured to be asked to become Dean's best man, again. Adam also looked forward to it and was planning to bring his new wife Lorna along for the experience. She'd never yet been to Greece in her life. Christine was confirmed as a guest and Dean promised that she wouldn't have to find any money for the trip. He would sort that out, even buying her tickets and reserving her hotel room for her. Alyson communicated with Flight of Fancy, where Anthoula and Sally assured her that they'd oversee all the legal arrangements, plus book Brian to play at the reception, along with a bass player and drummer he'd become acquainted with during the winter of 2005-6. That way they could play some rock and roll for the wedding party to dance the night away to.

Christine began a regular communication with Brian, at first by e-mail, after Dean bought her a laptop and gave her a few lessons on how to do all the basics, like surf the net and send and receive e-mails. Since Dean was a designer, the laptop was a Mac of course. Christine took to using it like a duck to water. She'd told Brian that for the time being e-mail would have to do, as she wanted to adjust to the idea of actually talking to him after such a long separation period. "Call me weird," she'd told him, "but be patient with me and who knows what may develop eventually?" Brian was more than happy to agree and was cock-a-hoop to once again be directly in touch with the woman about whom he began to entertain high hopes.

As of the end of February 2006, Dean and Brian still hadn't met face to face. Well, in truth they had, in fact, but neither of them knew it yet. Had they actually become acquainted, perhaps future events would have turned out quite differently.

4. Return to Lindos, July 2006.

Saturday 8th July saw the excited wedding party of Dean Waters and Alyson Wright waiting in the departure lounge at Cardiff International Airport for the Rhodes flight that evening. In the party were of course the prospective bride and groom, Dean's best friend Malcolm and his girlfriend Helen, Dean's business partner Adam along with his wife Lorna, Christine (who was flying for the very first time) and her youngest child, twenty-three-year-old Gemma, also an air-travel virgin, who'd turned into a very beautiful young woman. She privately entertained hopes of being swept off her feet by some swarthy Greek youth. Of course Christine knew this, but wasn't going to tell her daughter that. Claire had agreed to meet them in Lindos, as she was flying out from Bristol and staying with a friend in Lindos village itself.

The flight was only slightly delayed and they found themselves, later that same evening, exiting the plane into a warm Rhodean night, with a temperature of around 30°C, just after midnight. The small group travelling with Dean and Alyson didn't find it so difficult to adjust to the warmth of the Rhodean night, since the early part of July this year had been exceptionally warm in the UK. They'd even experienced temperatures in the lower thirties Celsius just a few days before departure. As they walked down the plane's steps toward the tarmac of the airport apron and the waiting transfer bus to take them the few metres to the glass doors leading into the Passport control and baggage reclaim section of the terminal building, Christine cried tears of excitement and disbelief that finally, after dreaming for so many years of coming to the 'land of the gods', she was here. She was actually here and so she immediately smelt the air. Despite the wafts of aviation fuel, the Greek air has a distinctive aroma from the native flora that grows everywhere and quite excites the head with its potency. The air itself reminds the visitor from the UK that they are somewhere different, somewhere perhaps ever so slightly exotic. It's full of promise of what's to come.

'Here I am, at forty-six years of age, travelling abroad for the first time. I may have left it a bit late, but I sure hope to make up for lost time' she told herself. She was also both excited and trepidatious about her forthcoming meeting with Brian, whom she now hadn't seen for twenty-eight years. 'Will he like what he sees, or perhaps be so disappointed that we end up just agreeing to keep in touch?' she asked herself. But then, she also thought, 'I suppose I might not like the look of *him* now. After all, he is ten years my senior. Perhaps he's gone to seed.' Deep down she knew that this wasn't going to be so, because Alyson had gone to pains to describe him to her and she was expecting him to look not dissimilar to how he had when they'd last faced eachother. 'Maybe a few laugh lines and a fleck of grey in the hair around the temples, but that's OK, it makes a man look distinguished,' she thought.

Before long they were on a coach heading south and both Christine and Gemma were glued to the windows looking out. Despite the darkness of the hour, they wanted to drink in everything they saw along the way. As the coach made a few stops in Faliraki, even detouring into Haraki as well, they were only too happy to get a little time to stare at hibiscus plants as big as trees, and at the oleander which they'd never seen before. They stared through undergrowth at hotel pools and large terraces out at the front of the bars, some of which still held a few knots of people, just whiling away the night hours in pleasant company. After just over an hour they were driving up the road above the bay of Vlicha and rounding the bend beside the Amphitheatre Club, where one is afforded the most breathtaking view of Lindos village, perched as it is on the shoulder of land between Krana and the imposing Acropolis, which was all lit up and demanding of their attention as the coach began its slow descent to the village itself. 'It's like a huge Christmas cake,' thought Christine, 'and somewhere down there is Brian Worth, well, well, well.'

"Well have to come up here and take some photos!" declared Gemma. Dean replied from the seat in front,

"Don't worry, we'll take a load of wedding shots right there at the parking area where you get the best view when we're on our way to the reception. You'll have plenty of time for photos, probably for checking out the local talent in the club too I shouldn't wonder."

"There's a very good photographer who works with F-o-F," interjected Alyson. "Well, it's actually a husband and wife partnership called Gallery Photography. Chris and Karen run it, lovely people. I'll show you some of their work on their website when we're at the hotel."

A few minutes later the coach pulled into the parking area in front of Reception at the Lindos Gardens Hotel, the rep jumped off and ran into the building to prime the member of staff manning the desk that they had some new arrivals and the group were all piling off the coach and crowding around the driver, who was already lugging heavy cases out from the coach's baggage bay underneath. Towing their respective luggage behind them, accompanied by the rumbling of plastic suitcase wheels on asphalt, they finally arrived at the place where they planned to stay for a fortnight, during which, in six days time, they looked forward to seeing Dean and Alyson finally tie the knot. There'd been 'many a slip' as the old saying goes, but it looked finally as though things were going to end happily ever after.

Oh dear, oh dear.

5. Brian and Christine - Lindos, July 9th 2006.

Sunday dawned bright, clear and sunny, as had every other day for more than two months. Brian arose at around 11.00am, having played the bar the previous evening and finally having climbed beneath his single, clean bed-sheet at around three o'clock in the morning. He was excited about two things. 1. Somewhere, not more that a few hundred yards away, was Christine Wright. Christine, whom he'd not clapped eyes on since January 1978. Christine, whom he'd not ceased to think about even for a day in the intervening twenty-eight years, was here in Lindos and they were soon to meet up and stare eachother in the face for the first time in more than a quarter of a century. 2. The other thing that excited him was the prospect of playing Dean and Alyson's wedding reception with his new band, who'd rehearsed for quite a while now and had finally put down a few tracks, his own material mainly, in his friend's studio up in Rhodes town. He had still to meet Dean, or so he thought, and hoped that they'd get on OK. 'Why shouldn't they?' he'd reasoned. After all, Dean sounded like a guy with good taste in music, from what Brian had learned in his communications with Christine by e-mail and from his chats with Alyson the previous year. If he likes the right kind of music, he must be a good bloke. It stood to reason.

Brian took a long time showering and shaving. He hadn't shaved off his five o'clock shadow for many years, but today he wanted to make himself look as young as he could. There was a lot riding on it. First impressions and all that.

He pulled on a pair of long khaki shorts and a sleeveless, plain white cotton t-shirt. No logos or slogans all over the front, just chic and assured, not 'last-chance-trendy". He needed to look youthful without looking like he was trying too hard. He didn't want Christine seeing him as some sad old hippy who'd lost his youth but didn't accept the fact. No, he had to look full of vigour, whilst carrying his years well. Fit, without looking like the whole thing preoccupied him. At least he still had a good head of hair. Boy it was hard. It was such a science getting the whole thing right, finding the correct balance. A woman doesn't like a man to be too vain.

Why on earth was he so nervous? Didn't he know this girl? Well, yes, he did, but this was a rather exceptional reunion. She had e-mailed him a couple of fairly recent photos, so he had a pretty good idea that she was still going to be looking stunning. He'd told her he didn't have any of himself and that she'd just have to make her mind up once she saw him. He also knew that Alyson had given her mother a good description, which he had every reason to believe put him in good stead.

He was sitting in a bar in the village eating a full English breakfast when his mobile phone finally chimed *"Money"* by Pink Floyd. He pulled it out of his leg pocket and noticed that it was Alyson's Greek mobile number, which she'd been sensible enough to keep from the previous year. He knew that it would be Christine, calling to arrange their first meeting in decades. Somehow he couldn't prevent the sweat from breaking out in his palms, and it wasn't only due to the temperature of the air around him. Pressing the green phone symbol, he held the device to his left ear and spoke.

"Hello?"

"Hello Brian. How are you?" It was Christine, he knew. She hadn't needed to tell him that. His excitement level was that of a fifteen-year old boy when he replied, trying hard to stop his voice from cracking,

"I'm good. I'm fine. How about you kiddo?" He hadn't called her that for many, many years. Yet back then in Bath he'd often used the term when implying that they were close, that she could always rely on him, that he'd move heaven and earth to look after her interests.

"I'm OK. I'll be much better when I clap eyes on you though, 'big Bri'. Where are you? Give me directions, and I'll walk down into the village. I want to walk everywhere, to savour each second. You know I never thought I'd actually ever make it out here to Greece."

"I remember, Kiddo. I remember like it was minutes ago when you and I used to talk and you'd tell me about your plans to come over here some day. Look, just walk down the hill from Krana, by the place where all the coaches park, I'll be under the tree in the square at the bottom. Do you think you'll recognise me, after all these years?"

"I only have to look for a plonker, I'll spot you!" She said those last few words with a chuckle in her voice and he hung up too, feeling apprehensive, yet elated. He threw some coins on the table for his breakfast, and rose to stroll to the square. He knew that he'd get there long before she arrived, but simply couldn't bear now to be anywhere else than at that spot under the tree. He had to be there to stare up the hill and get his first glimpse of Christine the moment she came into view. He walked briskly, even though he had plenty of time.

Some twenty minutes later he saw her. He fixed his eyes on her and everything around him faded away. Could it possibly be an interval of twenty-eight years? Christine looked from fifty metres away exactly the same. Her figure was still fantastic, even after four children. Her hair was loose, shoulder-length and blowing ever so gently in the light breeze; whether it was still her natural colour, or from a bottle, it certainly looked the same. He even noticed right away the way she placed her feet on the ground as she took each step. His little Chrissie. His little Kiddo. He couldn't help it, all his plans for staying cool having gone out of the window in a trice, he was on his feet and running. It was like automatic pilot had taken over. He ran, almost knocking over a couple of tourists from the Far East in the process, almost somersaulting over the bonnet of a taxi, totally zoned in on this vision from his past.

She spotted him, smiled that so familiar smile and then assumed a look of amazement as she saw what he was doing. She opened her arms and he ran into them, at the same time lifting her high off the ground and planting a huge kiss on her forehead. Not the mouth. Not yet. He knew that it had never been that way all that long time ago and now it would take a while. That didn't matter. She was here. Christine Wright, the little beauty he'd secretly adored when he was only in his twenties and she was sixteen, seventeen and finally eighteen, was here in his arms. She even smelt like she used to.

"Woa! Brian, you're squeezing the breath out of me you dozy old sod!" Christine cried.

Realising the truth of her words, he put her down, placed a hand on each of her shoulders and straightened his arms. She stood looking at his face. "You know, you don't look so bad for an old 'un!" She quipped. He realised right away that, if she'd changed at all, it was in the sense that she now had more self-assurance, more self-confidence. She'd never have been so cheeky all those years ago. This actually pleased him. He answered,

"Don't be so cheeky you little minx. But YOU! You haven't altered at all. Got a picture in your attic or something, have you?" He felt on top of the world. This girl was forty-six, but she looked twenty-eight. He couldn't believe his luck.

"No, just a lot of hard work. It doesn't come easy keeping your shape when you get into your forties. Now, seriously, let me look at you again. Yup, you'll do." She took the initiative now and, shocking him, she planted a huge kiss right on his lips. "Brian, let's face it, there's not much time to lose, my boy. You and I are going to be an item, aren't we?"

He found himself answering, "If you say so, Kiddo, if you say so."

"That's assuming there's no one else in the frame." She added.

"Kiddo, there never has been. Yea, all right, I've had a few flings, but I've always kind of thought that if I couldn't have little Chrissie, I'd be single 'til I went toes up."

"Anyway, are we going to stand here until some bus, taxi or car runs us over? Show me around. I want to see it all." Sliding her arm through his, she spun him around until they both faced the same way and began walking into the village of Lindos.

As the day progressed they walked all the way up to the Acropolis, where Christine gazed for ages from the battlement wall, built by the Crusader Knights hundreds of years before, at the view over St Paul's Bay, then down to Pallas Beach. Then they strolled along the main beach, barefoot, sandals in their hands at the water's edge until they reached the Palestra Taverna, where they ate a lunch of mussels and salad and washed it down with some retsina, which Christine had never tasted before. She may not have liked it, he wasn't certain, but she assured Brian that it was heavenly, enhanced is it is with the resin from pine trees.

All the while they strolled or sat they talked. He told her

everything he'd done since leaving Bath, including how he'd almost 'made it' several times whilst playing the pubs and venues around London. She told him about her three other children, making Brian particularly happy to learn that George, whom Brian had seen as a babe in arms, was now playing in a reggae band. Thoughts of them playing together some time flew through his mind fleetingly as well. She told him how she'd never really wanted to form a permanent relationship either, although with the passing of the years she'd finally come to understand why she'd been torturing herself when she'd been young. Had she been able to turn the clock back she told him she'd never have been so profligate in matters moral, but that it had taken her some years to acquire the self respect which she finally *had* acquired. Now, before learning that Alyson had come across her old friend and the guy she'd had a 'thing' for, she'd settled into a frame of mind that told her that she'd prefer to stay alone and go into her dotage as a spinster, rather than get it wrong again. Then, how strange, her daughter calls her from Greece and says that an old paperback book had been the reason why she was now here, in Lindos, keeping company with the guy she'd thought she'd lost forever.

"Thanks, Jean Paul Sartre," she said, staring at Brian. They walked from the Palestra back along the beach and up into the village again, finally arriving at Brian's modest abode in the late afternoon hours. There, they went inside and did something that both had dreamed of doing with the other almost thirty years before.

6. Alyson and Claire - Lindos, July 10th 2006.

It had to be the Ikon Bar. Claire and Alyson had so often sat there in the early evenings when they'd lived here. 11.00am arrived and so did the two women, from opposite directions. Both approached at the same moment, exchanged a genuinely warm hug and sat and ordered frappes.

"So, Alyson, it looks like miss Wright has really made it up with her Mr. Right. I've been looking forward to meeting him properly. Strange, us living only fifty miles apart in the UK and yet not actually having gotten around to meeting up. Still, it was my fault as much as yours, I hadn't expected to be so busy."

"Has the painting done that well then, Claire? I'm so glad for you. Has it created the desired effect?"

"Which was what, exactly? Do you know I can't remember what I told you last year when I left."

"You told me that you were lost. You said that with your life having reached the stage it had, that you felt an emptiness. I think, if my memory serves me right, that you even said that to return to painting would be like anaesthetic, it would dull the pain of the purposelessness of it all."

"Ah, yes. Well, it's been partially successful. I have been able to do several small-scale exhibitions. You know, wine cheese and grapes on launch evening and do the rounds of the punters who came. Shake a lot of hands. Give them a story about each work and hope they'll get their sticker on it to indicate that they're buying. Not that the money's of any importance of course.

"You know Alyson, I'm fifty-five now. That means that the only way is down. There are some species of tree that live for thousands of years, even a giant tortoise that can live for a hundred and fifty years, and here we are, little old mankind, with a brain that can do amazing things – well, when applied in a positive way, of course – and we're lucky to get past three-score and ten. Does it make any sense to you? I've read that the average human doesn't employ point one of a percent of his or her brainpower in an average lifespan. So what's all that grey-matter up there for then?"

"Is it worth torturing yourself with such stuff, Claire? Isn't it better to try and lead the kind of life that you can be satisfied with when it reaches its end?"

"Well, that's just it, Darling. It's not satisfying to me. However virtuous one is, however much good one tries to do for others, one is gone and soon forgotten. All this 'I live on through my children' rubbish is poppycock. It's just another way of trying to deal with the fact that, although none of us wants to die, we have to, so we make up ideas to help us deal with it.

"Alyson, you're still a young woman. When I was your age, I thought that it was everyone else that grew old. I was destined to be one of the young and beautiful forever. Suddenly, far too many years are on the clock and you're getting more and more preoccupied with your mortality.

"I'll tell you something else. I've dabbled with a few religious systems of belief, but, by and large, they don't make enough sense for a logical person to commit to them. Take reincarnation, for example. The whole idea is that you learn from each incarnation and eventually – when you're thoroughly cleansed and virtuous – you can break the cycle and reach nirvana. But if it were true, why are there seven billion humans on this planet today, when there were only about a billion at the end of the eighteenth century? Doesn't that strike you as rather a giveaway? Where did all these extra souls come from? Plus the belief is that with each incarnation, you'll have learnt to be a better person, so why isn't the planet now full of virtue and altruism? It's going in quite the opposite direction, to further decadence and chaos.

"Then there are all the so-called 'Christian' churches. What a farce they are. You remember those talks we used to have when we were island-hopping, don't you? You already have a fair idea of my mind on that subject."

"We had a meeting of minds on that one, Claire. I could never subscribe to a religious organisation either, that has so much material wealth, yet professes to follow a man who lived hand to mouth. Jesus was the first communist I suppose. Yet communism, by and large, doesn't work, does it."

"Greed, darling. Afflicts us all. But I wouldn't describe the man Jesus as a communist, really. If you read the gospels, which I have been doing frequently of late, it's noteworthy how often he refers to the Kingdom of God as some form of government, some form of future government. Long time coming, that's the problem.

"You can't tell people either, by and large, that you read the Bible. It's odd how if you say you're, for example, a Buddhist, people go, 'Oh, right. How interesting,' and kind of see you as some sort of intellectual. If you say 'I'm Zoroastrian', they'll fall over backwards to commend you for your beliefs and even feign interest. Mention the Bible or Jesus in conversation and see where that gets you. You can see it on their faces, 'Poor sod.' They're thinking, '...must be a bit soft in the head. They need this crutch to get through.'"

"I know what you mean."

A brief silence ensued, both sipped their iced coffee through their straws and eyed the passers-by. Alyson continued, "Claire."

"Yes, darling?"

"Well, you know I do enjoy such conversations, but, well, it's the week of my wedding. I'd kind of like to be happy, if only for a few days."

"Oh, yes. I'm sorry Alyson. I'm so selfish, aren't I? Getting all heavy on you like that. Are you two really good together, then? Must be so nice to have such companionship. My days of enjoying such intimacy ended when Charles went over the parapet above the Avon Gorge."

"Dean and I do have something special. If I told anyone now, that before we'd known eachother a couple of days I was off from Bath over the Severn Bridge to share a flat with him all those years ago, they'd say we were far too impetuous. But I had no roots to speak of. My mother, though I love her dearly, didn't really provide the kind of home environment that was conducive to making one want to stay around any longer than necessary. She's the first to admit that too.

'Yes, I think that I was just waiting for life to take me by the scruff of the neck and throw me in some direction or other. And to be frank, it worked at first. Dean and I found that we had a connection almost immediately. Yes, I found him incredibly attractive right from the 'off', yet the first few times we were together we used to talk. In fact, all the time we'd talk. We'd have so many things to talk about and we'd really enjoy getting into eachother's brain. How do you explain such a connection between two individuals? I can't. I only know that, young though I was, he was the man for me. If his father hadn't been such a monster, I'd never have sacrificed Dean the way I did back then in 1998.

"Anyway. You know most of the story. I bored you with it often enough."

"Dear, you've never bored me. You give me an infusion of the youth I've begun to lose my grip on. But, there I go again. Listen, why don't we walk out and have a chat with old Kleo, that'd be fun, yeh?"

"Brilliant idea."

7. Lindos Gardens Hotel - Lindos, July 12th 2006.

Linda turned up as promised at 2.00pm on Wednesday. She knocked on Alyson's hotel room door and the women were all present and correct to have their trial run. Alyson, Christine, Lorna, Gemma and, of course, Claire had all assembled in the room and all wanted their hair to be 'up' owing to the heat. Linda, who'd lived on Rhodes for some years and was a well-experienced hairdresser, was also very personable and soon had all the girls involved in animated conversation. She kept them falling about too with tales of past weddings she'd 'done'. She was probably older than Claire, a fact which reassured Claire a great deal, since she was also very modern in appearance. She was able to put them at their ease about the big day too, another bonus.

Alyson was probably the quietest among the group during the course of Linda's visit, largely due to the fact that she couldn't get out of her mind the occasion just a year earlier when she'd knocked on Fiona Kyle's door in similar circumstances. It wasn't lost on her either, the fact that the groom for both marriages was the same man, her very own Dean. However much she struggled to tell herself that this time it would all pass off without a hitch, she couldn't remove her feelings of guilt about Fiona's ruined visit to Lindos. She couldn't too shake off the thought that something was going to ruin her wedding too. She'd take herself in hand and say, 'Don't be stupid. What could possibly go wrong this time? Dean's father is out of the picture. None of the women here this time would cause problems and why should any of the men? NO, it's just silliness. Snap out of it girl,' she told herself.

But she just couldn't.

8. Lindos, July 13th 2006.

During the morning Dean and Alyson spent an hour in the office of Flight of Fancy, down in the village, being instructed about all the paperwork that was required in order for the wedding to proceed without any last minute hitches. They were also to do a kind of dry run of the whole ceremony, which required the presence of Malcolm as prospective best man, and Christine and Gemma as maid of honour and bridesmaid respectively. That evening Dean was intending to have a quiet stag night, one which, this time, he fully intended to turn up for. The men were going to start at the Rainbird Bar at nine, then see where the mood took them. They intended to finish up out at the Amphitheatre Club, because for once Dean had acquiesced and agreed that he'd not complain about the mindlessly repetitive music that they'd be playing.

He and Alyson snatched an hour for a light lunch at the Palestra out at the far end of Lindos beach. Whilst they sat with that beautiful vista of Lindos Bay and the Acropolis stretched out before them, Dean sipping his Mythos and Alyson running her fingers around the condensation on her glass of chilled white wine, he asked her,

"Is everything OK, Ally? You seem not quite yourself. Bit nervous, are you?"

"No, love. It's not nerves. You'll think I'm silly."

"I never think you're silly. Come on, tell me. What's up?"

"Oh, it's nothing, just a mixture of memories of last year and other stuff. I mean, I was so amazed that we saw eachother. I was so unable to resist the chain of events. I mean, I'm glad Dean, I'm more than glad. You and I are the ones for eachother, I'm convinced of that. Nothing would shake me on that score. But I can't stop my mind going over poor Fiona's experience, her desperate disappointment, the fact that you're no longer part of a family – all because of me. I so wish I hadn't run into those girls at Flora the next day.

"See, I'm just being silly. You can't stop your mind sometimes. You know what I mean?"

"Ally," he took her hand and squeezed it, "Don't worry, OK? Yes she was in a state, who wouldn't have been? But if I were to go where I know I'd find her now, in the horsey set of south Gloucester, Somerset and Wiltshire, I know she'd be well into another relationship with some hooray-henry or other. If I drove through Castle Combe, I'd bet a penny to a pound that she'd saunter out of the White Hart in her jodhpurs with her girly mates, full of stories about her 'lucky escape' from the dipstick she almost married. Ally, there's no harm done, only good in the long term."

"But what about your parents? I know you're not bothered much about your father, but your mother! She loves you and I know she wants to see you."

"And she will, Ally, she will. Once we get back I'll take you over with me and we'll have coffee at Cribb's Causeway together. I'm quite sure that she'll find ways of getting to see us quite regularly. You see, love, there's nothing to fret about. Nothing at all."

At just after nine o'clock that same evening, Dean and his two closest friends were ordering their first drinks of the night at the Rainbird. The light was just beginning to fade, but they still had a pretty good view across Lindos Bay. Dean drew the attention of his two friends to the circular stone structure out at the headland on the other side of the bay.

"You know what that's called?" he asked them.

"Nope," they both replied in unison, "but you're going to tell us."

"It's called the Tomb of Kleoboulos. He lived two and a half thousand years ago. Apparently he used to rule this village."

"Still got a pretty good view of it by the looks of things," replied Adam.

"I don't believe that either of the two of you have been out there, have you?"

"Nope," came the reply, once again, in unison. "And I don't think I'm gonna rectify that situation this evening my old mate," continued Malcolm.

"Oh, I dunno," said Adam. "Maybe a good idea to finish up out there. We could leave Dean in his underpants and scarper back here at dawn. It'd be fun, eh?"

"Why leave him his underpants, then?" suggested Malcolm.

"I've already spent one entire night out there, thank you very much. I think we'll take a raincheck on that this time."

"Raincheck? Here? Not much chance of that happening in June."

The conversation continued as the three men slipped into comfortable mode, the kind of relationship that develops as an evening wears on between friends who've known eachother a while. The sense of bonhomie grew with each drink and before long they'd been to two or three other bars before Dean reminded them that it was approaching eleven and he thought it would be a good idea to go to the bar where Brian was playing to see him do his last few numbers before he joined them for the remainder of the evening. The profile of their group would then change, since Brian was an unknown quantity to all of them. The previous year they hadn't run into him at all and were now including him because they'd agreed that it would be a nice gesture to extend the warm hand of familial friendship to the man who bore all the hallmarks of becoming Dean's stepfather-in-law some time soon.

They found the bar and went in. It was packed and they had to stand. This didn't bother them, once they each had another beer in their hands, that is. They watched Brian and listened as he played the song *"May You Never"*, by John Martyn. Dean was especially amazed at Brian's dexterity with the instrument. His instrumental breaks demonstrated that, when it came to guitar playing, he had all the ability of the song's composer and more. When he finished the song with a flourish, the audience clapped politely and the three friends all agreed that this bunch of plebs didn't appreciate a talented musician and singer when they saw one.

Brian announced that he was going to finish off with a song by a little known artist, Keith Christmas, who'd been a hero and indeed friend of his for thirty years. The song was called *"Song For a Survivor"* and Brian joked at the mike that it could have been written for him. He invited a drummer and a bass player to emerge from the shadows to join him, which they did. The drummer slid behind the kit and the bass player slung the strap of his bass over his head and Brian began the song with a series of vigorous strums of his strings and they were under way. As the song progressed, containing as it does a lengthy jam section in the middle, the entire crowd were gradually brought under the spell of this little combo wedged into the corner of this courtyard under the Greek night sky. Something magical was happening, the kind of thing that only happens when a band or artist connects with the audience. On the original version of the song, which goes on for something like nine minutes, there is a much larger band and the solos are shared between keyboards, saxophone and electric and acoustic guitars. Here, there was just one guitarist, backed by a pretty dexterous and fluid bass player and a very proficient drummer, but the sound they were making was so full that no one present could quite accept that it was only the three instruments producing the sound.

When they finally wound up the song with a few delicate final chords, the place erupted and those seated all rose to their feet. Brian bowed a few times, waved a grateful hand toward his rhythm section and bade everyone goodnight, with the suggestion that they come back again on Saturday, when they'd be playing a different set. One or two shouted out their disappointment that they'd be going home on Saturday and so Brian replied that there were a few CDs of his music now available from behind the bar, modestly priced at nine Euros. The bar staff did a brisk trade for fifteen minutes or so following Brian's departure from the limelight.

After he'd gone behind the bar to the tiny storeroom to change and stow his guitar safely, he re-emerged dressed in baggy linen khaki trousers and white cotton shirt, looking every inch the cool artist. He looked around to see Dean and his friends and was able to find them when all three beckoned with their hands.

Approaching the friends Brian extended a hand to shake all of theirs in turn. Dean did the honours,

"Well Brian, at last we meet properly. This is Adam, my business partner, and this is Malcolm, whom I've had the misfortune to know ever since I was eleven in first form at school! Boys, meet the man that will probably become my stepfather-in-law, that's if my mother-in-law has anything to do with it!"

Brian shook each hand warmly, but couldn't shake off the niggling feeling that Dean was somehow familiar. Oddly enough, Dean was struggling with a similar thought.

"I've heard the full story about what happened last year both from Alyson and from Christine. It must have been a mega-bombshell for you to see Alyson here in Lindos like that. You know, she'd told me quite a lot about you."

"You could say that. Still, having bolted within hours of my last attempt at getting married, I'm not likely to pull the same trick this time. Tomorrow afternoon I'll have a wife for the first time and Malcolm will actually have performed his duties as best man, just a year late, that's all! It's weird to think that you'd been meeting with Ally during the days leading up to our bumping into eachother. She told me about the book. You saw her with it, right?"

"Right. In fact, she was perched just over there," Brian gestured toward the bar with his arm, "on that bar stool while I was playing my set. If I remember right, I stopped slap in the middle of a Bob Marley song because I was so gobsmacked. She looked so much like Christine. It was spooky."

"Yea, I know. Now having met her mum I can agree, they're very alike. It's a bit hard for me to think of Christine as Alyson's mum, to tell you the truth. She looks so young. More than I can say for you, though." Dean looked straight at Brian with a smirk, to be sure that Brian got the joke. He did.

"Thank you and goodnight, eh?"

The four men decided that it was time to find a quieter bar in which to sit and discuss the next day's big event, among other things. So they strolled up through the village to the Atmosphere Bar. When they finally got there it was a little after midnight and Brian was rather disturbed at what his memory was telling him. He knew that he'd have to ask Dean a few questions. He needed to get something clear.

If he was wrong, which he so hoped that he was, then everything would be fine. If his suspicions were confirmed, it didn't bear thinking about.

Part Eight

Deconstruction

1. Haraki – July 13th 2006.

Alyson, along with her mum and younger sister, plus Claire, Helen and Lorna, had decided to have a quiet hen-night at Haraki. They had to go somewhere where they wouldn't run into the men, but didn't want to go all the way to town. Besides, it would have been uncomfortably similar to the arrangements for Dean's aborted wedding of the previous year.

Haraki is a well-kept secret. Situated on the east coast of the island at the north end of Kalathos Bay, it's accessed by a road that leads from a crossroad at the bottom of a huge hill, which comes down from Arhangelos to the north. Coming up from Lindos and Kalathos further south, one takes the right turn at the crossroad and simply follows the road a couple of miles right down to the village. When you reach the village it's nothing to look at. There really isn't very much of it anyway. Notable to one's right as one reaches the point where there's a t-junction, since at this point you're right behind the "promenade", is the Italian restaurant called Da Vinci's. What the visitor has to do is leave the car and walk the few metres through to the sea front, where you then get the "wow" factor. You suddenly find yourself on a gently curving pedestrian promenade, above and behind a horseshoe-shaped beach composed of small pebbles, shingle and sand. The bay is usually so calm it's like a mirror, since it's very sheltered from the prevailing winds, which are north-westerly. The front is lined with a clutch of bars and tavernas and is watched over by the "kastro", which dominates the village from the headland to the north. It's called Feraklos Castle and bears the dubious distinction of having been the very last stronghold on the island of the Crusader Knights of St. John, when Suleiman the Magnificent invaded the island in 1523 and finally ousted them after a three hundred year occupation.

The six women headed straight for the bar called "Bottoms Up" and sat as close to the edge of the bar and of the promenade as they could. They all wanted an uninterrupted view of the castle as the sun went down, so that they could watch as its lights came on threw its reflection into the still waters of the bay. They were soon immersed in animated conversation when Alyson noticed an attractive woman standing near the lane that leads to the front from the road behind. She was gazing around as if looking for someone, which in fact, she was.

The woman was wearing an off-the-shoulder white sundress, which clung to her very slim body. She wasn't so slim as to look thin, she was simply the kind of shape that most women would kill to see in their full-length mirrors. Her hair was pulled up and fastened with a huge ethnic-looking wooden pin, but whisps hung down in a way that any male observer would find very becoming indeed. There was a touch of the Goldie Hawn about her. Goldie Hawn in her heyday that is.

Quite why Alyson couldn't stop looking at her she couldn't rightly explain, but just when she had decided that she ought to give her fellow "hen" girls her full attention, the woman seemed to have registered that Alyson's group ought to be her first target. She briefly locked glances with Alyson, registered a kind of acknowledgement and began walking toward the six women.

"What's caught your attention my girl?" Asked Christine, "We've been talking to you for ages with no response. The lights are on, but no one's home." Alyson didn't answer, but rather inclined her head as if to say, 'what do you make of her then?'

They all turned to look at the suave, chic woman with the gold clutch-bag as she walked slowly towards them, an air of hesitancy about her. Eventually, she drew up to their table. They waited. She spoke.

"I'm so sorry. I may be wrong, but would you be the hen-group for Alyson Wright? The Alyson who's marrying Dean Waters in Lindos tomorrow afternoon?"

"We are, yes," replied Alyson, "but I'm sorry, who… I mean, what can we do for you?"

"Would you mind awfully if Dean's mother added to your number? I'm very lonely and dying for a G&T."

2. Atmosphere Bar, Lindos – early hours of July 14th 2006.

Brian knew that the alcohol was having an effect on all of them. But what now preoccupied him was having a tremendously sobering influence. He leaned towards Dean and asked in a half-whisper,

"Dean, could we talk? Alone I mean. There's something I need to clear up."

Dean looked puzzled. Was this man who was over a decade and a half older than him going to ask something about women? Or perhaps he just needed to know something about Christine. He wasn't sure that he could be of any assistance, but nodded and turned to Adam and Malcolm, who were busy arguing in a friendly way about the virtues of the Wales and England rugby teams.

"Guys, Brian here needs a little fatherly advice! We're just gonna walk around the car park awhile. If anyone comes, we'll have the same again, OK."

Both men nodded in assent, although slightly bemused by the situation. At this stage of the evening though, with an inky black Greek sky above them, punctuated by those little stars like diamonds that glowed intensely, like sparklers behind a dark cloth which was full of pin-holes, a couple of seven-star Metaxas already warming their blood and their cheeks, they were cool about it. Dean arose and beckoned for Brian to come too. They walked out of the bar into the parking area, both gazing across the shallow valley, in which glinted the village below them, to the Acropolis above, all yellow in the sodium lamps which illuminated it against the blackness of the night ocean and the night sky.

Once they were safely out of earshot, which wasn't far, something made a little easier by the music that was playing in the bar, Brian began.

"Dean, do you know that we've met? Extremely briefly it had to be said, but we have met before."

"We have? You've got me there Brian. When? Where?"

"Last year, the day before you were to marry the other girl. I'd been up to see Alyson to ask if she'd spoken to Christine about me. When I left,..."

"You bounded down the steps!" Dean had suddenly pieced it together, "...and almost fell over me. I was sitting on my suitcase. It was you! Now I remember, yes. It was you. Well, I'll be a..."

"Dean, that's not all there is to this. I remember walking through the village, on my way to work the previous evening, when I passed

Yanni's Bar. I think I caught sight of your mates who were waiting to start your stag night. Was it Yanni's where you were supposed to meet them?"

"Yes, it was. What's this about, Brian? I can't for the life of me work out..."

"Was your father in the party? Was he one of the group?"

"Why, yes, he was. But what's this...?"

"Dean, was he the only one of his generation in the group? Were there any others of his age range?"

"No, no. Fiona's father was at the hotel, because stag nights aren't his thing. Bit below him to tell you the truth. I fancy my dad only came because he wanted to keep an eye on me. Didn't work, as it happened."

"I feared that you'd say that." Brian was struggling to decide quite how to continue. He sat on the wall above the village, parked cars to one side, the illuminated village of Lindos below.

Dean was perplexed, he was pacing back and forth a little. "Brian, please. What's the problem? I thought you wanted to talk about Christine. What's all this about my father? How come you even know who he is?"

"Dean, I know him. I know your father. When I saw him that night I did a double-take. It took me a long time to realise where I knew him from. When I passed you near Alyson's the next day, I was even more baffled, because I certainly hadn't ever met you. Yet you too looked familiar. It was only tonight that I put it together. I thought that I knew you simply because you look a lot like your father. It's him I know, or rather knew.

"I never liked him, but I didn't really know him well. I knew that he was married though, oh yes. That was what made things worse."

"Brian, cut to the chase. I'm baffled and a bit woozy too. But where are you going with this? Tell me in words of one syllable, please."

Brian let out a long, desperate sigh. "Dean, Alyson was born in August of 1978, right?"

"Yes, of course. So?"

"Which means that she was conceived during December of 1977, right?" This time Brian didn't wait for Dean to agree, he went on, "Dean, the only man I knew who would call for Christine after she finished at the bar during December 1977, in fact most of November too if I recall correctly, was your father, it was Francis Waters. Yes, he was a lot younger, but he's worn well and hasn't really changed a great deal. I'm certain it's him. I wouldn't forget a man like that because, at the time, I was crazy for Christine and it used to cut me up inside to see this 'suit' calling in, having a drink while he waited, even pretending to watch and listen while I played, then slipping Christine's coat over her shoulders and holding the bar door open for her as they went out at the end of the evening. When were your parents married, Dean?"

Dean was breaking out into a sweat borne of dread. He'd begun to understand the nightmare scenario that Brian was attempting to paint for him. He struggled to keep his cool.

"April 1974. That's when they got married. I was born in June of '76. Brian, let me get this straight. Are you telling me that my father was taking other girls out when I was only eighteen months old and my parents had only been married a few years? Well, ARE YOU?"

"Dean, please. Don't shout. Perhaps there's some other explanation. But, do you see what I'm saying? Do you understand what is probably, sadly, the case?"

Dean's eyes were filling up and his heart was near to bursting. His brain was racing and getting to the logical conclusion before his emotions could assimilate the situation that was forming before his eyes and ears. His father, Francis Waters, the great moralist, the great family man, the great provider, he who talked continually of loyalty and moral fibre. He'd been taking Alyson's mother out when his own sweet mother had been at home nursing him as a babe in arms, in the belief that her loving hubby was working hard, burning the candle to provide for his fledgling family.

In short, he'd fathered Alyson.

Alyson Wright, the one true love of Dean Waters' life, was his SISTER.

3. Haraki – July 13th 2006.

Alyson, leapt from her chair in shock. It toppled to the floor behind her.

"You're Dean's MOTHER? Are you sure?"

"Of course I'm sure. I only wish that I wasn't the trophy wife of Dean's rather irritating father. You must be Alyson. You're even more beautiful than I'd imagined." Turning to look at the others present, she looked at Christine, "Ah, Alyson's mother, am I right?"

Christine nodded, "Yes, I'm Christine, and you are?"

"Oh, yes, sorry, Julia Waters. I wouldn't miss my son's wedding for the world. I've never agreed with the way my darling husband treated our son, I hope you believe me. If I'd had my way we'd have welcomed Alyson into the family right from the 'off'. Sadly, my husband's values do not concur with my own. Excuse me ladies, but do you think I may sit down?"

The girls all rallied to rustle up another chair, Gemma managing to bring one from a neighbouring table, after asking its occupants if the chair was free. They beckoned to Julia to sit and all began talking at once...

"Dean will be so thrilled."

"How wonderful, you came!"

"Does your husband know?"

"Actually, I've left him. As of two days ago," replied Julia. "I finally realised why I hadn't been happy for so many years. I haven't been able to live my own life for so long that it frightened me, the prospect of getting by on my own. But I turned fifty and began thinking, 'Look here girl. Are you going to be this man's piece of eye candy until you finally lose your looks?' I began salting away cash and, after two years I finally had enough to get started on my own. I called Dean and Adam's office and demanded that the girl tell me the date and location of the wedding. Dean hadn't told me the details. I suppose he didn't expect me to be able to come anyway. But we have been communicating for the last year or so. Not that Francis knows, of course. And not that it matters any more anyway."

The women were all ears. Claire reached across and placed her hand over Julia's. She said, "You know, Julia, I think you and I may just have a lot in common. Claire Mason, pleasure to meet you. I think I can speak for all of us when I say, it's a delight to have you as one of the girls."

The others nodded and uttered their assent. The waiter arrived and more drinks were ordered. Julia was looking forward to that gin and tonic. She believed now that she could finally begin looking forward to seeing her son on a more regular basis.

But then, what we believe and what is actually the case are not always one and the same.

4. Francis Waters – Limpley Stoke, July 13th 2006.

It was late, probably around 11.00pm. Francis Waters was slouched into a sumptuous Chesterfield sofa, glass of Laphroaig in his right hand, the bottle, half-empty, on the coffee table in front of him. The TV was burning in the corner of the room, but he wasn't watching it. His mind was turning over and over again the words his wife had spoken to him just two days ago, when she'd lain his breakfast before him and said, cool as a cucumber, "By the way, I'm leaving you today. You can go to hell. Thanks for a life of misery. I'm going to see my son."

She'd then pulled her jacket on and steadily walked along the hallway, opened their heavy hardwood front door and closed it quietly behind her. He didn't know that her case was already packed and in the boot of her Audi. Francis had only lightly registered her words, since he'd been studying the financial pages of his newspaper at the time. By the time he's said, "Hmm, what?" She was starting the engine and engaging first gear. What she had said filtered through just in time for him to leap out of his chair and race along the hallway. Throwing open the front door, he watched as her car drove off, gravel crunching beneath its tyres as it sped away toward their wrought-iron front gates, which were already swinging open automatically for Julia to drive through.

"Bitch'll be back. You see," he'd told himself. As he'd walked back along the hallway, the house seemed strangely quiet, his daughter Aimi having left to go off around the world some months before.

He reached for the bottle of Laphroaig, poured himself a generous one and slumped back into the couch. He was rather surprised that Julia hadn't yet returned. She hadn't even called. Silly mare. She soon would, she soon would, he was quite sure.

"You know where your bread's buttered my girl, am I right?" he muttered.

Francis' Mio A701 3G phone chimed on the table in front of him. "Aha!! Knew it, you silly tart." He reached for it, but the display betrayed a number that he didn't recognise. This threw him a little.

"Hello? Francis Waters."

"You absolute bastard. You nasty, sneaky, hypocritical, sleazy…"

"WOA!! WHAT THE BLAZES? Is that my former son's voice? I don't have to stand for this. What the devil are you doi…"

"Before I slam the phone down on you I have a couple of words for you. - Porky's Bar."

"Porky's what? What the devil are you talking about?"

"Don't give me that. Porky's Bar, Bath, circa November, December 1977. Christine Wright, teenager."

"Oh, …oh. How did you learn about that? Dean, it's not…"

"Shut up!! Not content with destroying my life once, it looks like you're going to do it again. How could you, you stinking, cheating bastard?"

"But Dean, hold on. Let me…"

"THAT'S why you wouldn't even entertain the idea of me and Alyson, isn't it? You KNEW who she was. You KNEW that you and Christine had been up to it in the back of your car all those years ago, didn't you?!"

"Dean, maybe we should meet and talk, I…"

His phone went dead.

5. Haraki – July 14th 2006, early hours.

By the time they'd talked for a couple of hours Julia had won the women over completely. She was the total antithesis of her social-climbing husband. She was down to earth, not 'affected' at all and very witty. The time was well after midnight when Alyson asked Julia,

"By the way. How on earth did you find us? How did you know that we'd be in Haraki tonight?"

"Easy, dear. I'd checked into the Melenos, but I knew from Dean's secretary that the wedding party was staying at the Lindos Gardens. I checked in, showered, changed and strolled over to the square and took the courtesy bus up to Krana, where I'd left the car. Then I drove up to the Lindos Gardens and asked if anyone knew where the hen night was being held? The receptionist told me that he'd ordered a taxi for the Wright party to go to Haraki. I have a map!!"

"And, more importantly, a car!" said Claire.

"Yes, of course. I got it at the airport when I arrived. Incidentally, how are you all planning to get back to Lindos? Do you have a car or are you planning to order another taxi?"

"Taxi," they all replied, like a girl band.

"No need girls, I'll drive you."

"You'll drive us? But Julia, in case you haven't noticed, there are already six of us. With you that makes seven," said Christine, "a bit of a squeeze don't you think?"

"Not a problem. The only car they could let me have at the airport was an MPV, it's high season and they didn't have anything else. It's a seven-seater, so it shouldn't be too much of a problem, should it?"

With general exuberance, the girls all agreed. They were even happier when Julia insisted on picking up the bill, "It's my way of thanking you all for accepting me at such short notice." She declared.

Throwing a few large denomination notes on to the table, to more than cover the tab, she arose with the rest of them and all seven walked unsteadily back to the car park, next to Chef Tommy's Taverna, behind the village.

To a woman, they couldn't wait to see Dean's face when he saw his mother among the guests later that same day at his marriage to Alyson.

6. Atmosphere Bar, Lindos – early hours of July 14th 2006.

Malcolm and Adam had been watching the exchange between Brian and Dean, without, of course, having heard a word. It looked to them as though Brian had upset Dean, but why, they had no idea. They'd seen Dean take out his mobile phone and make a call, during which he appeared very agitated, but as he'd talked he'd also walked off down the hill into the village and was soon lost to sight.

Brian walked slowly back into the bar, a very sullen look on his face. He flopped down into a chair, took a deep gulp from the glass of Metaxa which had been waiting for his return and sighed. The other two looked at eachother, then at Brian. Perplexed, Adam spoke first,

"What's all that about Brian? To say the least, it didn't look good."

"Guys, I don't know where to start. It's all totally horrible. You won't believe what I've got to tell you. But now Dean knows, I'd better put you both in the picture." He sighed again, a deep sigh from his very insides. It was evident that it wore him out to carry the information that he was going to share with them, information that the two men were eager, yet at the same time reticent to hear.

"Dean's father, you know him I presume." Both men nodded, Malcolm replied:

"Wish I didn't, but of course we both know him."

"What do you know about him?"

Adam spoke this time, "That's a strange question isn't it? Brian, it's probably best to just spell it all out."

"Yes, yes, you're right, of course. It's just, …I don't know, where to start. Look, Dean and Alyson are both from Bath, right? Alyson's mum was only a teenager when she gave birth to her first child, Alyson's older brother George. She was still only seventeen when she fell for Alyson. Guys, I was working with Alyson's mum at the time. We were both working in the same Bar. I used to play in the corner and help out behind the bar when I wasn't 'entertaining' the ignorant few, but Christine worked behind the bar all the time."

"You don't mean that you're…"

"No, I don't. Please, let me get through telling you what you need to know. It's terrible, just terrible. Christine Wright was a sweet girl and I loved her, yes, but we never got it together. I was ten years older than her and she always saw me as a big brother, or even a father figure. I'd try and offer her advice, I'd try and protect her from herself, but with little success I'm afraid. The last time I saw her she was pregnant with Alyson. I'd have loved to have been the father, I really would. But the fact was that Alyson's mum was torturing herself over her past. She had so little self-respect that she was in the habit of, you know, 'entertaining' different men. Sometimes they'd give her money, sometimes they'd string her along with all kinds of false promises. I so wanted to take her home with me, to protect her, to stop her sliding down this slope into, into… You know what I'm saying?"

Both of the other two men nodded solemnly.

"Well, at the time when Christine conceived Alyson, there was only one man I saw who would come regularly into the bar late in the evening and take her away when she knocked off from work. That man, guys, that man …was Francis Waters, Dean's father."

The import of what Brian was telling them sank in. Brian stopped and just stared at them both in turn. "What was I supposed to do guys? I only put two and two together this evening. I was hoping that somewhere along the line I'd find out that I was wrong. But when Dean confirmed that the man I recognised in Yanni's Bar last summer was his Dad, there was no longer any room for doubt. I had to tell him. You do see that, don't you?"

Both nodded, but both remained speechless. They stared at Brian, then they stared at their drinks, then they stared at eachother. How could this be happening? How could one man, for the second time in a year, be unable to marry his girl? How could he find out at this late stage in the proceedings, that his one true love was his own sister, or half-sister, as if it made any difference? How must he be feeling about all of this? Who had he phoned as he'd walked away?

"Dean!" shouted Adam. "Where's he gone? We'd better get after him."

"Shouldn't we call the women, let them know what's going on?" Asked Malcolm.

"No," replied Brian. "There's a chance that we'll find him and perhaps calm him down a bit. Then we can all talk tomorrow morning. There might still be some way to salvage the situation."

"Brian," said Malcolm, "you're probably right. I just wish, though, that you hadn't said anything. May have been best to let sleeping dogs lie."

"And let a brother and sister marry eachother?" Said Adam, "No, Brian did right. It can't have been easy, especially when he's in love with Alyson's mother. But if they'd got married and then she'd got pregnant, what would have happened then? However bad this is, it would have been ten times worse if Brian hadn't spoken up."

They decided to split up and try and cover every nook and cranny of the village. Both Adam and Malcolm suffering uncomfortable memories of just a year ago, when they'd done something similar after Dean had encountered Alyson for the first time in seven years. Things were very bad the following morning but, at least in the time that had elapsed since, they'd all developed a much more optimistic outlook. All that was out the window now. Who knew, though, what Dean was going to do? How could any of them put themselves in his shoes? This kind of stress drives people to…

They both strove to put the thought out of their minds and got on with the work at hand. Soon three men were to be seen relentlessly running through the narrow Lindian streets and alleys. The village gradually went to sleep as the night wore on, yet still they ran. Occasionally one would bump into another and they'd try and make some sense of what areas they'd covered, but with no success.

To be honest, none of them had any idea where Dean might have gone. Brian climbed all the way to the Acropolis, leapt the gate and searched the entire area within the walls. Adam inspected every sunbed and every taverna terrace along Pallas Beach, still nothing. As the sun rose at 6.00am all three men were standing by the water's edge on the main beach. Just for a few moments the three of them stood and gazed out over the sea to the grand spectacle that nature was presenting. Just for those moments, it seemed to each of them that everything was so trivial. Everything was of so little account. How many centuries had this village witnessed this show? Just a few short centuries ago a knight would have stood guard atop the acropolis and wondered about the brevity of his life whilst observing the same grand beauty of the dawn. Perhaps in late December of 1522, that guard would have been quaking from the reports of the Ottoman successes to the north of the island. Just a couple of months more and the knights would be evacuating.

'Funny how the whole thing about the knights was framed in this romanticism about shining armour and chivalry,' thought Brian. 'They were simply a bunch of religious zealots who charged across Europe raping, plundering and killing Moslems, when it comes down to it.' His reverie was cut short by Adam's voice.

"Guys, there's nothing more for it. We may as well go back to the hotel. Maybe he'll be asleep in his room after all."

That's about as likely as Christine or Alyson ever forgiving me," replied Brian.

Malcolm spoke up, Wait guys! Of course! Why didn't any of us think? Where did he spend the night last year when he went A.W.O.L. with Alyson? Out there wasn't it?" As he said those last few words, he pointed out to their left to the headland on which stood the Tomb of Kleoboulos.

7. Lindos Gardens Hotel – mid-morning, July 14th 2006.

Adam and Malcolm were already sitting at a table near the pool when the women began to emerge, slightly sore-headed from their night out the previous evening. The girls had all agreed that they'd say nothing about the presence of Dean's mother until they actually went to the far end of St. Paul's Bay for the wedding ceremony during the afternoon. They wanted Dean, whilst standing at Alyson's side, to look along the modest line of wedding guests and see his mother smiling approvingly at him.

Brian had insisted on being there when they explained to the girls the events of the previous night. He felt entirely responsible for what had happened and knew that he had to be the one to try and offer an explanation.

First Christine, then Alyson and, finally Gemma, Lorna and Helen arrived, all puzzled to see Brian there at the hotel with them at that hour. Claire was staying with a friend in the village and so not present. Once they were all seated, Brian began. One or two had already enquired where Dean was, but the men had simply told them that all would be revealed, whilst trying to keep cool heads and not giving too much away until the time was right. The girls all concluded within themselves that, either Dean was hung over, or that the men had a ruse set up as a morning diversion.

"OK," began Brian, his voice betraying that all was not right. Heaving a heavy sight, he continued: "There's been a bit of a hitch. Dean's gone missing again."

The girls all took this as a joke, albeit in pretty bad taste, but they laughed and Alyson spoke up first,

"Yea, very good, fellas. But not the best stunt to pull now is it?"

Brian looked Alyson in the eyes and she knew, she understood from his face, that this wasn't a wind-up, that this was serious. Her heart sank and she began to shake. Brian struggled against a huge urge to cut and run, and went on.

"Look, Christine, love, I don't know if you're aware, but up until last July I'd never ever met Dean's father. I didn't know him from Adam. Let's face it I hadn't even met Dean until yesterday evening. Well, correction, I'd seen him for about ten seconds last year, we'd passed in the street and I'd registered something in my mind, but I didn't know why. The day before that I'd seen Dean's father in the bar where they all waited for him when he didn't turn up. But you've all got to remember,

I only knew Alyson then, I didn't know any of the rest of you."

"Brian, please. I'm getting very wound up."

"Look I'm sorry, but I have to give you the story properly. Maybe then you'll all understand what's happened and why." His audience were rapt, yet all the women carried expressions of dismay and perplexity. They'd not touched their orange juices or croissants since Brian had begun.

"Last night, as you know ladies, we met up when I finished my set and that was the first time I ever really had a chance to get to know Dean. Only then, at somewhere not far short of midnight, did I realise what had been bugging me for the best part of a year. The man I'd seen in Yanni's Bar had been Dean's father, but I hadn't known that. Only when sitting and talking with Dean did it come back to me. I realised that I knew him from a long time ago."

"Pleeeease, Brian! Where's this going?" asked Alyson.

"I think I know." It was Christine's voice. All eyes turned to look at her, "I've been telling myself that it's nothing, but ever since meeting Dean I've had this feeling that he looked like someone from the distant past. Brian, is Dean the son of Francis?"

"I'm afraid so, yes. But why didn't you register this months ago Christine?"

"Because I never ever knew Francis' surname Brian. I only ever knew him as Frank or Francis. Plus I've never met Dean's father since meeting Dean. Why should I ever have made the connection? He was so desperate to keep me on the straight and narrow that young man." At this comment, Brian registered a look of incomprehension, nay disbelief.

Lorna, Adam's wife, now chipped in, "Am I the only one who hasn't the faintest idea what's going on here?" Gemma and Helen muttered comments to the same effect. Alyson said once again,

"Please!!! The two of you, stop talking in riddles!! My fiancé's missing, why? What's going on here? Someone tell me in words of one syllable."

Both Christine and Brian made as if to speak. Then she deferred to Brian to continue with his story.

"Alyson, I had to tell Dean something of vital importance. Your mother will have to forgive me when I say that I knew Dean's father from 1977." Alyson looked as if to say, 'SO?' but Brian pressed on with the story, "He was the only man I remember seeing your mother with during the whole period of time when she could have conceived YOU. Do you understand what I'm saying?"

Alyson's face contorted into something resembling that of someone who's just seen all the atrocities of war at close quarters. She let out a whine and buried her head in her hands. Christine leapt to put her arms around her daughter and said, with great lumps catching in her throat,

"No, NO!! Love, it's all right. Frank's not your father. Francis Waters is NOT YOUR FATHER!! I SWEAR ALLY!!! I SWEAR."

"He's NOT?" shouted Brian. Other guests were beginning to stare now. "How on earth can you say that Chrissie? He MUST be, surely."

"Oh, Brian, Brian!!! I know you did what you thought was right, but why didn't you speak to me first?"

"How could I have? I mean, it was only last night. I still don't have a number for you and, anyway, I didn't quite expect him to react the way he did. I don't know. I just did what seemed right at the time. But, Chrissie, I don't understand? How can Francis not be Alyson's father?"

"Because, you dope, Francis told me that his family had known my mother's family before I was born. He may not have told me his surname, probably so that I couldn't give anything away to the wrong people, but his family were from just around the corner from my mother's. It was my mum who'd asked him to help when she knew that I was getting into the wrong company, the wrong habits. He put himself out, at great expense to himself, to take me home from work as often as he could to keep me out of trouble. He told me that his family owed my mother for something going back years before, when his dad had done a potato round or something.

"There was no way I could have equated Dean's elusive father with the Frank I'd known. From all that Dean told me, his father was a well-to-do Jaguar driving, golf-playing toffy-nosed sort. The Frank I knew was working class and had absolutely no airs and graces, not a chance."

Brian's face now took its turn to register dismay, anguish and shock at the damage he'd caused, albeit with the best intentions. "So, but… who, I mean how did you fall pregnant with Alyson?"

"Bri, Bri, my 'big Bri'. You know what I was like. I just hooked up with some good-for-nothing in the winter of seventy-seven for one night. It got a bit frantic and he forced himself on me. No protection, nothing. I decided that it was best to tell no one. I just hoped that nothing would come of it. Tell the truth, it was tantamount to rape really. Only two good things came of it. One was this little girl you see with her head buried in my chest now. The other was that I realised just how close I'd come to really being stupid. I lived to tell the tale, although until today I never have. But it was enough to make me finally change my habits.

"Of course, Frank finally decided that he could leave me to my own devices when it seemed to him that I'd finally learned. He stopped coming to the bar before I began to show with Alyson. He never saw me again, but retreated in the delusion that he'd set me straight, and that he'd repaid my family a favour that his family owed mine.

"See, the trouble is, while you were busy telling me all about your plans to make it big and become the next big thing, you omitted to ask me about where Alyson had come from. It didn't even dawn on me to tell you about Frank or what had happened with that thug who was her real father. It really doesn't matter now anyway. I still love you and Alyson's turned out to be the best of the best. Anyway, if I'm right, I was probably only a few months when you left, wasn't I?"

For a moment, there was silence while everyone tried to assimilate what had just happened. Then they began to wonder how they could put things right. One thing was for sure, they had to find Dean and tell him that it was OK, that he and Alyson weren't brother and sister.

From among her sobs, Alyson spoke up, with some difficulty, but she spoke nevertheless. "Guys," sniff, "I know where he'll have gone."

"Oh, Ally," replied Adam. "You're going to say the Tomb aren't you? We went out there." She nodded, hope fading already from her eyes, "We found nothing, except these. Beneath the table was a plastic bag, which Adam now lifted on to his lap, opening it he lifted out a pair of Adidas trainers. "These were placed neatly beside one another at the top of the cliff the other side of the tomb. Nothing else, no clothes, no signs of Dean having been there."

Part Nine

Redemption

1. July 2006 – April 2007.

Dealing with what life throws at you isn't so hard when what it throws is roses. They smell lovely, they look lovely, but prick you just now and then. OK, so you can deal with that.

For Alyson Wright, what life had thrown at her, a young woman still not yet thirty years of age, was enough to leave permanent scars on anyone. Her life had risen to a crescendo of impossible hope not once, but twice, and on both occasions her emotions had been wrung out and hung up to dry. In the days immediately following Dean's disappearance the helicopter had been out and swept the ocean for signs of a body. They'd found nothing. This didn't mean much, the uniformed Greek officer had told Alyson, when he'd visited her and told her that the helicopter would be returning to base and the search scaled down, in fact there were lots of reasons why a body need not be found. He may have been swept many miles away, even to another island, by currents and winds. He may have deliberately weighted himself to be sure that he was dragged all the way to the bottom, plus there were several other potential explanations. The one he didn't mention was the possibility that the person who'd gone missing did not actually want to be found. Why raise false hopes?

Brian and Christine had talked through the misunderstanding. At first there was anger, then forgiveness. Christine came to the conclusion that, after having lost this man for nigh on three decades, she was not going to let his arguable lapse in judgment cause her to lose him again. She spent every possible moment with Brian, he even coming over to the UK to stay with her while they talked over all the possible permutations of a future together. They weren't going to rush it, but they did want to keep talking and making plans. During the winter months he didn't really have to work and so took advantage of the fact to spend December through April in Bath. It was quite an emotional rollercoaster, strolling through the city's streets again after so long. He went more than once down the narrow cobbled street where Porky's Bar used to be, only to discover that it was now an antiques shop, one of seemingly hundreds to be found in the city nowadays. He and Christine also went to the Salamander together, Brian being totally amazed to find that it was still there and that it still had a great atmosphere.

He even went to see his old mate Keith Christmas play at the Cheese and Grain, in Frome, then surprised him afterwards by showing up while Keith was packing his gear away. They'd played together many times on the folk club scene way back in the early seventies in and around the Bath and Bristol area.

Adam carried on running the business. He wouldn't change the name of the firm from Hastings-Waters Design, since it would have been admitting to the possibility of Dean never turning up again. He couldn't bring himself to believe that Dean had thrown himself from that cliff out at Kleo's Tomb. He preferred to believe that somewhere on this earth, there was this tortured soul who'd one day turn up at a place where someone would be able to tell him the truth about the situation. His one true love was not in fact his half-sister. She was still waiting for him, a fact that Adam knew, because he kept in touch with Alyson regularly by e-mail, occasionally tiptoeing around sensitive questions, but always expecting to hear one day that Dean was right next to her and they were together again. The other designer whom he'd recruited didn't have Dean's flair or work as quickly as Dean, but it suited Adam well enough that she always treated him deferentially as her boss and always got the job done. Adam also ensured that the business continued to pay rental on Dean's apartment in Cardiff. He visited it once or twice a month just to check the mail and see if anything needed attention. Plus he held on to the hope that one day he'd go there and find Dean reading a newspaper and asking if he'd like a coffee. Anyway, the entire place was a memorial to his missing friend and he knew that it would be a long time before he could bear to go there and actually clean the place out.

Malcolm and Helen produced their first child and rejoiced. Their daughter Alyson would grow up hearing the story of how her namesake lost her love, the man who'd been her daddy's best friend through life right back from their schooldays. Malcolm, too, didn't believe that Dean was gone forever. There was nothing to say that he wasn't still living and breathing. Although on occasion Malcolm found himself short of breath when he contemplated how Dean must be feeling, every minute of every day of every week of his troubled life. Now and then he and Helen would drive over to Wales and spend a pleasant Sunday afternoon and evening with Adam and Lorna. If nothing else came out of this whole awful affair, it was a new friendship that was forged between the two couples, who really did get on well.

Another new friendship developed quickly between Claire and Julia, Dean's mother. Being of similar ages they had much in common.

When Claire finally opened her own modest gallery in Clifton, Bristol, Julia was its manager. It proved successful and both women would joke about becoming old maids together. Julia did contact her ex-husband though. She had no intentions of going back to him, yet she couldn't help allowing him a warm feeling in her heart about the way in which he'd tried, at great risk to his fledgling marriage, had she found out at the time, to get Christine on to the straight and narrow. Where had that young man gone, she wondered? How could he have turned into the man she left? But she did want him to know that it had all come out and that she'd been quite impressed by what he'd tried to do.

The first time she'd called Francis, early one Saturday evening in September of 2006, when she knew he'd most likely be alone at home, a woman's voice had answered the phone. This was the primary reason why Julia would never go back to him. Yet she had asked to speak to him and been almost sorry for him when he'd told her about Dean's phone call on the night before his son's second aborted wedding. He assured his ex that he'd tried to explain, but that Dean was too wound-up to listen and had hung up. He'd tried calling back, but got no answer.

He wasn't to know that Dean had thrown his mobile phone to the stone floor of a Lindos street and quite slowly and deliberately ground it to pieces with his foot.

Alyson? Well she was given her old job back with Flight of Fancy, just as they'd promised. So she once again settled into life in Lindos. She was also able to secure her old apartment in which to live, the place where Dean had come when he'd walked out on his marriage to Fiona, the place where Brian has come to ask her if there was any news about Christine's feelings for him. She was especially grateful to be back there, since the view from the terrace outside was some kind of solace for her.

Not only could she see the Acropolis in all its glory, but she could also see the bay and the path which led out to the Tomb.

The Tomb of Kleoboulos. This place had burned into Alyson's soul. She'd spent many a happy time there with Claire, laughing, talking, wondering what life would bring for them both, having pretend question sessions with old Kleo himself. Once they'd even thrown all of their clothes off and danced around the thing, pretending to be ancient Nymphs. This may have had something to do with the bottle of Ouzo that they'd taken out there with them on that particular occasion. Of course she'd also spent all night out there talking with Dean on that July night back in 2005. What a night that had been though, July 18th-19th 2005. How could she ever have foreseen bumping into Dean after all those years?

With the advent of winter in 2006 she once again adopted the habit of going out there to the tomb, each time all alone, to think and talk things out with old Kleoboulos. Her preferred time was early mornings, whilst the sea was still calm, looking almost as if one could walk out on to the surface. The light was usually clearer then too, a fact that made her think that perhaps her mind also would be clearer. A vain hope, as it turned out.

She yearned to see Dean again, to talk to him and tell him that perhaps his father had some redeeming qualities after all. She, Alyson, even felt that she had Francis Waters to thank for her mother's change of heart and way of life. If he wasn't totally the cause, he certainly, by his diligence in calling by the bar to see her home without getting into trouble again so regularly, deserved some recognition for his virtue and concern. What would the baby Dean's mother have said if she'd heard what her husband was doing before coming home after working late in the office? He'd always told Julia that he was boning up for his next round of exams in some financial field or other, and that, since they had a two-year-old at home, he could better concentrate at the office, where once the telephones stopped ringing at 5.30pm he had total peace and quiet to concentrate. He'd admit to having stopped by a bar to have a single pint before coming home and she always allowed him that little luxury. After all, he was working to secure their future, so didn't he deserve it?

After receiving that call from his irate, nay, furious son, Francis had gone down into a pit of despair. Just one year earlier he'd been on the brink of uniting his family with that of Charles Kyle, eminent barrister. The potential boost to his income, as a result of the expected referrals from his daughter-in-law's father, were beyond calculation. The outcome of his dear son's doing a bunk and abandoning Fiona at the altar had seriously damaged Francis' credibility and his client base hadn't increased at anything like the rate that he'd have forecast before the fiasco. Kyle had left him in no doubt that he didn't like being embarrassed in this manner and also that a daughter as beautiful as his would also suffer a blow in her social circle after having been stood up so unceremoniously.

Francis had spent a long while licking his wounds. Then, to cap it all, his great image as a well-settled happy family man was further dealt a blow when his wife hit him with a bolt from the blue and walked out on him. There were people at the golf club, who used to sip their single malts beside the clubhouse fire with him, but now stood or sat further away, chatting with others and throwing knowing glances toward the man whose career was, in their opinions, on the skids. Then, just a couple of days after his wife had gone, his son calls him and lays into him with vitriol. Hadn't he always done what was best for his wife and family? Hadn't he been a good solid provider? He'd never been unfaithful to Julia, but didn't she know how many chances there had been?

Why, by the end of the year 2006 his own daughter, Aimi, had called him just once to say that she was settling in New Zealand with some fairly well-heeled sheep farmer bloke who'd swept her off her feet. 'I mean,' he thought to himself, 'New Zealand. She could hardly have found anywhere further away, could she?'

Alyson lapsed into a kind of numbness. Once the end of October had come and gone she had no work to do, and so she'd spend long hours reading a novel in the chair outside her front door. Both women at Flight of Fancy had pitied her her plight and allowed for her sullenness, plus, as long as she did the jobs she was assigned to do to the satisfaction of the clientele, they were happy to keep her on. She was a good hairdresser, plus she had the knack of suddenly brightening up whilst busying herself over the heads of the wedding parties that she 'did'. Once she'd closed the hotel room door on them though, her blackness of mood would return. She didn't seek out company and few others sought out hers. The days drifted into weeks. Christmas and New Year 2007 coasted by without her really noticing. She slept a lot too, since it was the best way for her to keep warm during the cold nights of the winter period. She received the occasional e-mail or phone call from Claire, telling her all about how she and Julia had hit it off and were going into business together. Alyson was genuinely pleased for the both of them and told Claire as much. Claire didn't try to cheer her friend up, she knew better than to try. Instead, during their telephone conversations, she'd listen as Alyson talked, on the rare occasions when she wanted to do so, and simply say that she was always thinking of her and would continue to hope that Dean would eventually show up again.

The only thing that Alyson could count as a kind of pleasure, was her regular walk out to old Kleo's tomb. The exhilaration brought on by the bright, beautiful deep blue-sky days when she'd make the walk simply made her feel lighter of mood. It wouldn't last long, but whilst she was out there on the sunny days she could almost imagine that things were all right with the world. The sheer vitality of the environment would rub off on her mind for a while. She would walk out there as often as she could, usually in the early morning and often before she'd eaten anything.

She loved the solitude. She loved the feeling of being away from the 'system' as it were. It was simply her communing with the natural world around her. The vastness of the sea below would have the effect of putting everything into perspective. What were we all anyway, us humans? We're here, then we're gone. Can that be all there is to it? Claire had often spoken of the evidence in nature for design. That there had to be a mind of infinitely greater capacity than that of us puny homo sapiens behind it all. Whether we'd ever find out any more than that, she couldn't say. The record of the world's religions had done a grand job of putting most rational people off ever pursuing the answers any more, since the explanations they gave were wholly illogical and usually involve a large degree of, "we're not meant to understand these things", and "just put some money in this box", that kind of stuff.

One warm morning in April 2007, eight months and counting from the night when Dean had gone, Alyson was sitting on Kleo's tomb, staring at the view northward along the Bay of Kalathos towards Haraki, when she was conscious of someone approaching from the direction of the old windmill. At first she was annoyed. Didn't they know that this was her territory, her place of refuge, where she could find enough strength to cope with another day or two before absolute despondency threatened to descend upon her again? She was used to sharing the place with a few goats, but humans? Apart from during the tourist season, when she herself didn't venture out here quite so often, she needed to know that this was where she could be alone with her thoughts.

She pretended not to notice the person's approach. From the corner of her eye, the periphery of her vision to the left, she felt them climbing the few metres of rocky ground up to the tomb's entrance. Was there something slightly familiar about the way this person walked? No, surely not. She heard the unmistakable sound of the intruder circling the tomb to the side above the cliff, where it was easier to climb up on to the roof, where she herself sat on the cold stone, arms around her knees, gazing northward.

The new arrival gently approached and sat beside her. Still she didn't look. There was no way she wanted to be engaged in conversation and no way she could deal with it being anyone other than Dean, whom it surely couldn't be. Well, if it could perhaps be Claire, maybe she'd cope. Otherwise, she just hoped that they'd go away as quietly as they'd come.

"Ally." Said a male voice.

Alyson was frozen in her position, arms around her knees, head facing straight ahead. She was finally going crazy, now she knew. That voice was so like Dean's. Yet, how could it have been his?"

"Ally," the voice repeated, "please look at me. If you'll grant me one look, then I'll go away contented. Well, all right then, not contented, but a little more able to cope."

Now her mind began to race. Could she be wrong? Could this actually not be madness, but the impossible come true? Had he come back? It took a huge effort, and already her eyes were flooding with tears, but she turned her head through ninety degrees to see a familiar face staring, imploring her to grant him a smile.

It was Dean's face. His hair was shorter, cut into a rather grungy no. 3, and he had a full beard, one like most painters would give to their images of Christ. He looked like an eco-warrior, but that face was unmistakably Dean's. For a further fleeting moment she told herself 'no', this must be her mind playing tricks on her. But then he placed an arm around her shoulder and began to sob, quietly at first, then more loudly, until his whole body was racked with spasms, which went along with his laboured breathing. He placed his lips against the side of her head and breathed deeply of the smell of her hair.

Finally, she let herself accept the truth. Dean had come back from the dead.

2. Christine – Bath, April 2007.

"I'll get it!" called Christine to both Gemma and Brian, both of whom were bumping into eachother in the kitchen, trying to sort out breakfast together. Laughter was interspersed with the sound of their two voices, as was so often the case. The telephone was jangling its electronic tone, demanding attention. It was 9.00am. It was also Monday.

It pleased Christine immeasurably that Brian and Gemma had become fast friends very quickly. Things would have been much more difficult to resolve, plans more tricky to formulate, had the two of them not got on well. Brian and Christine had of late been finalising plans for the coming summer, since Brian would either have to return to Rhodes to play in the bar again, or seriously think about either – heaven forbid – getting a proper job, or finding an agent to procure him some gigs. Either option meant his putting down roots back in the UK.

They were giggling loudly when they heard Christine call out that she'd get the phone. Neither Gemma nor Brian had intended to get it anyway. As Brian poured boiling water into a cafetière and Gemma spooned yogurt on to her muesli, they were brought up with a start as they heard Christine call out from the sitting room,

"BRIAN! GEMMA!! COME HERE, QUICK!"

The two of them looked at eachother and exchanged that look of 'what is it NOW?', put down what they were doing and marched into the other room, where Christine was standing, one hand pressing the cordless to her ear, the other waving vigorously at them both.

"HE'S COME BACK. GUYS, DEAN IS BACK!!"

Alyson was talking almost incoherently to her mother down the phone, but the gist of it was that she wanted her to open up the laptop and launch Skype, pronto. Christine shouted to Brian, even though he was only feet away, "Open Skype, Bri!! Quick, they want to see us!!" Brian complied and within a couple of minutes they were staring in disbelief at both Alyson and Dean, who were evidently sitting side by side in a bar with Wi-Fi in Lindos village. At first the three of them weren't too sure that it was Dean, but he himself could see from their faces that they were puzzled at his appearance and so began to explain.

"It IS me, honest! How are you folks? I'm sorry if you've been worrying about me. To be honest, I always worried about everyone I'd left behind as well. But I couldn't deal with it. I've been through hell and only came back to Lindos to catch a glimpse of Alyson. I knew where I'd probably find her. I really wanted to kill myself when Brian told me what he thought. It was too much to bear. I don't blame you, Brian. I know that you did what you thought was right. I'd have probably done the same myself. Plus the way you'd been living, Chris, kind of meant that Brian's conclusions made perfect sense at the time. Oh, Sorry, I didn't…"

"It's OK, Dean," answered Christine. I'm entirely to blame. My lifestyle left a lot to be desired at the time, I know. Forget all that. Where have you *been*? How have you lived? Are you OK? Has Alyson explained all…"

"Yes, yes. I'm so glad that I actually came up to her to touch her. I almost stayed back so that she wouldn't see me. I'd been hiding in the old windmill when she walked past on her way to the tomb. I almost bottled out. I still thought there was no hope. It's just, well, something drove me back to Lindos. If I couldn't have her, at least I could look at her.

"But when I saw her sitting there, on top of that building, all alone. I couldn't stand it," Dean was now finding it difficult to continue. Alyson had already dissolved into a flood of tears and was clutching several paper serviettes to her nose. All three at the Bath end of the conversation too, had begun to sniff and snort in tears of happiness and disbelief. Dean swallowed hard and went on, "I didn't think about what I was doing. I just left the windmill and went up to her. I was in a daze. My mind would have told me to keep out of sight, but I'd quite lost it by this time. She told me the truth about my stupid father. All those months! If only I'd not run off like an idiot!"

"Dean," it was Brian talking now, "You didn't behave like an idiot. How could any of the rest of us have even known how we would have reacted if it had been us in your shoes, eh? Nothing matters now apart from the fact that you're back, you know the truth and Alyson waited for you."

They talked on for over an hour, during which Alyson found her voice and was able to tell her mum that she'd told Dean, the instant that she'd accepted that it really was him, about what his father had really been doing for her mother. Dean also went on to tell the others what he'd told Alyson while they were still sitting on the tomb.

He explained how he'd gone out to the tomb as soon as he'd

smashed his phone after talking to his father. He'd fully intended to throw himself off from the clifftop behind the tomb but, when he got there he'd stood for a while, literally on the brink, before realising that he didn't have the courage to do it. So he'd stumbled on across the rough landscape until eventually, he didn't even remember how, he reached the road, the Lindos-Rhodes main road, somewhere above Vlicha Bay. Then he'd begun walking north. He'd walked right through Kalathos and was a kilometre or two along the road north of the village when he'd started waving his thumb at any passing vehicles. There hadn't been many, as it was the small hours of the morning, but eventually a car had stopped and there was a young couple inside who were returning to Rhodes Town after a session at the Amphitheatre Club. They'd taken him to town, where he'd thanked them and assured them that he'd be OK if they left him near one of the gates into the Old Town.

His mind has been in such a turmoil that he really was fearful that he'd go completely mad. There was simply no way out and he'd been delirious about what to do next. Finally he'd fallen asleep in a dark doorway deep in the Old Town and awoken next morning to find a black and white cat in his lap. What was he going to do now? He remembered that when they'd been there some years before on a yachting holiday, they'd enlisted the services of some guy who'd worked in a chandler's store near the commercial harbour to do some minor repairs to the boat. So, getting his direction wrong several times, he'd finally emerged from the Old Town by the gate nearest the chandlers premises, as he remembered it, and made his way to the store.

Inside he'd asked if there was still someone working there called Fotis. Yes, the man replied, there was, and Dean was talking to him. He didn't know how he'd dreamt this up, but he made up some cock and bull story about bumming around Europe and how he needed a place to stay and some kind of work and could Fotis help him? The two men slowly began to recall eachother better, having met only briefly some years before, but Fotis had told Dean that it was highly unlikely that there'd be any work, or even anywhere to stay and so he'd stumbled off into the Old Town yet again. Finally he'd persuaded a taverna owner to let him sleep in the upstairs stockroom and wash up just for his room and meals. He hadn't really cared what was going to happen to him, but it drove him almost insane just to realise that when he was hungry he needed to eat and that he couldn't simply sleep in the streets without getting picked up by the Police, which would only mean one thing. He'd have been eventually shipped back to Lindos and he couldn't face that. Anything else could happen, but he couldn't bear to see Alyson and know that they could no longer carry on as lovers.

Until the season ended he worked his socks off for the taverna's owner Babis and was content to be given food and somewhere to doss down overnight. His stomach was in a constant state of agitation, yet he still would grow so hungry that he just had to eat. His mind was entirely blown and he was running on automatic pilot. Babis and the staff concluded that he was perhaps a little simple, owing to the blank way he'd look at someone when he was being spoken to. Dean didn't mind, he didn't want to communicate with anyone anyway, he simply wanted to get through however much time was left until he died and found some rest and relief from the pain. When Babis had told him that the taverna would be closing for six days a week during the winter months, only opening on Sunday lunchtimes, Dean's reaction had softened his 'employers' heart and so he'd suggested that Dean may like to harvest olives with him and his family. Dean nodded, having no idea at all what he was getting into, yet once in the olive groves, which the family owned, he'd thrown himself into the work with ferocity. When the others broke for bread, cheese and a little retsina at midday, he simply pressed on, beating branches and shaking nets and ramming olives into the sacks for transporting to the mill. Hard work was good, hard work temporarily took his mind off the torture.

Babis was turning into a saviour of sorts for Dean and had begun to be quite concerned for this young man. By now he'd concluded that Dean wasn't 'thick', but that he'd been dealt a mean blow by this life and was grieving over something, perhaps a death. Babis didn't want to pry, but did want to see this young man alright. So he'd persuaded his mother to let Dean have his old room at her house, since Babis was now living somewhere else with his own wife and two children. During the winter he made a point of finding things for Dean to do, all of which he'd do with diligence and never once did he give his 'employer' reason to complain. Babis was getting used to having his helper around and was well impressed with how well and how carefully Dean had emulsioned the inside walls of the taverna during January. Dean had also fixed a couple of appliances and revised the taverna's menus, setting to work on Babis' own computer, to transform the menus into a much more professional-looking affair.

By mid-March Babis' curiosity had begun to get the better of him and he plucked up the courage to ask Dean if he wanted to talk about things. Dean replied with a 'no', but then thought better of it. He had begun to deal with the constant gnawing grief. It would never go away, of that he was certain, but he found various ways of getting through each day, usually by totally focussing on whatever Babis had given him to do. He expertly repaired numerous chairs and tables at the taverna using tools from Babis' toolbox, he even serviced the moped that his Greek benefactor would use to gad about Rhodes town. In return he was quite content to be fed with whatever Babis' wife or his mother would cook for him. He spoke to Babis a few days after Babis had asked about his troubles. This was the first time that he'd initiated a conversation apart from when he'd turned up asking for work and lodging back in July.

Dean told Babis the whole thing. In return the Greek assured Dean that as long as he wanted to live either at his mother's house or, once the season started, upstairs at the taverna, it was fine by him. His benefactor's heart was truly touched and he felt desperately sorry for this young man. That was basically it. That was how Dean had lived from July of 2006 until April of 2007, when he took a bus down to Lindos and dossed down rather uncomfortably out at the old windmill near the Tomb of Kleoboulos, in anticipation of seeing his love walk past at some time during the following morning. He'd shivered during the night, plus he'd awoken several times to find things scuttling about on his clothes, but he was warmed by the first rays of the April morning sun and the thought of just seeing Alyson's familiar form as she walked past on her way out to the tomb. He had no guarantee that she'd come that particular day, but his luck had been in for once.

Once Dean had recounted all of this to Christine, Brian and Gemma, Alyson suddenly remembered something.

"What about that pair of trainers the boys found out at the tomb on the morning after the night you went missing? Weren't they meant to make us think you'd..?"

"What trainers?" asked Dean, "I didn't leave any trainers."

"Oh," replied Alyson, we thought.., it doesn't matter."

Postscript, June 2007.

June 8th and 9th of the year 2007 saw the second ever Lindos Floydfest, held at the far end of St. Paul's Bay in Lindos. It was such a resounding success that the decision was made to make it an annual rather than a biennial event. Well, to be precise, so many other bands approached the organisers with requests to be included, that in 2008 it was re-branded as Rhodes Rock, featuring the Lindos Floydfest as the final night. The day after Dean, Alyson, Christine and Brian had watched and listened, mesmerised by the brilliance of Think Floyd, as they'd performed Pink Floyd's music so well that all four found their eyes filling up with the joy of the occasion, there was a double-wedding at St. Paul's Bay.

This time both bridegrooms were present for the ceremony, which went without a hitch.

Well, there *were* two "hitches", but both were intentional, of course.

Page 16. "Let Your Love Flow" by the Bellamy Brothers. Written by Larry E. Williams. 1976.

Page 42. "Redemption Song", written and performed by Bob Marley & the Wailers. Album "Uprising" 1980.

Page 136. Lyric "Everything comes and goes" from the song entitled "Down to You", written and performed by Joni Mitchell. Album "Court and Spark" 1974.

Page 136. Lyric "Nothing comes from nothing..." from the song entitled "Something Good", from the musical "The Sound of Music", written by Richard Rodgers and Oscar Hammerstein II. 1965.

Page 213. Both lyric extracts from "Tower of Song" written and performed by Leonard Cohen. Album "I'm Your Man". 1988.

Page 166. Harvest is a real store, situated in Walcot Street, Bath, UK. Website: http://www.harvest-bath.coop/home.htm

Page 231. Gallery Photography is a real photography partnership based on the island of Rhodes. Chris and Karen are their real names. They have a website: http://www.gallery-photography.net/
They are also on Facebook.

Page 246 & 273. Singer-songwriter Keith Christmas is real. His website is: http://www.keithchristmas.co.uk/

Page 289. Rhodes Rock actually takes place annually at Lindos. Having evolved out of the original Lindos Floydfest. More details here: http://www.classicrocktours.com/

All other bars and tavernas mentioned on Rhodes by name are real.

Interview with John Manuel, author, December 2012.

The first question has to be, where did you get the idea from for the plot of VFK?

I actually knew a young couple, many years ago in Cardiff whose experience gave me the idea for what was to happen to Dean and Alyson. Only in their case, it was really so.

Why haven't you written fiction before now, having authored four books of Grecian travel memoirs?

I have always envied fiction writers who can come up with plots again and again. I've always fancied writing fiction, but held off from doing so until I found a plot that I thought would work. The worst thing one can do is attempt a novel without a decent story line, hopefully with a few twists in there too.

Do you set out to teach a moral point, bearing in mind the fact that you preface the book with a thought from the Bible book of Proverbs?

Only that so often in life, huge disasters could probably be avoided if we all listened a little more before drawing conclusions or, even worse, taking action.

Is there a degree of autobiography in VFK?

A smidgin, yes. I did work in a similar environment to Dean whilst he was in South Wales. But largely it's just that I've used knowledge of places and people in my life to flesh out the content of VFK.

And the characters, are they based on real people you know or have known?

Without exception they are conglomerations. For example: I've used what sketchy knowledge I've gleaned from both my wife's brother and a close friend to create the career for Dean's father, but his character is most definitely not a reflection of either of theirs (hope you're reading this Paul or John!).

Other characters are a mixture. There is, for example, a piece of me in Dean, but also in Brian. Quite a few friends and relatives have had their thoughts, appearance and ways plundered in order to create the characters here, but there isn't any that fully mirrors someone I know or have known. Too dangerous!

You are one of Jehovah's Witnesses, correct?

For my sins, yes. Pun intended by the way.

So, how do you square the tenets of your beliefs with those of the people in this book?

The answer I suppose is that you don't have to approve of, or indeed live similarly, to any of the people you write about when you write fiction. Although, quite a few of the musings or conversations which take place in VFK do reflect perhaps how I used to feel before becoming a JW. There was simply, for me, a story I wanted to tell, so I set out to tell it.

You don't come across as a typically religious type of person, if that's not too personal?

I take that as a compliment. As a general rule I hate religion. Many eyebrows are raised in conversation when I say that but, by and large religion divides, robs and decieves people and I continually marvel at how gullible so many of the members of the established religions are. One of the first things that I found interesting about the JW's in my initial chats with them was how they do their *homework*. They are not, in the usual sense of the word, religious but, rather, they are studious. Their propensity to study is what actually *deters* some from joining them. Yes I do know many among them who do come across as "religious" in the usual sense, these being by and large those members who've come to the movement from other religions. But I'd say that the majority are well adjusted regular kinds who take their beliefs seriously. Suffice to say that I have a strong aversion to all things "religious", but a deep-held trust that there is a creator and that there is a purpose to us being here.

Any little idiosyncrasies you slipped in that you could share with us?

There are, yes. I've always been a Pink Floyd fan for example, right back to the pre - *Dark Side of the Moon* days. In fact my favourite PF music is still on the albums *Meddle, Atom Heart Mother* and *Ummagumma.* So I thought it would be fun to use surnames of band members for the hero and heroine, also for Claire. I couldn't use Gilmour, of course, because that would have been too obvious, but Waters, Wright, Mason, they're all in there.

Can we expect more fiction from you? Perhaps a sequel?

I have absolutely no idea!

*

Note regarding the spelling of "Kleoboulos"

I have chosen the most common English spelling of the name as found most often on-line and in other reference works.

The actual Greek pronunciation however, is in fact *Kleo'voulos*, with the accent on the first 'o'.

31862749R00162

Printed in Great Britain
by Amazon